image comics presents

CHEW

BLOOD PUDDIN'

created by **John Layman & Rob Guillory**

written & lettered by
John Layman
drawn & colored by
Rob Guillory

Color Assists by Taylor Wells

IMAGE COMICS, INC.
Robert Kirkman – Chief Operating Officer
Erik Larsen – Chief Financial Officer
Todd McFarlane – President
Marc Silvestri – Chief Executive Officer
Jim Valentino – Vice-President

Eric Stephenson – Publisher
Corey Murphy – Director of Sales
Jeremy Sullivan – Director of Digital Sales
Kat Salazar – Director of PR & Marketing
Emily Miller – Director of Operations
Branwyn Bigglestone – Senior Accounts Manager
Sarah Mello – Accounts Manager
Drew Gill – Art Director
Jonathan Chan – Production Manager
Meredith Wallace – Print Manager
Randy Okamura – Marketing Production Designer
David Brothers – Branding Manager
Ally Power – Content Manager
Addison Duke – Production Artist
Vincent Kukua – Production Artist
Sasha Head – Production Artist
Tricia Ramos – Production Artist
Emilio Bautista – Sales Assistant
Jessica Ambriz – Administrative Assistant
IMAGECOMICS.COM

Dedications:

JOHN: To Poyo, who stole the show, and had to pay the ultimate price.

ROB: To my daughter, Amelia, who was born during the making of this volume. If I do my job as your father, you won't read this until you're 17.

Thanks:
Taylor Wells, for the coloring assists.
Drew Gill, for the production assists.
Tom B. Long, for the logo.
Comicbookfonts.com, for the fonts.

And More Thanks:
David Brothers, Kelly Sue DeConnick, Valentine De Landro, Jeff Krelitz, Tom Long, Theresa Peterson, and Katheryn & Israel Skelton. Plus the fine foks at Image, especially Eric, Jonathan, Emily, Ron, Corey, Kat, Meredith, Randy and Branwyn.

Chapter 1

CONTENTS: MINT, SUGAR, HIGH FRUCTOSE CORN SYRUP, CRACK.
MINT.
"YOU STANK."
MINT.
"WHAT DID YOU EAT?!!"

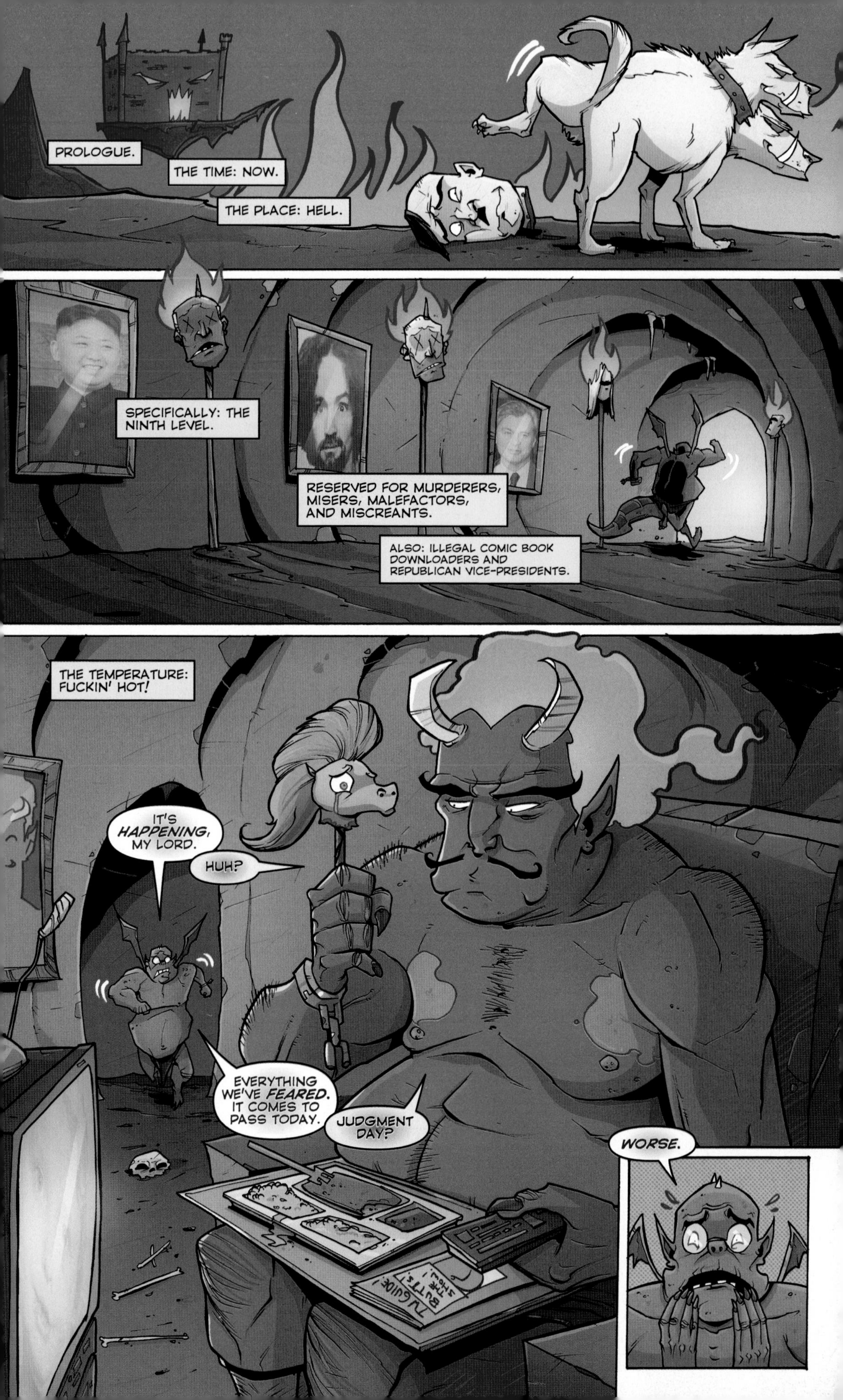
PROLOGUE.
THE TIME: NOW.
THE PLACE: HELL.
SPECIFICALLY: THE NINTH LEVEL.
RESERVED FOR MURDERERS, MISERS, MALEFACTORS, AND MISCREANTS.
ALSO: ILLEGAL COMIC BOOK DOWNLOADERS AND REPUBLICAN VICE-PRESIDENTS.
THE TEMPERATURE: FUCKIN' HOT!
IT'S HAPPENING, MY LORD.
HUH?
EVERYTHING WE'VE FEARED. IT COMES TO PASS TODAY.
JUDGMENT DAY?
WORSE.
TV GUIDE! THE BUTT'S SHOW!

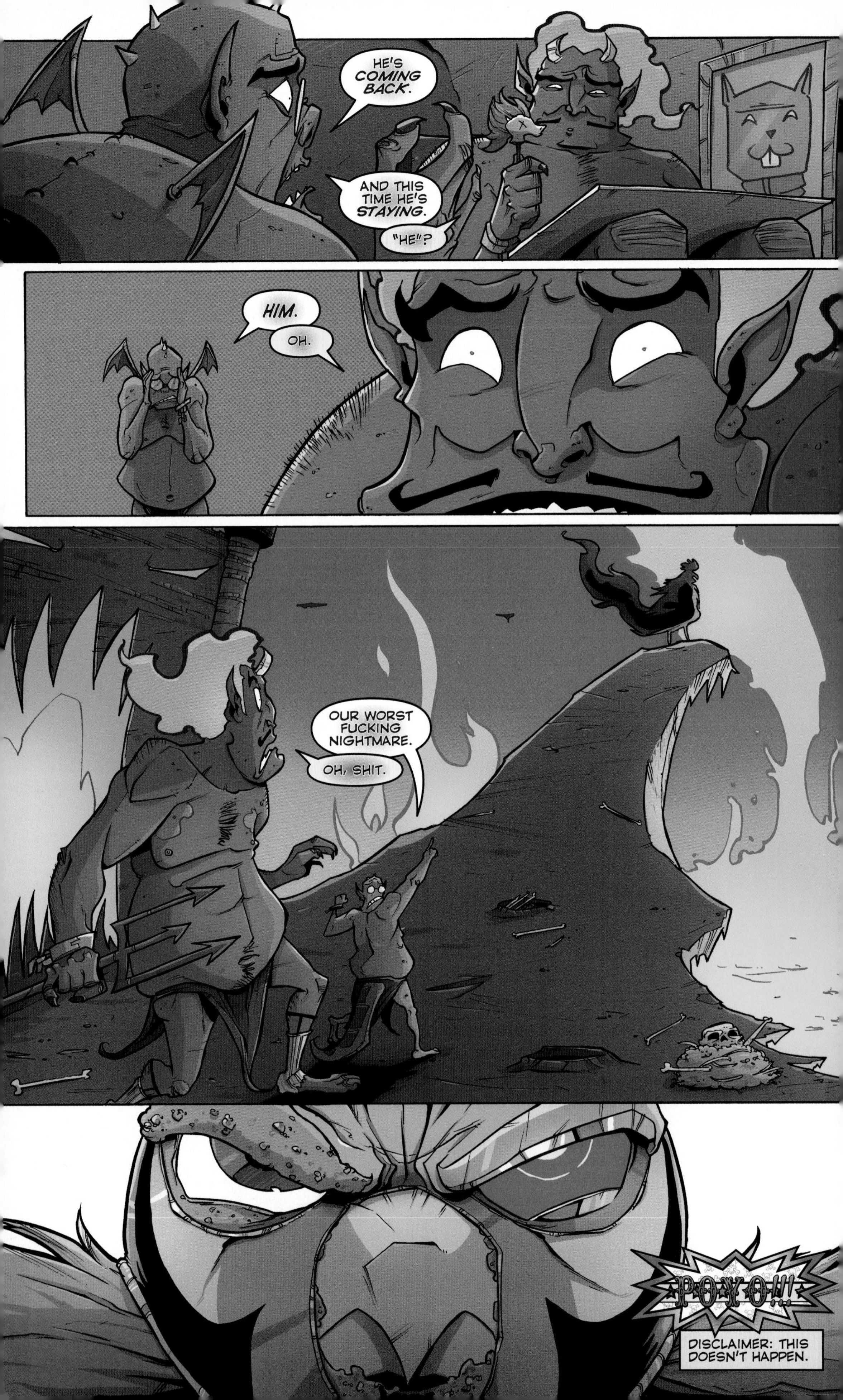
HE'S COMING BACK.
AND THIS TIME HE'S STAYING.
"HE"?
HIM.
OH.
OUR WORST FUCKING NIGHTMARE.
OH, SHIT.
POYO!!!
DISCLAIMER: THIS DOESN'T HAPPEN.

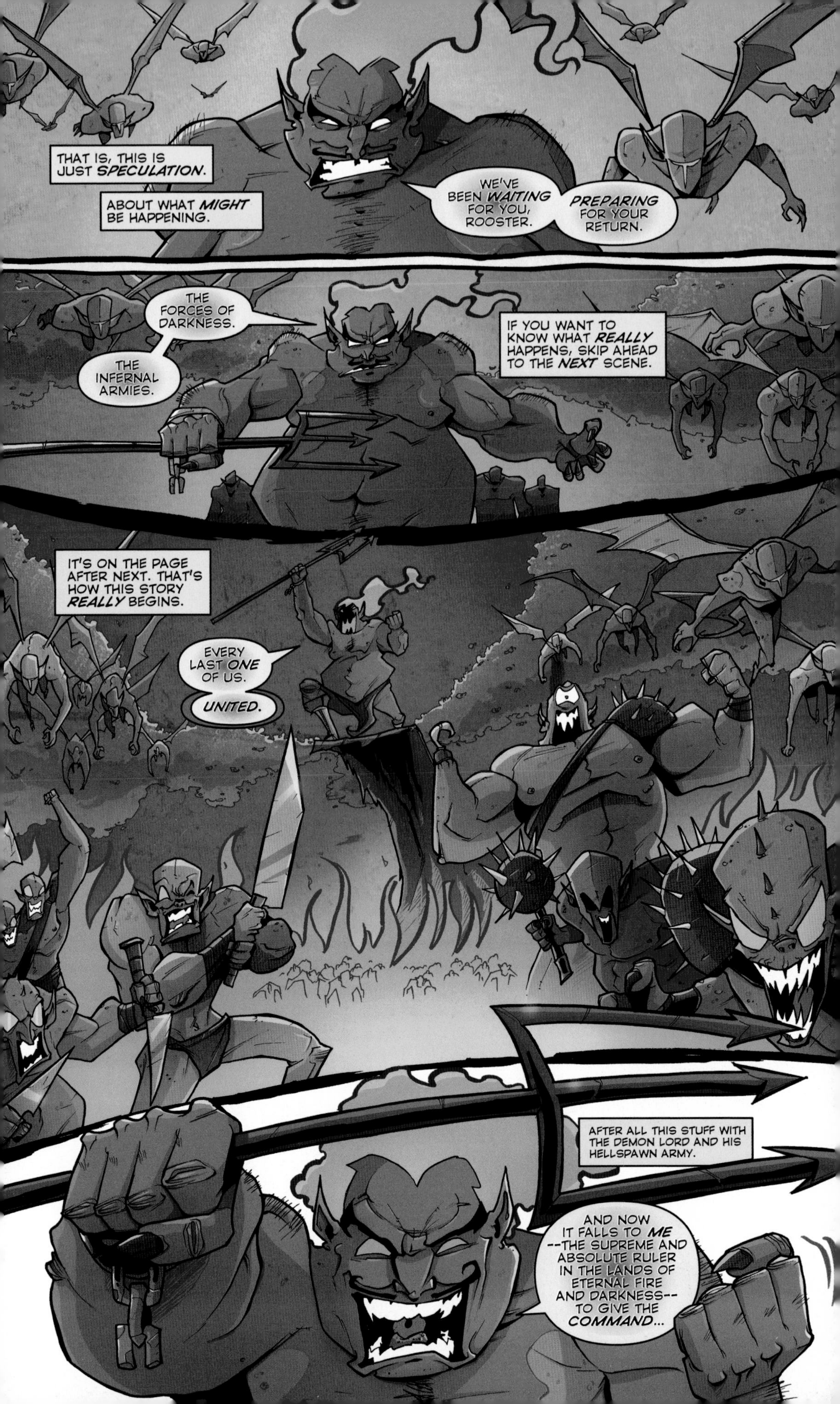

THAT IS, THIS IS JUST SPECULATION.
ABOUT WHAT MIGHT BE HAPPENING.
WE'VE BEEN WAITING FOR YOU, ROOSTER.
PREPARING FOR YOUR RETURN.
THE FORCES OF DARKNESS.
THE INFERNAL ARMIES.
IF YOU WANT TO KNOW WHAT REALLY HAPPENS, SKIP AHEAD TO THE NEXT SCENE.
IT'S ON THE PAGE AFTER NEXT. THAT'S HOW THIS STORY REALLY BEGINS.
EVERY LAST ONE OF US.
UNITED.
AFTER ALL THIS STUFF WITH THE DEMON LORD AND HIS HELLSPAWN ARMY.
AND NOW IT FALLS TO ME --THE SUPREME AND ABSOLUTE RULER IN THE LANDS OF ETERNAL FIRE AND DARKNESS-- TO GIVE THE COMMAND...

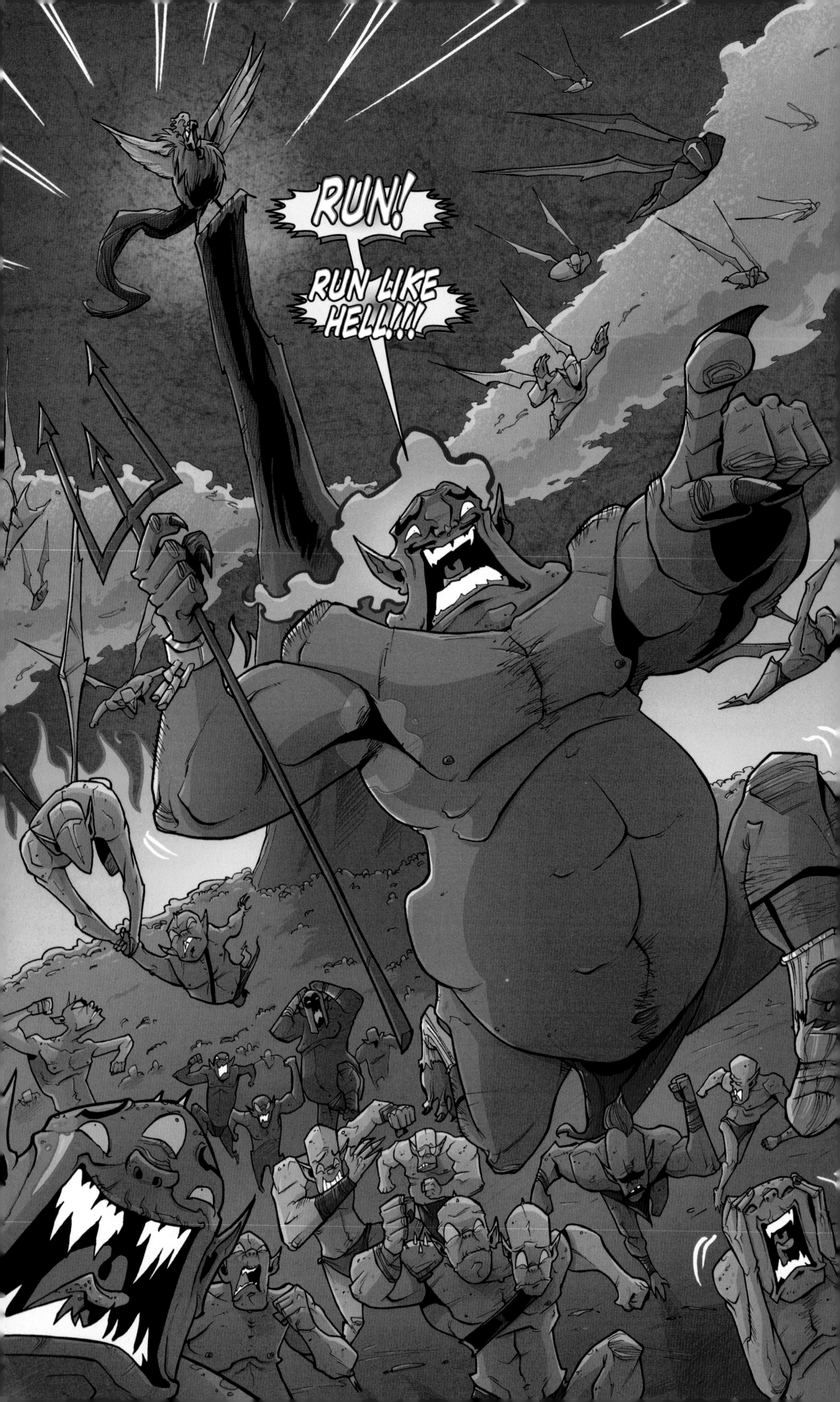
RUN!
RUN LIKE HELL!!!

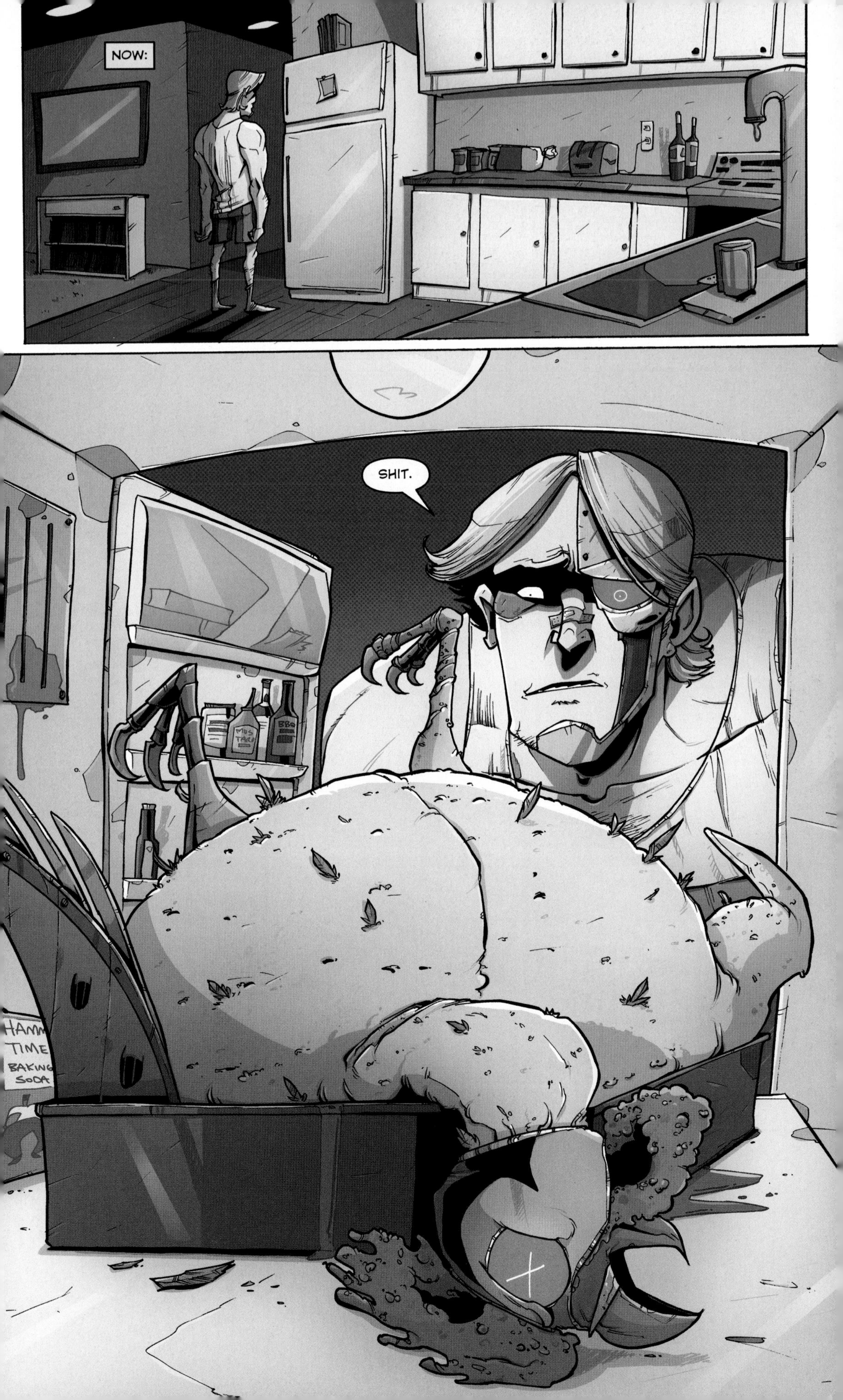
NOW:
SHIT.
MUSTARD
BBQ
HAMM
TIME
BAKING
SODA

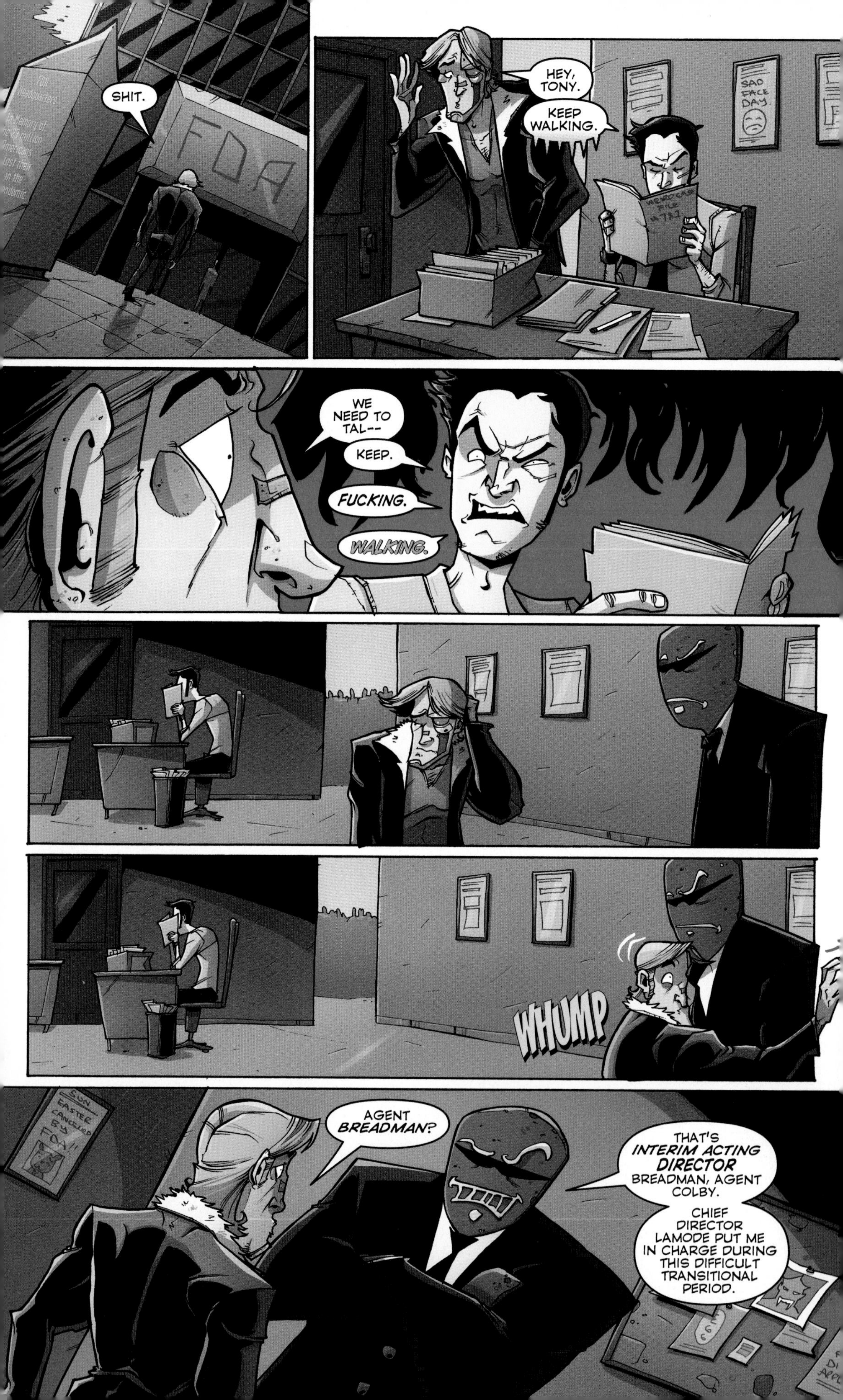
FDA
SHIT.
HEY, TONY.
KEEP WALKING.
SAD FACE DAY
WE NEED TO TAL--
KEEP.
FUCKING.
WALKING.
WHUMP
AGENT BREADMAN?
THAT'S INTERIM ACTING DIRECTOR BREADMAN, AGENT COLBY.
CHIEF DIRECTOR LAMODE PUT ME IN CHARGE DURING THIS DIFFICULT TRANSITIONAL PERIOD.

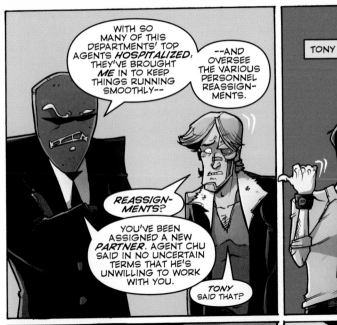

WITH SO MANY OF THIS DEPARTMENTS' TOP AGENTS *HOSPITALIZED*, THEY'VE BROUGHT *ME* IN TO KEEP THINGS RUNNING SMOOTHLY--

--AND OVERSEE THE VARIOUS PERSONNEL REASSIGN-MENTS.

REASSIGN-MENTS?

YOU'VE BEEN ASSIGNED A NEW *PARTNER*. AGENT CHU SAID IN NO UNCERTAIN TERMS THAT HE'S UNWILLING TO WORK WITH YOU.

TONY SAID THAT?

TONY SAID *THIS*:

NO FUCKING WAY.

YOU KEEP ME PARTNERED WITH COLBY, AND I *GUARANTEE* YOU END UP WITH ANOTHER AGENT IN THE HOSPITAL.

LAMODE'S PULLED SOME STRINGS TO GET YOU A *NEW* PARTNER.

HIGHLY DECORATED AGENT. BRAVE. SMART. TOUGH AS FUCKIN' NAILS.

ABSOLUTELY FEARLESS.

TRANSFERRING IN TODAY FROM THE *USDA*.

AND I'M TOLD YOU *ALREADY* HAVE A WORKING RELATIONSHIP WITH HIM.

YOU MEAN... **POYO**?!?

FUNNY. I WAS TOLD HE WAS *PUNCTUAL*. WONDER WHY HE HASN'T REPORTED IN YET.

I TRUST YOU CAN KEEP BUSY UNTIL HE SHOWS UP, CAN'T YOU, AGENT COLBY?

...

CHU. MY OFFICE.

NOW.

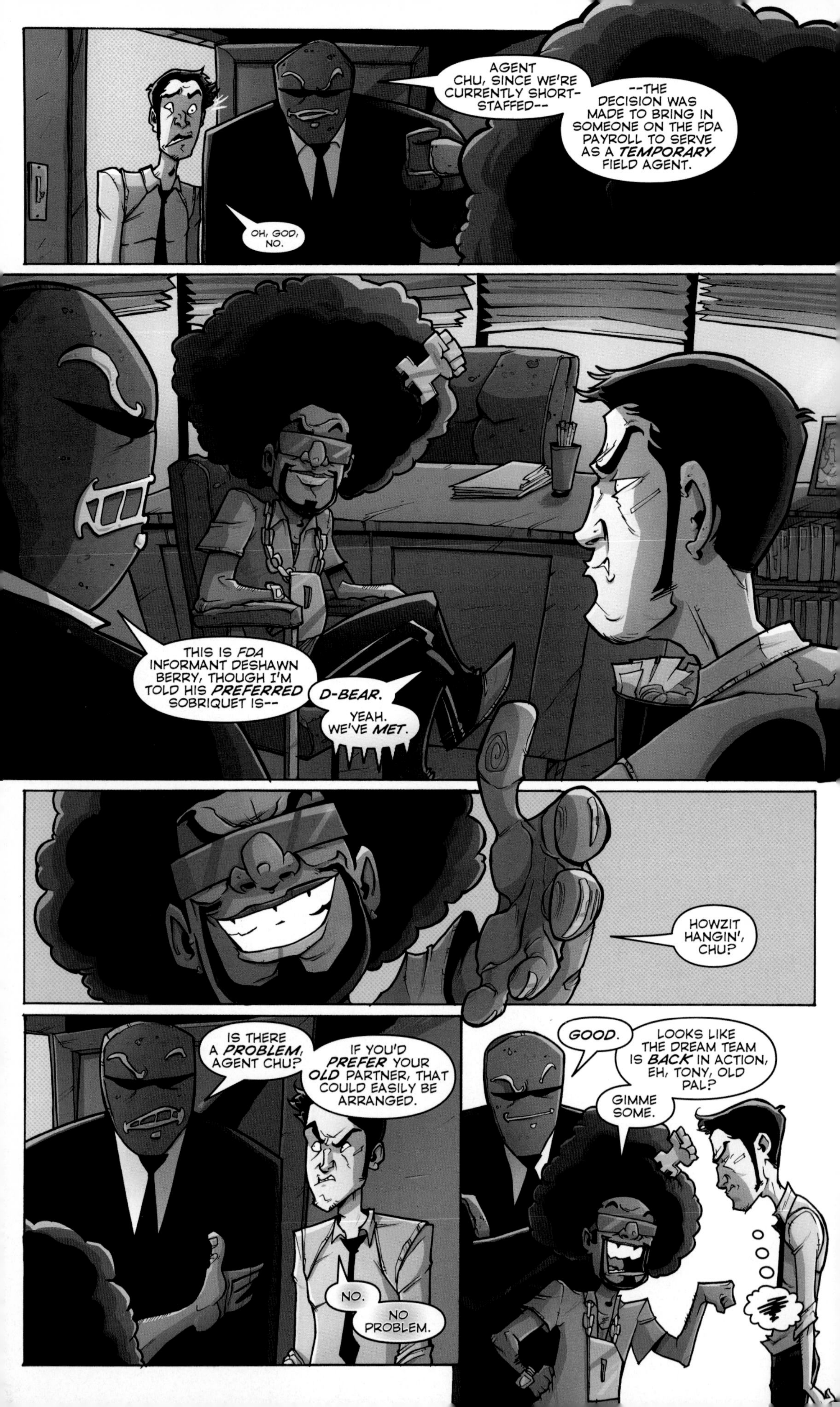
AGENT CHU, SINCE WE'RE CURRENTLY SHORT-STAFFED--
--THE DECISION WAS MADE TO BRING IN SOMEONE ON THE FDA PAYROLL TO SERVE AS A *TEMPORARY* FIELD AGENT.
OH, GOD, NO.
THIS IS *FDA* INFORMANT DESHAWN BERRY, THOUGH I'M TOLD HIS *PREFERRED* SOBRIQUET IS--
D-BEAR.
YEAH. WE'VE *MET*.
HOWZIT HANGIN', CHU?
IS THERE A *PROBLEM*, AGENT CHU?
IF YOU'D *PREFER* YOUR *OLD* PARTNER, THAT COULD EASILY BE ARRANGED.
NO.
NO PROBLEM.
GOOD.
LOOKS LIKE THE DREAM TEAM IS *BACK* IN ACTION, EH, TONY, OLD PAL?
GIMME SOME.

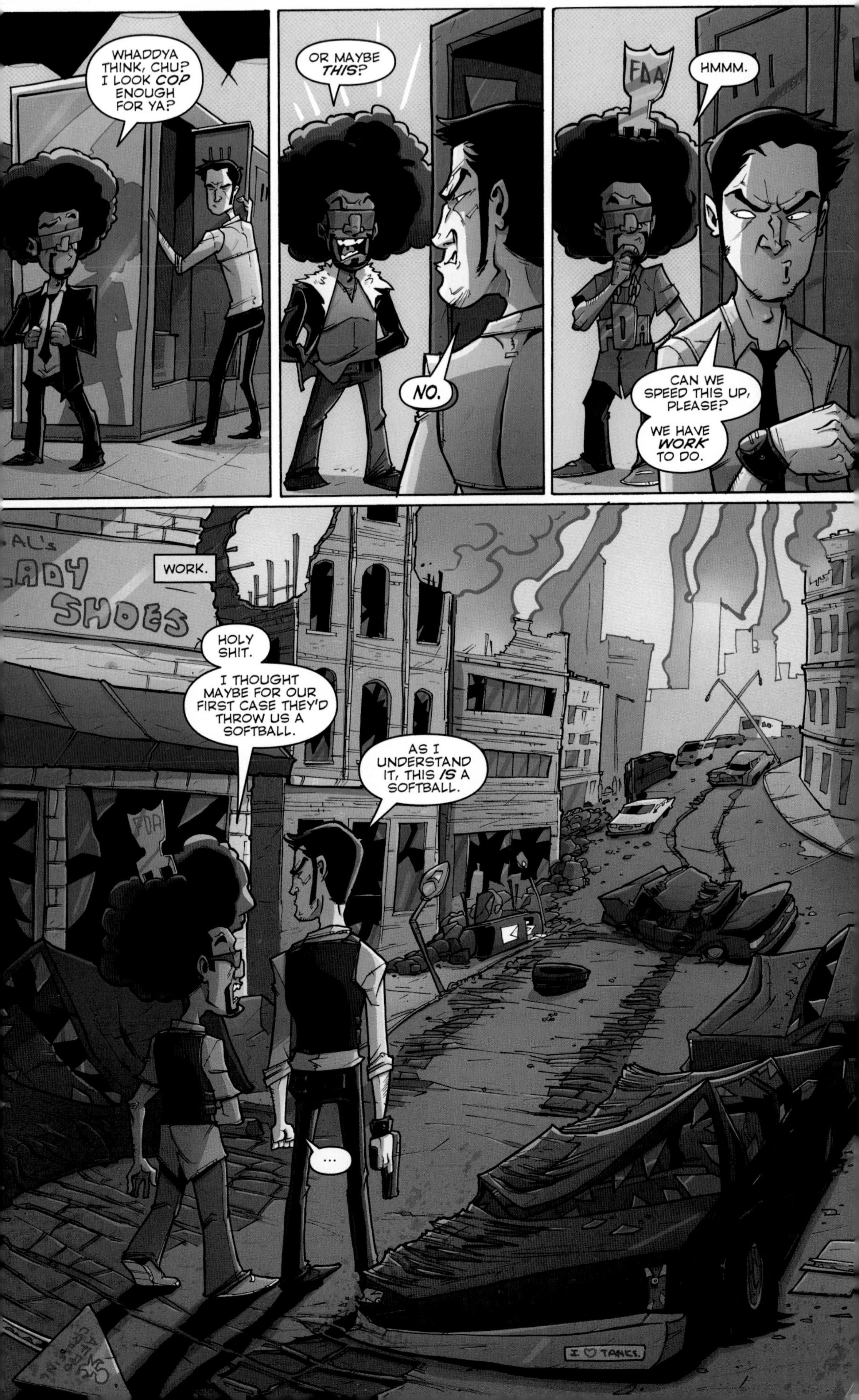
WHADDYA THINK, CHU? I LOOK COP ENOUGH FOR YA?
OR MAYBE THIS?
NO.
FDA
HMMM.
FDA
CAN WE SPEED THIS UP, PLEASE?
WE HAVE WORK TO DO.
AL's
LADY SHOES
WORK.
HOLY SHIT.
I THOUGHT MAYBE FOR OUR FIRST CASE THEY'D THROW US A SOFTBALL.
AS I UNDERSTAND IT, THIS IS A SOFTBALL.
FDA
...
I ♡ TANKS.

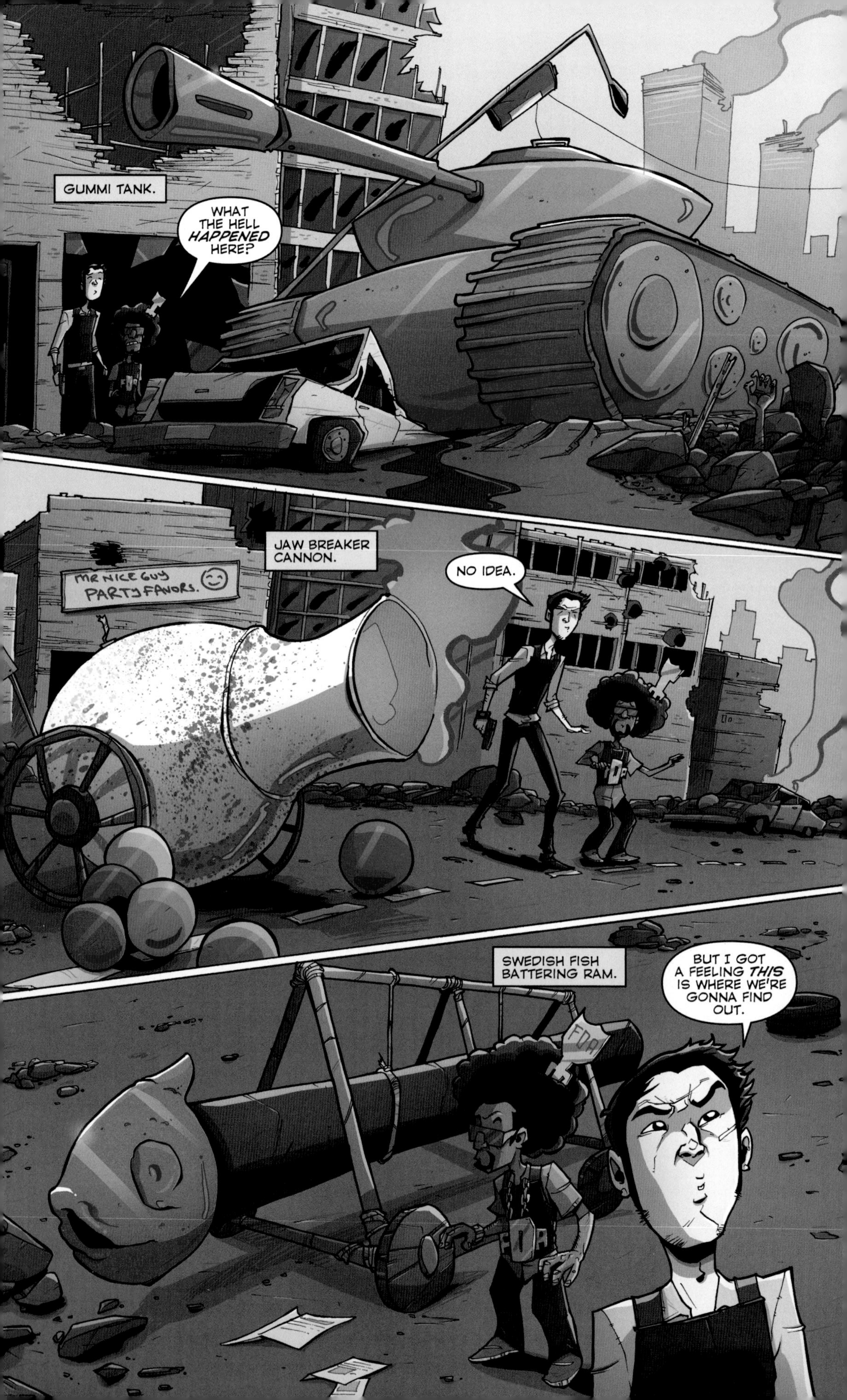

GUMMI TANK.
WHAT THE HELL *HAPPENED* HERE?
JAW BREAKER CANNON.
MR NICE GUY PARTY FAVORS.
NO IDEA.
SWEDISH FISH BATTERING RAM.
BUT I GOT A FEELING *THIS* IS WHERE WE'RE GONNA FIND OUT.

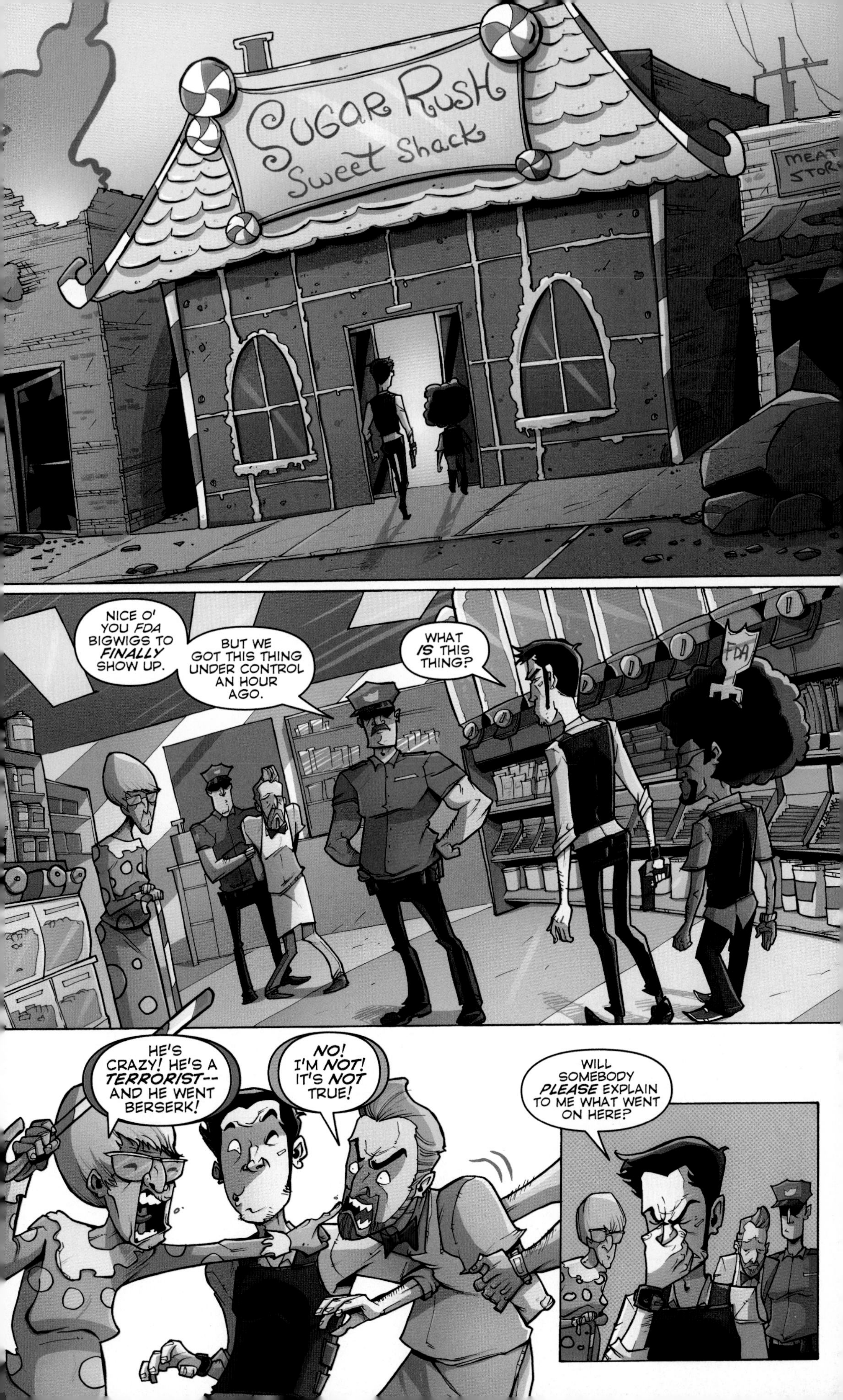
SUGAR RUSH Sweet Shack
MEAT STOR
NICE O' YOU *FDA* BIGWIGS TO *FINALLY* SHOW UP.
BUT WE GOT THIS THING UNDER CONTROL AN HOUR AGO.
WHAT *IS* THIS THING?
FDA
HE'S CRAZY! HE'S A *TERRORIST*-- AND HE WENT BERSERK!
NO! I'M *NOT!* IT'S *NOT* TRUE!
WILL SOMEBODY *PLEASE* EXPLAIN TO ME WHAT WENT ON HERE?

RAYMOND REECE IS A CREOSAKARER--

ABLE TO CRAFT ANYTHING WITH THE MONOSACCHARIDES GLUCOSE AND FRUCTOSE MOLECULES INTO WORKING, FUNCTIONING MACHINERY.

HE IS ALSO THE MOST RECENT HIRE OF THE SUGAR RUSH SWEET SHACK CANDY SHOP.

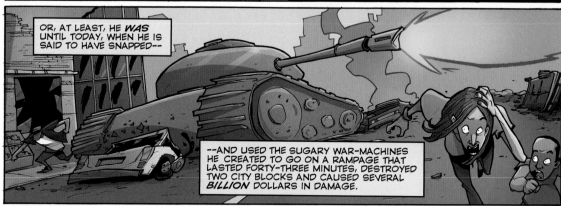

OR, AT LEAST, HE *WAS* UNTIL TODAY, WHEN HE IS SAID TO HAVE SNAPPED--

--AND USED THE SUGARY WAR-MACHINES HE CREATED TO GO ON A RAMPAGE THAT LASTED FORTY-THREE MINUTES, DESTROYED TWO CITY BLOCKS AND CAUSED SEVERAL *BILLION* DOLLARS IN DAMAGE.

AND THROUGHOUT HIS FRENZY OF DESTRUCTION, HE WAS HEARD TO UTTER THESE WORDS:

WAR IS COMING!

A WAR FOR THE TRUTH!

WE ARE E.G.G.!

WE'VE GOT A HALF-DOZEN WITNESSES, INCLUDING THE STORE-OWNER HERE, CONFIRMING THAT MR. REECE PERPETRATED THESE AC--

WAITA-MINUTE! HOW'S THIS CREOSAKARER POWER WORK?

HOW'S HE *DO* THAT?

AND HOW DO YOU SPELL "CREOSAKARER," ANYWAY?

D-BEAR, LISTEN. LET *ME* DEAL WITH THE PERP.

WHAT DO *I* GET TO DO?

I DUNNO. MAKE YOUR-SELF USEFUL. GET A STATEMENT FROM THE STORE OWNER.

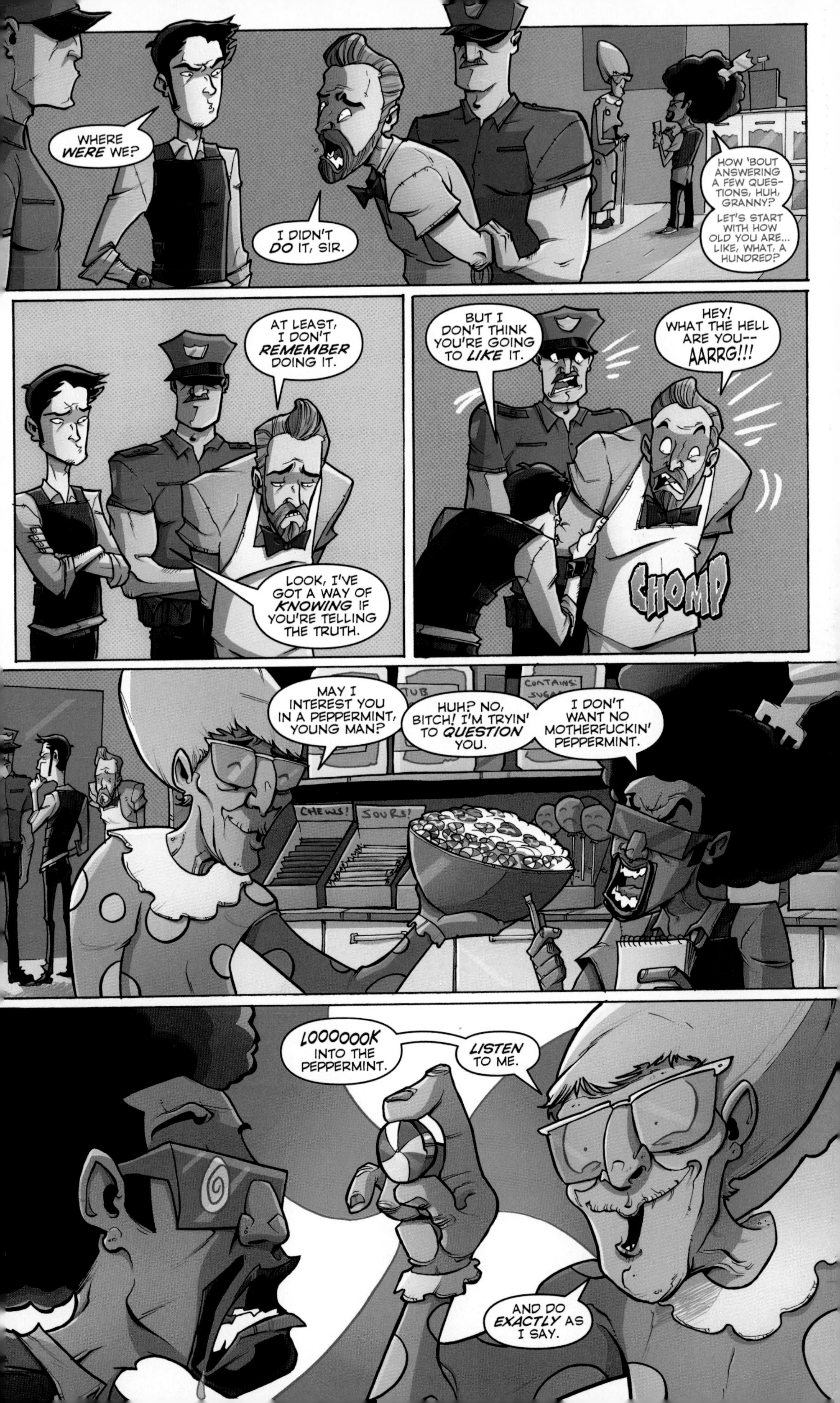
WHERE WERE WE?
I DIDN'T DO IT, SIR.
HOW 'BOUT ANSWERING A FEW QUES-TIONS, HUH, GRANNY?
LET'S START WITH HOW OLD YOU ARE... LIKE, WHAT, A HUNDRED?
AT LEAST, I DON'T REMEMBER DOING IT.
LOOK, I'VE GOT A WAY OF KNOWING IF YOU'RE TELLING THE TRUTH.
BUT I DON'T THINK YOU'RE GOING TO LIKE IT.
HEY! WHAT THE HELL ARE YOU-- AARRG!!!
CHOMP
MAY I INTEREST YOU IN A PEPPERMINT, YOUNG MAN?
HUH? NO, BITCH! I'M TRYIN' TO QUESTION YOU.
I DON'T WANT NO MOTHERFUCKIN' PEPPERMINT.
CHEWS!
SOURS!
LOOOOOOK INTO THE PEPPERMINT.
LISTEN TO ME.
AND DO EXACTLY AS I SAY.

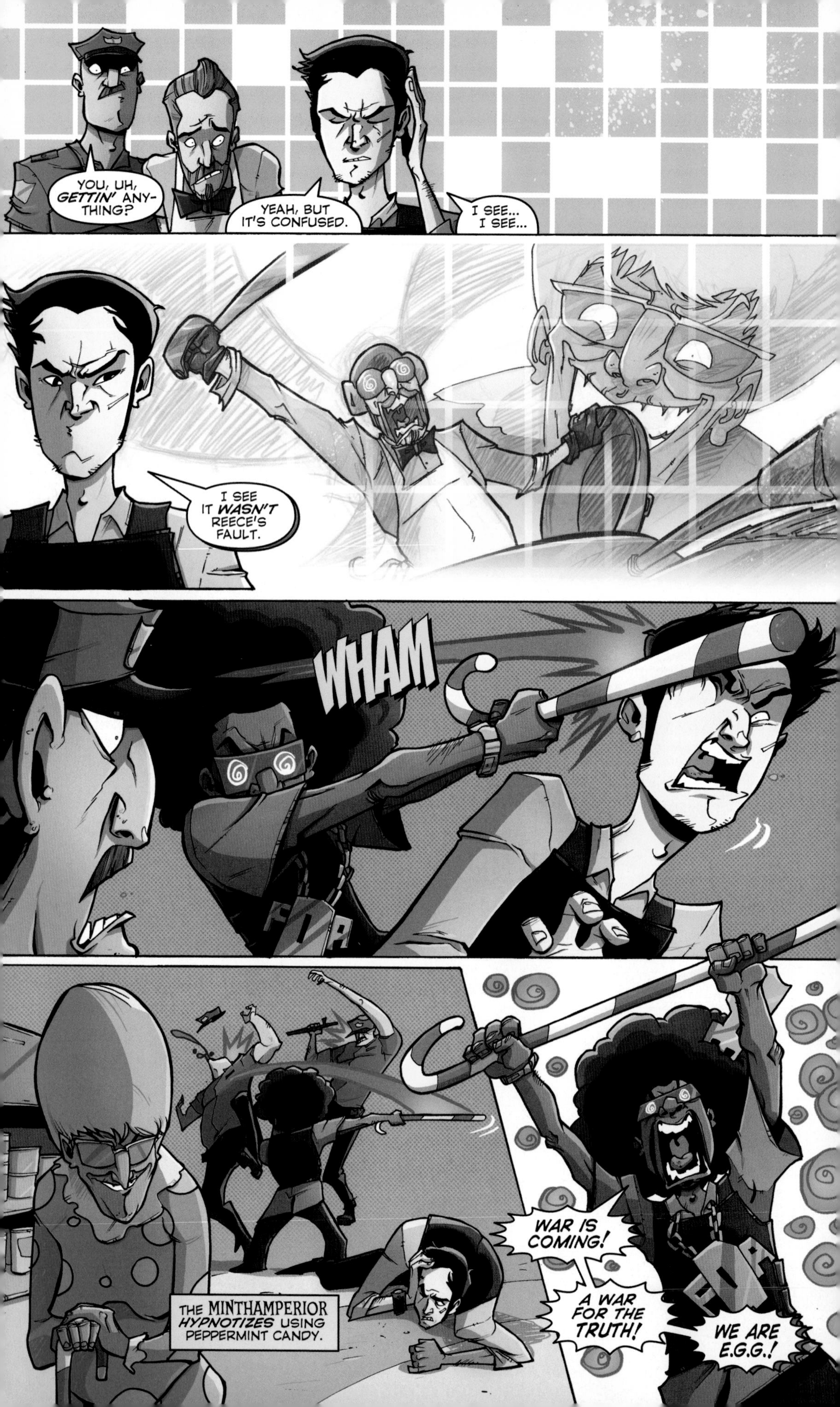

YOU, UH, *GETTIN'* ANY-THING?
YEAH, BUT IT'S CONFUSED.
I SEE... I SEE...
I SEE IT *WASN'T* REECE'S FAULT.
WHAM
THE MINTHAMPERIOR *HYPNOTIZES* USING PEPPERMINT CANDY.
WAR IS COMING!
A WAR FOR THE TRUTH!
WE ARE E.G.G.!

FWACK

I DON'T *THINK* SO.

SNAP *OUT* OF IT, D-BEAR.

AND *YOU*-- DON'T MOVE, LADY. YOU'RE *BUSTED*.

DOESN'T MATTER.

WAR *IS* COMING. AND YOU GOVERNMENT THUGS AREN'T GOING TO BE ABLE TO STOP IT UNTIL IT'S TOO *LATE*.

YOU CAN'T KEEP THE *TRUTH* FROM US FOREVER.

SUGAR EGGS SANCTIONE BY YOUR FDA OVERLORD

TAFFY STRIPS

SUGAR BITS

AS FOR ME, I'M EIGHTY-THREE. NO RECORD. FIRST OFFENSE.

SWEET DODDERING OLD NEIGHBORHOOD GRANDMOTHER, WHO'S MAYBE NOT ALL TOGETHER UPSTAIRS.

I FIGURE THE *WORST* THAT HAPPENS TO ME IS I GET A CUSHY CELL IN A PEPPERMINT-FREE *FDA* PRISON--

--RIDING OUT MY TWILIGHT YEARS WITH THREE MEALS A DAY AND A TAX-PAYER-FUNDED ROOF OVER MY HEAD.

tap tap

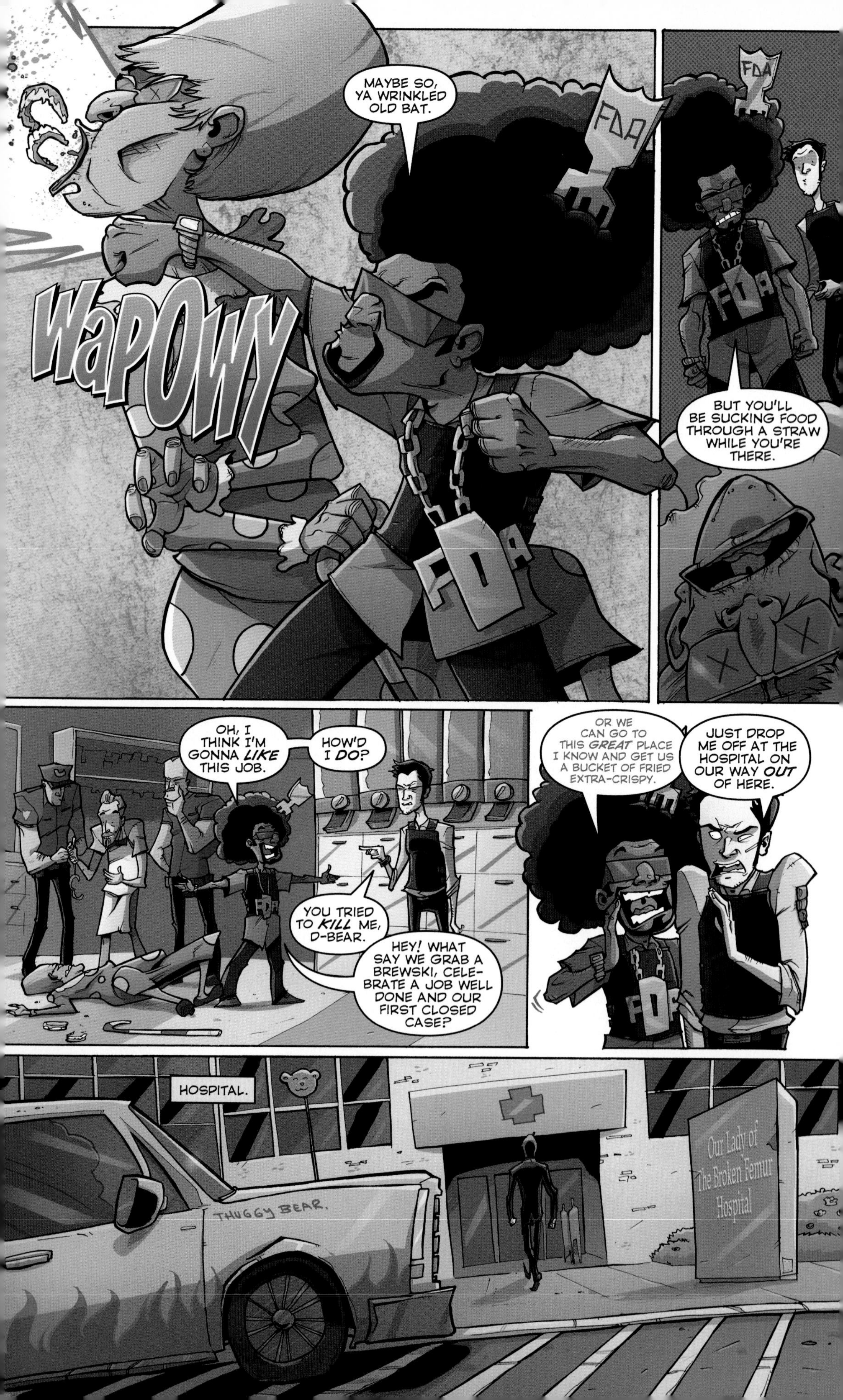
MAYBE SO, YA WRINKLED OLD BAT.
WAPOWY
BUT YOU'LL BE SUCKING FOOD THROUGH A STRAW WHILE YOU'RE THERE.
OH, I THINK I'M GONNA *LIKE* THIS JOB.
HOW'D I *DO*?
YOU TRIED TO *KILL* ME, D-BEAR.
HEY! WHAT SAY WE GRAB A BREWSKI, CELE-BRATE A JOB WELL DONE AND OUR FIRST CLOSED CASE?
OR WE CAN GO TO THIS *GREAT* PLACE I KNOW AND GET US A BUCKET OF FRIED EXTRA-CRISPY.
JUST DROP ME OFF AT THE HOSPITAL ON OUR WAY *OUT* OF HERE.
HOSPITAL.
THUGGY BEAR.
Our Lady of The Broken Femur Hospital

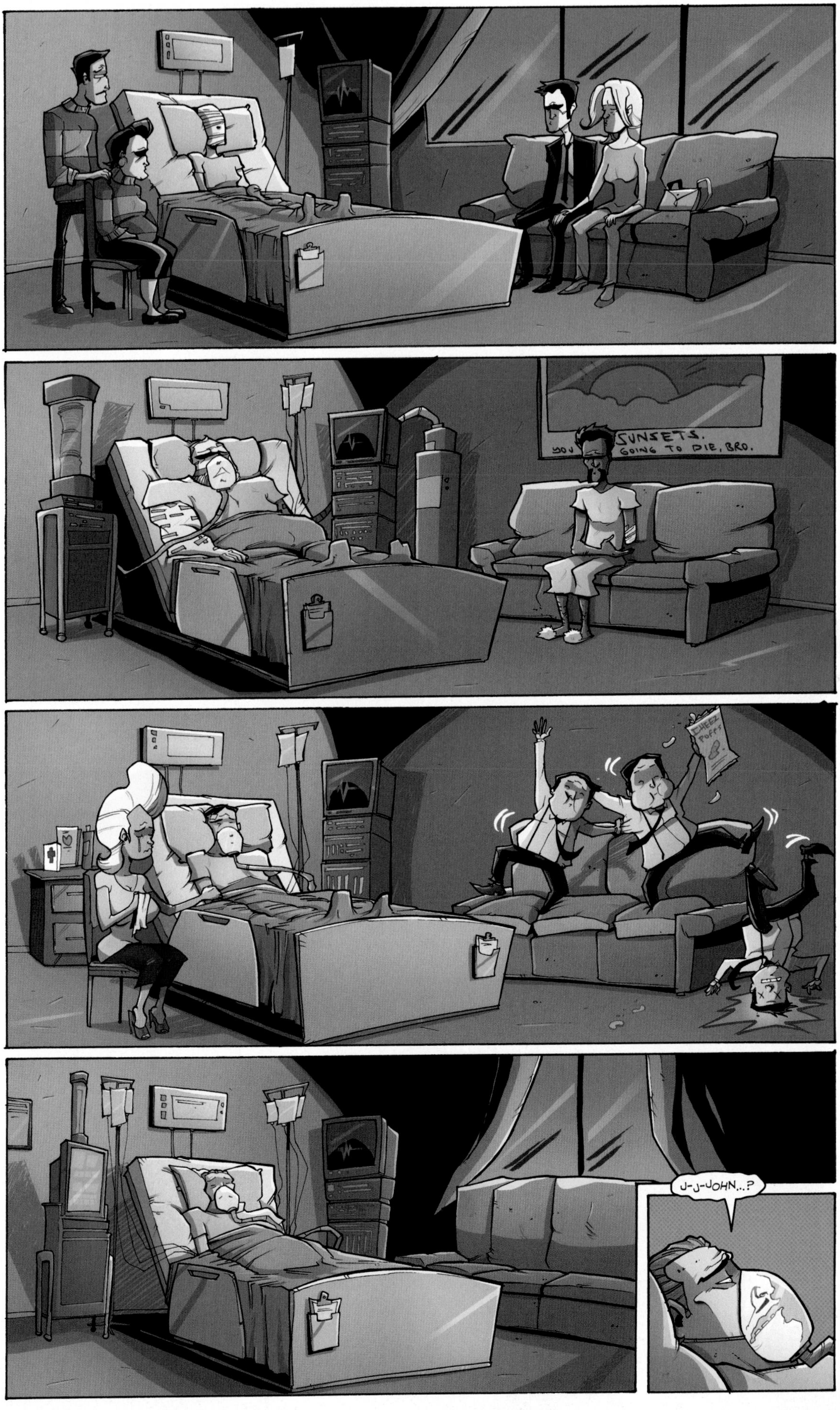
SUNSETS.
YOU
GOING TO DIE, BRO.
CHEEZ
POFFS
J-J-JOHN...?

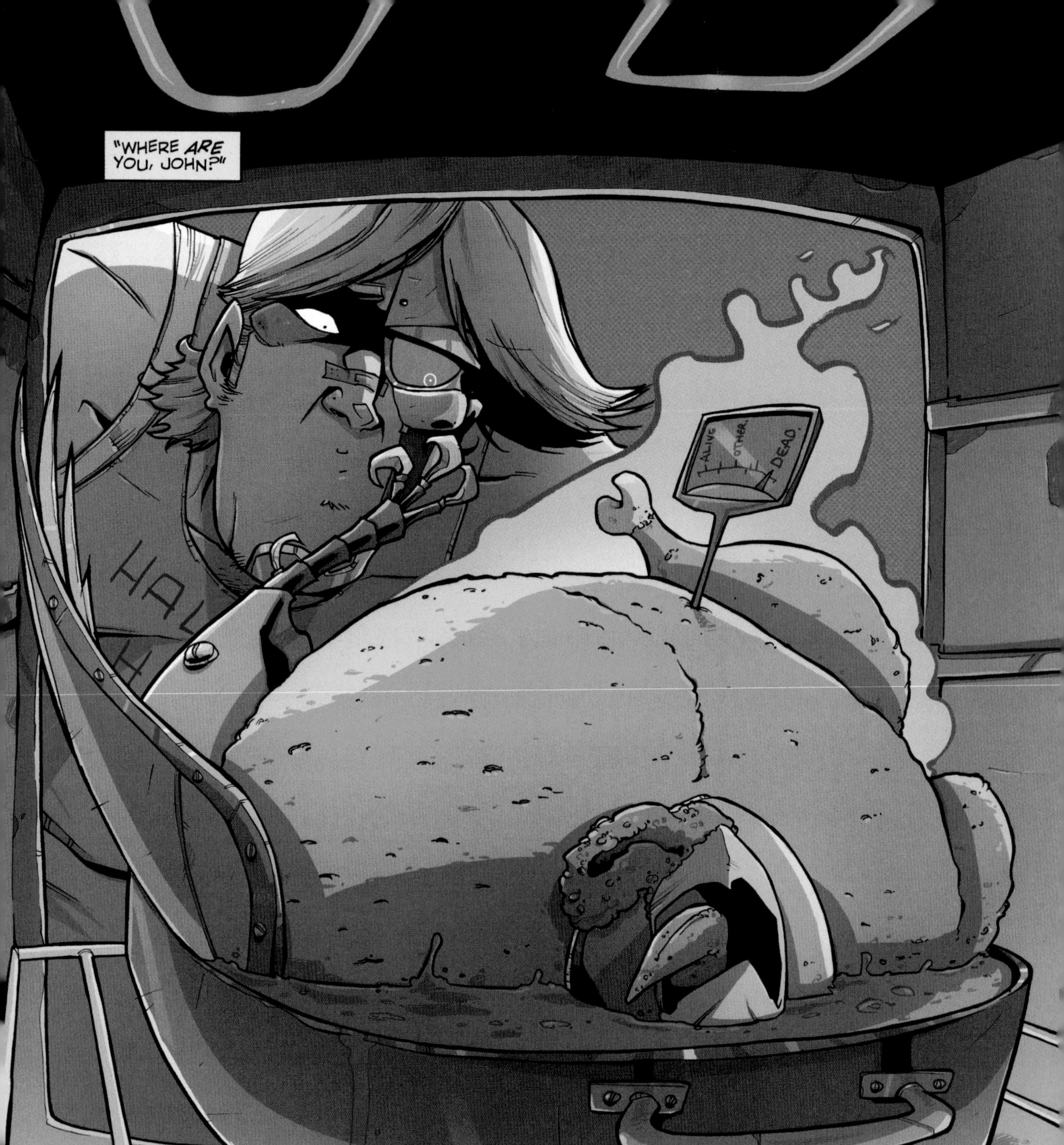
"WHERE ARE YOU, JOHN?"
ALIVE
OTHER
DEAD

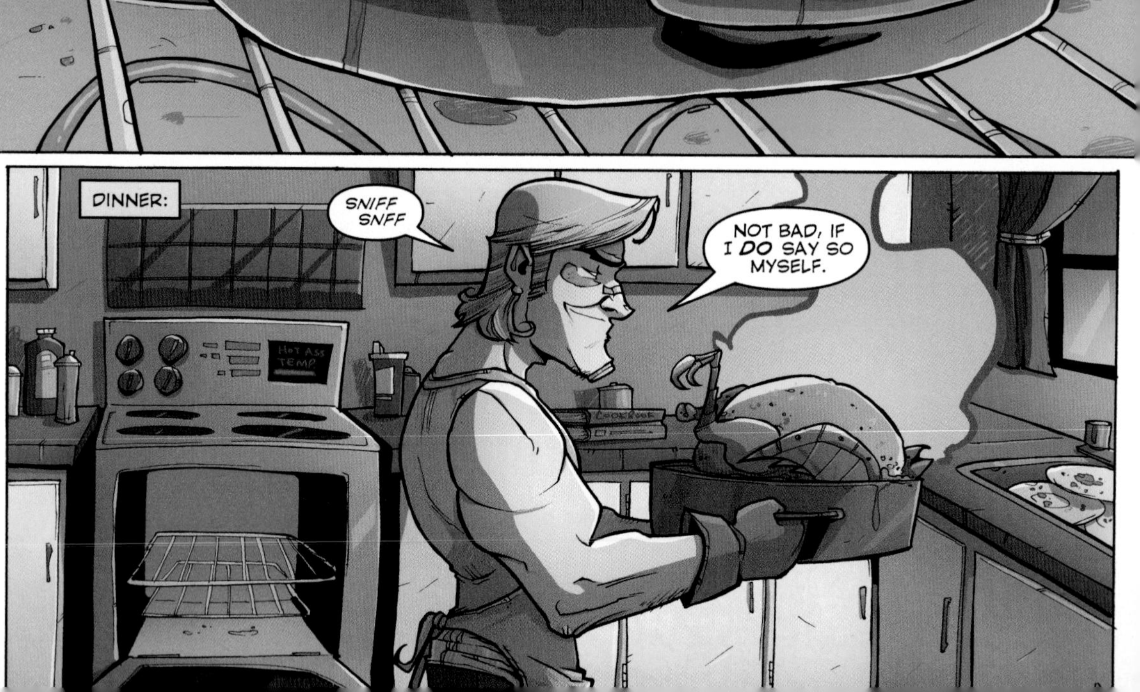
DINNER:
SNIFF SNFF
NOT BAD, IF I DO SAY SO MYSELF.
HOT ASS TEMP
COOKBOOK

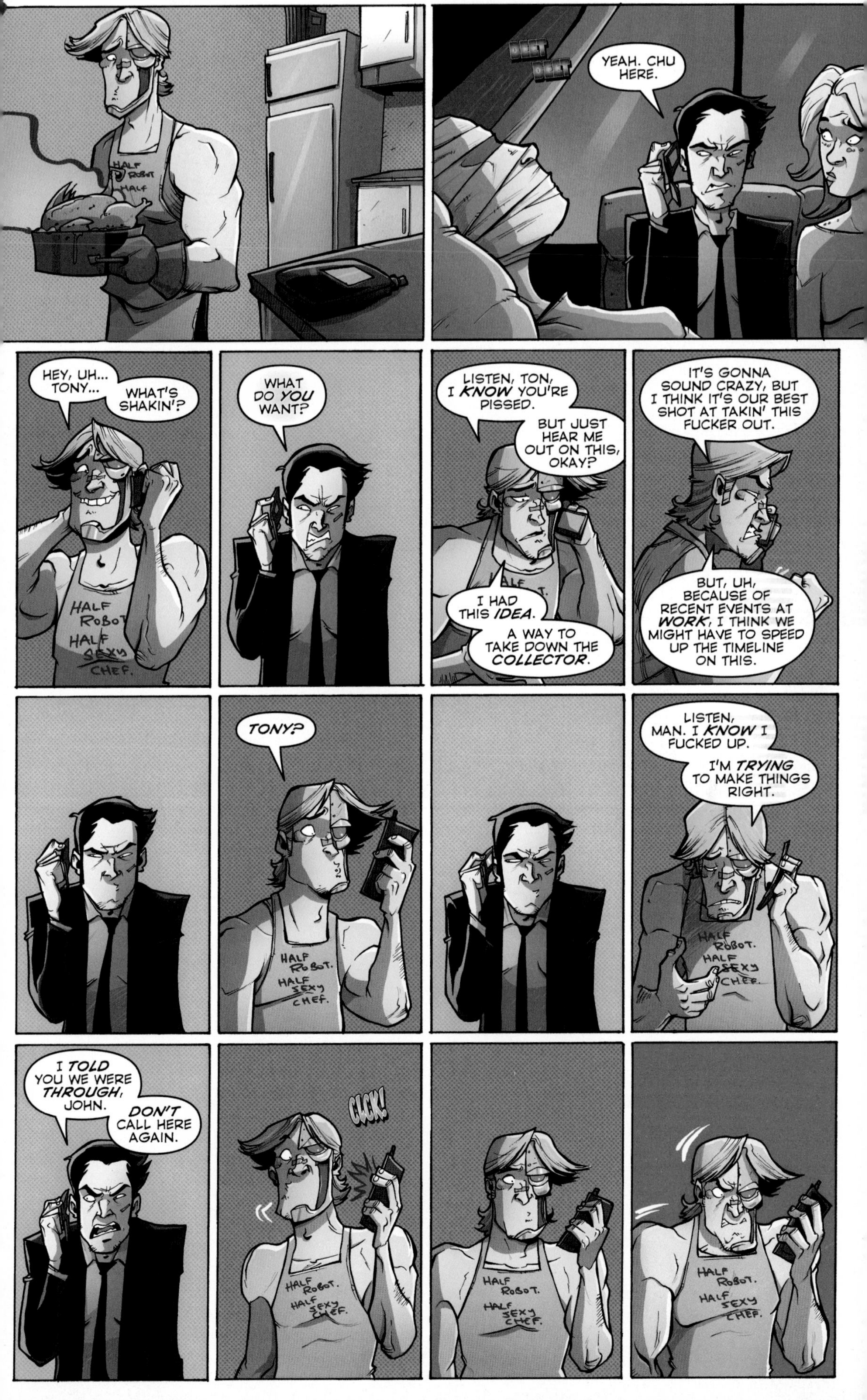
BEET BEET
YEAH. CHU HERE.
HALF ROBOT HALF
HEY, UH... TONY...
WHAT'S SHAKIN'?
HALF ROBOT HALF SEXY CHEF.
WHAT DO YOU WANT?
LISTEN, TON, I KNOW YOU'RE PISSED.
BUT JUST HEAR ME OUT ON THIS, OKAY?
I HAD THIS IDEA.
A WAY TO TAKE DOWN THE COLLECTOR.
IT'S GONNA SOUND CRAZY, BUT I THINK IT'S OUR BEST SHOT AT TAKIN' THIS FUCKER OUT.
BUT, UH, BECAUSE OF RECENT EVENTS AT WORK, I THINK WE MIGHT HAVE TO SPEED UP THE TIMELINE ON THIS.
TONY?
HALF ROBOT. HALF SEXY CHEF.
LISTEN, MAN. I KNOW I FUCKED UP.
I'M TRYING TO MAKE THINGS RIGHT.
HALF ROBOT. HALF SEXY CHEF.
I TOLD YOU WE WERE THROUGH, JOHN.
DON'T CALL HERE AGAIN.
CLICK!
HALF ROBOT. HALF SEXY CHEF.
HALF ROBOT. HALF SEXY CHEF.
HALF ROBOT. HALF SEXY CHEF.

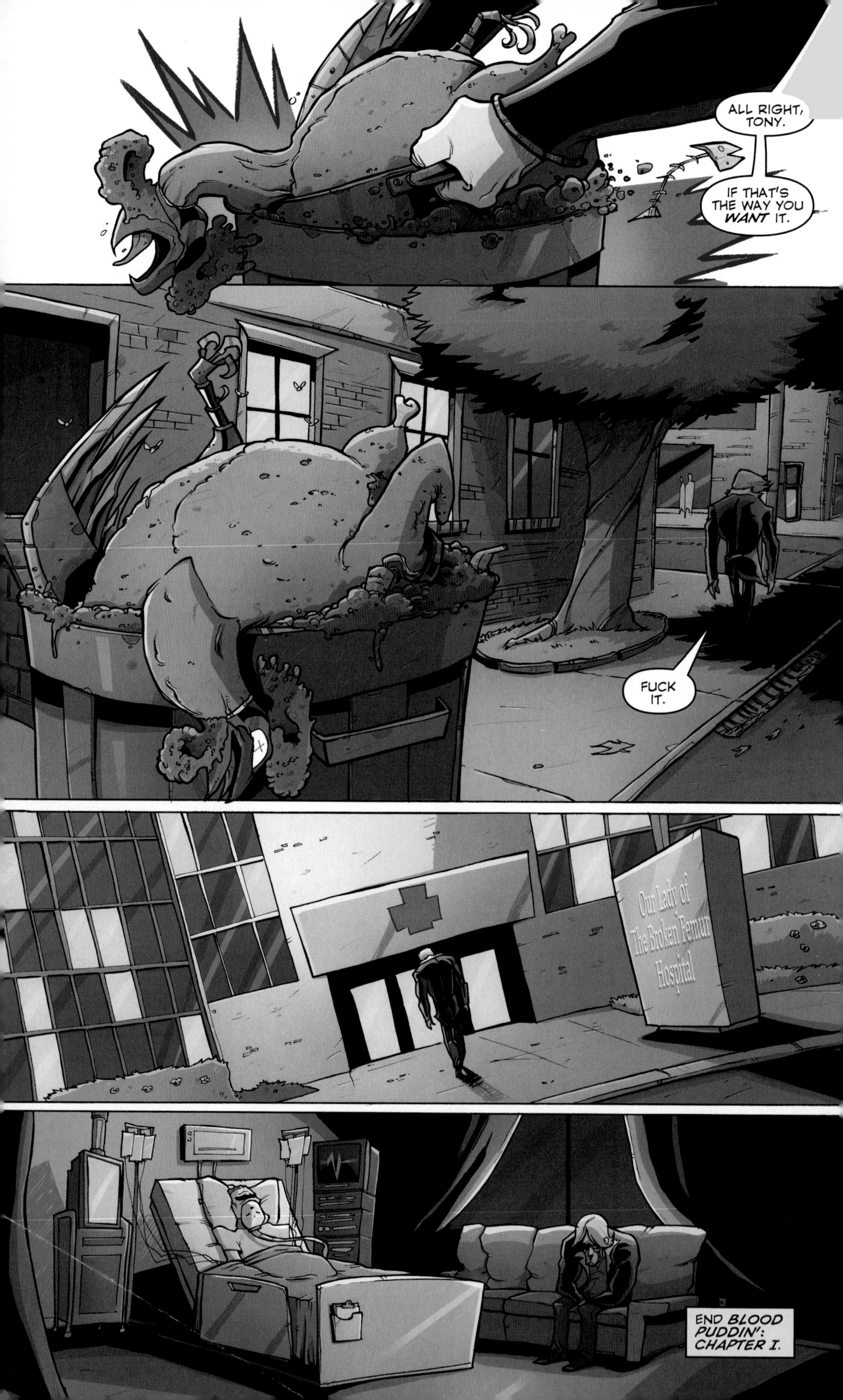
ALL RIGHT, TONY.
IF THAT'S THE WAY YOU *WANT* IT.
FUCK IT.
Our Lady of The Broken Femur Hospital
END *BLOOD PUDDIN'*: *CHAPTER I.*

Chapter 2

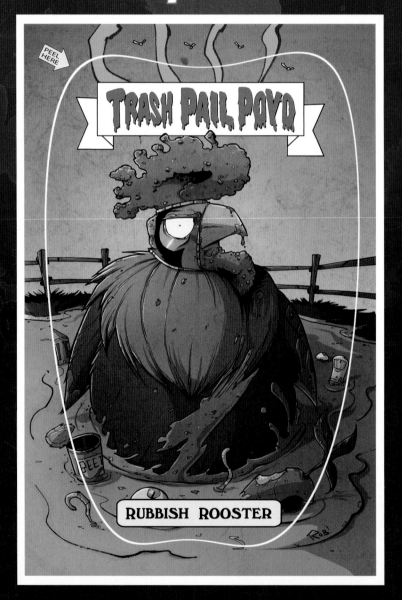

PEEL HERE

TRASH PAIL PAYO

RUBBISH ROOSTER

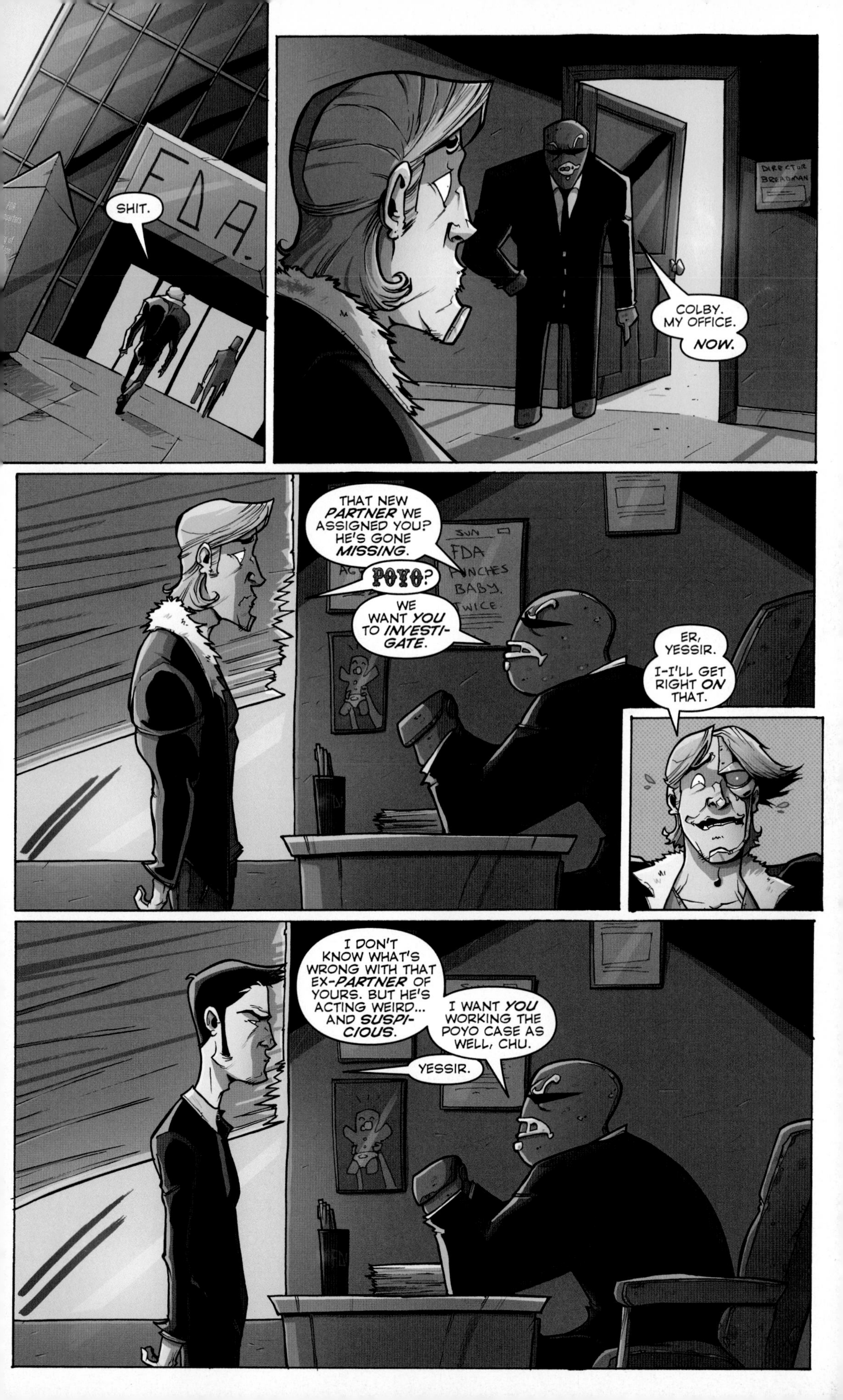
SHIT.
FDA
DIRECTOR BREADMAN
COLBY. MY OFFICE. NOW.
THAT NEW PARTNER WE ASSIGNED YOU? HE'S GONE MISSING.
POYO?
WE WANT YOU TO INVESTIGATE.
FDA PUNCHES BABY. TWICE.
ER, YESSIR. I-I'LL GET RIGHT ON THAT.
I DON'T KNOW WHAT'S WRONG WITH THAT EX-PARTNER OF YOURS. BUT HE'S ACTING WEIRD... AND SUSPICIOUS.
I WANT YOU WORKING THE POYO CASE AS WELL, CHU.
YESSIR.

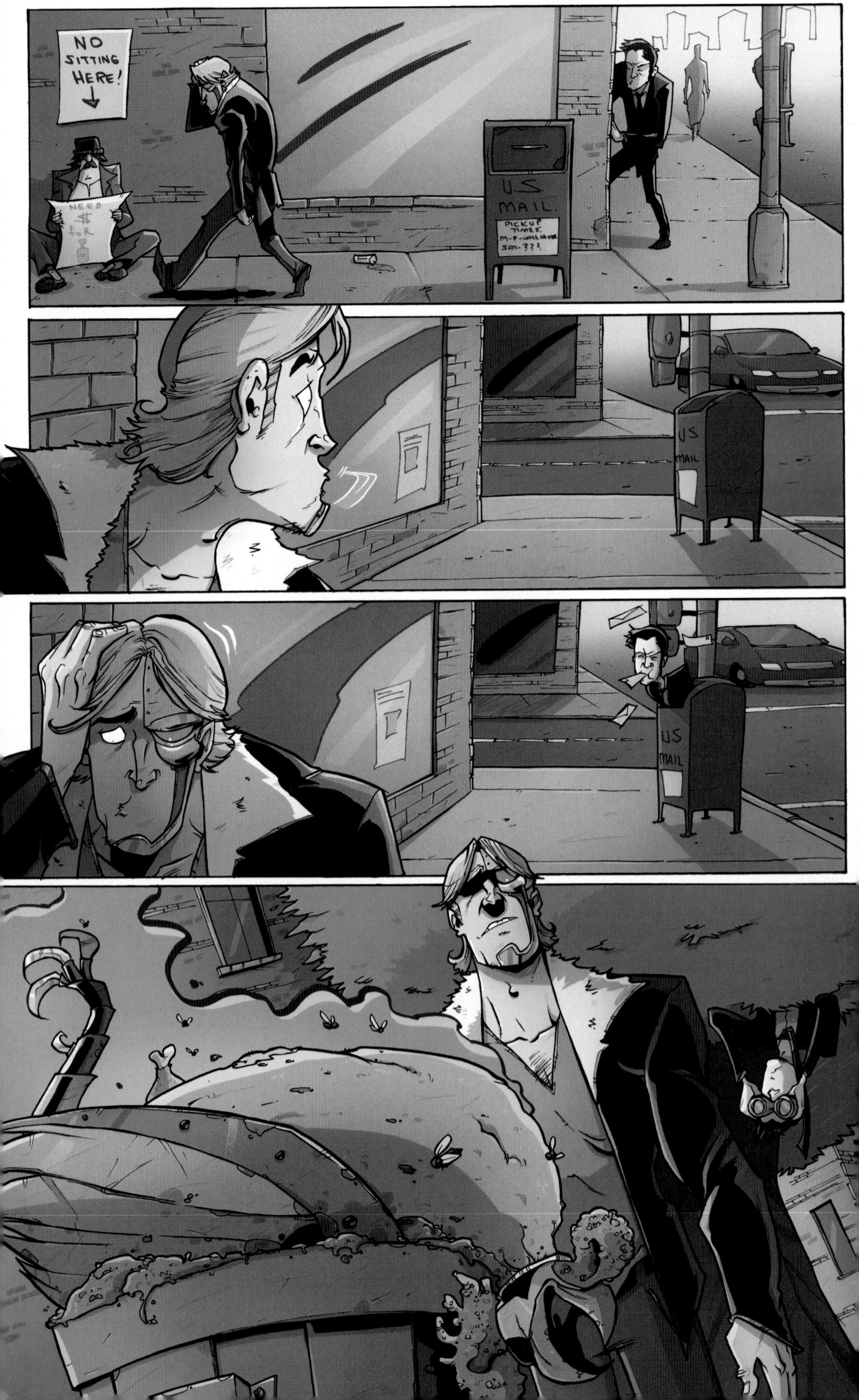
NO SITTING HERE!
NEED $ FOR
U.S MAIL.
PICKUP TIMES: M-F-WHENEVER SAT-???
US MAIL
US MAIL

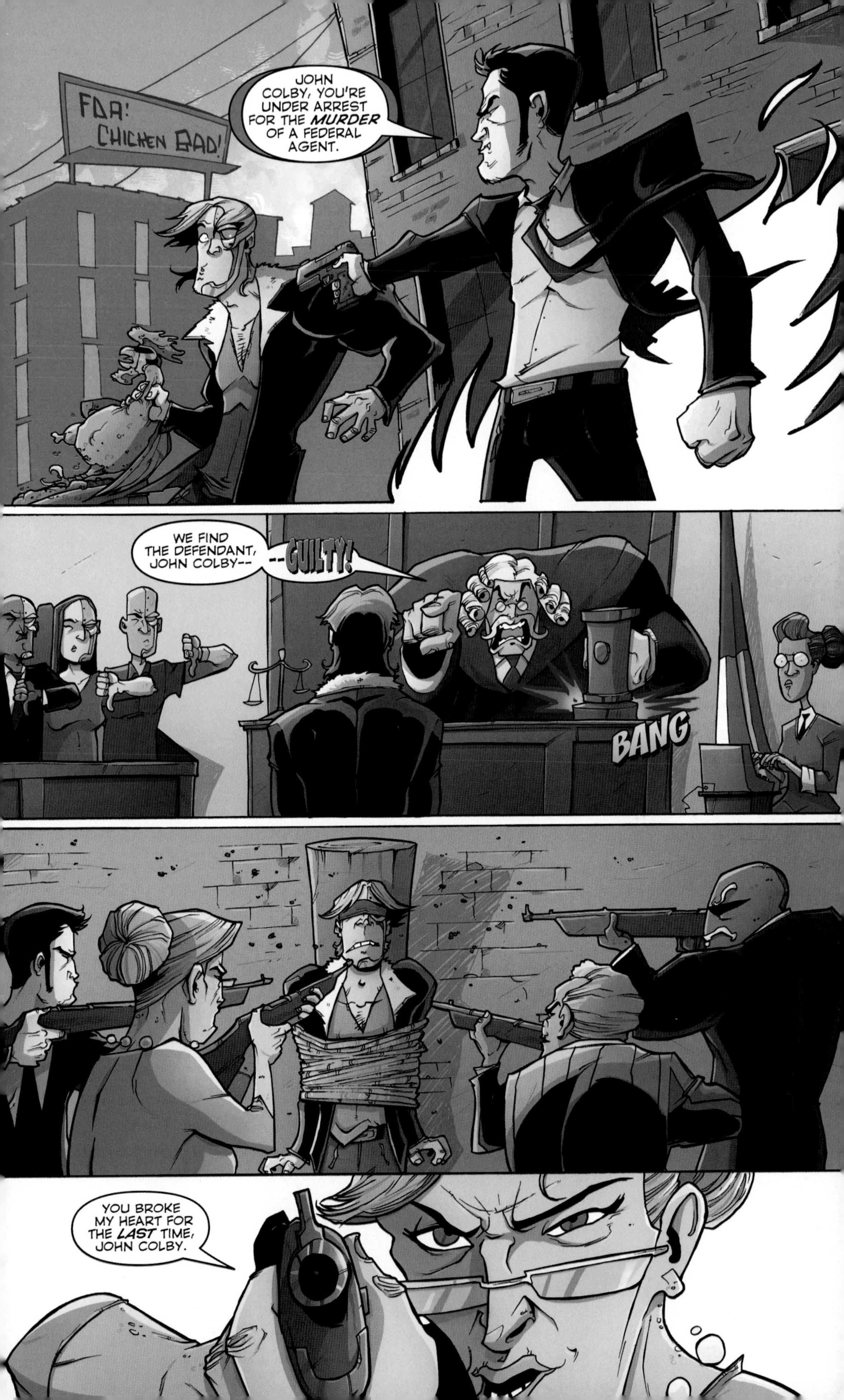
FDA! CHICKEN BAD!
JOHN COLBY, YOU'RE UNDER ARREST FOR THE MURDER OF A FEDERAL AGENT.
WE FIND THE DEFENDANT, JOHN COLBY--
--GUILTY!
BANG
YOU BROKE MY HEART FOR THE LAST TIME, JOHN COLBY.

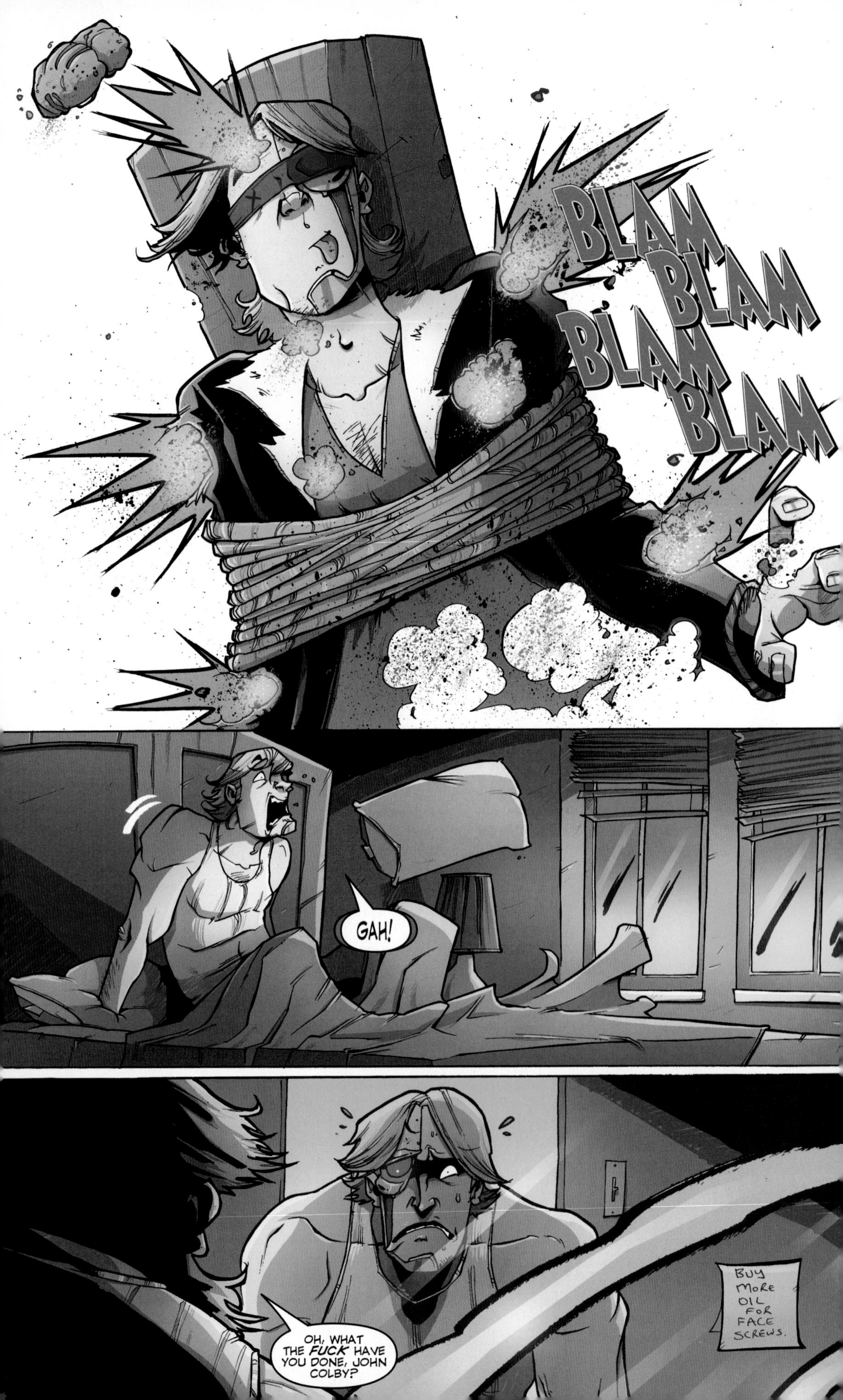
BLAM
BLAM
BLAM
BLAM
GAH!
OH, WHAT THE FUCK HAVE YOU DONE, JOHN COLBY?
BUY MORE OIL FOR FACE SCREWS.

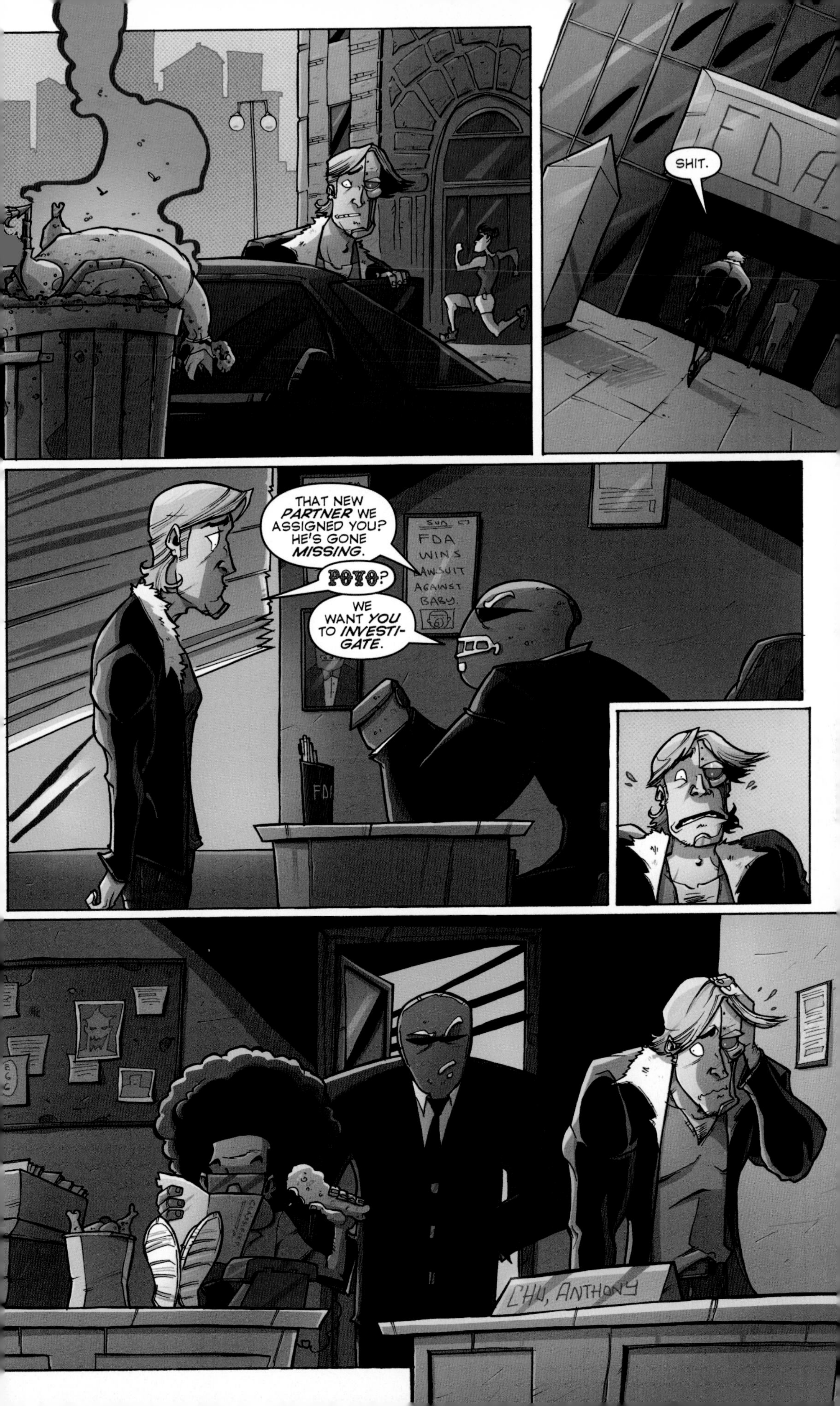

SHIT.
THAT NEW *PARTNER* WE ASSIGNED YOU? HE'S GONE *MISSING*.
FDA WINS LAWSUIT AGAINST BABY.
POYO?
WE WANT *YOU* TO *INVESTI-GATE*.
FDA
CHU, ANTHONY

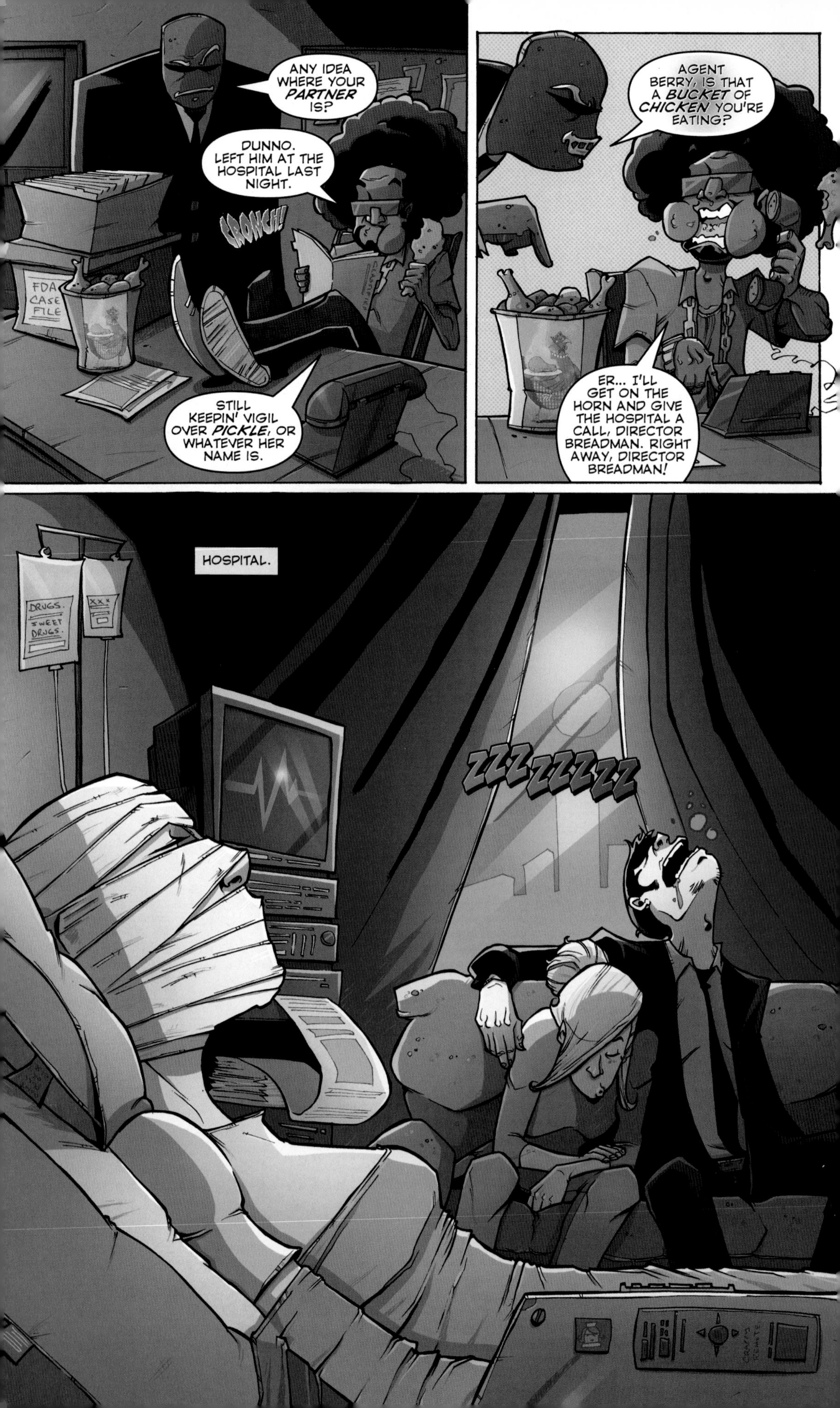
ANY IDEA WHERE YOUR PARTNER IS?
DUNNO. LEFT HIM AT THE HOSPITAL LAST NIGHT.
CRONCH!
STILL KEEPIN' VIGIL OVER PICKLE, OR WHATEVER HER NAME IS.
FDA CASE FILE
AGENT BERRY, IS THAT A BUCKET OF CHICKEN YOU'RE EATING?
ER... I'LL GET ON THE HORN AND GIVE THE HOSPITAL A CALL, DIRECTOR BREADMAN. RIGHT AWAY, DIRECTOR BREADMAN!
HOSPITAL.
DRUGS. SWEET DRUGS.
ZZZZZZZZ

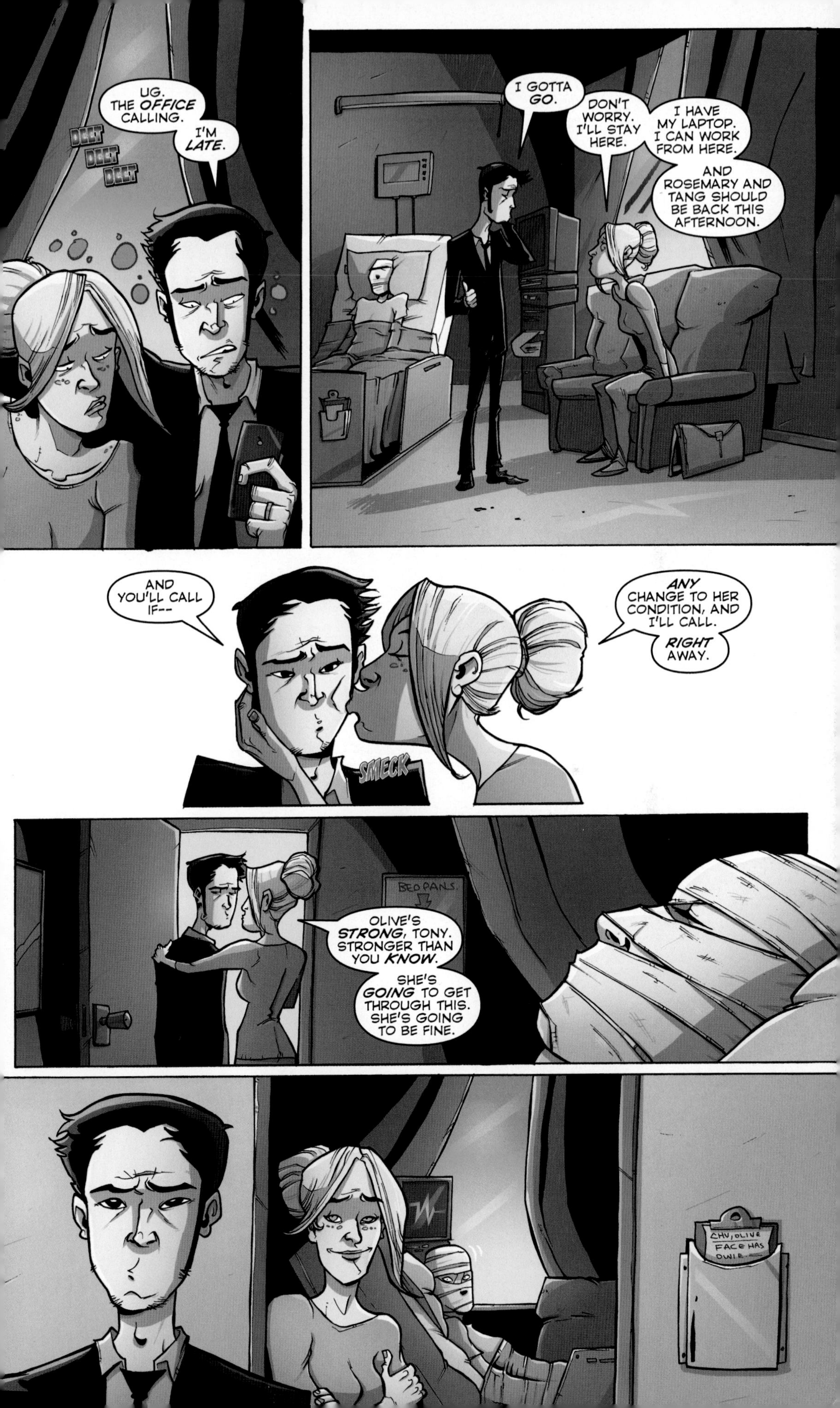

DEET
DEET
DEET
UG. THE *OFFICE* CALLING.
I'M *LATE*.
I GOTTA *GO*.
DON'T WORRY. I'LL STAY HERE.
I HAVE MY LAPTOP. I CAN WORK FROM HERE.
AND ROSEMARY AND TANG SHOULD BE BACK THIS AFTERNOON.
AND YOU'LL CALL IF--
ANY CHANGE TO HER CONDITION, AND I'LL CALL.
RIGHT AWAY.
SMECK
BED PANS.
OLIVE'S *STRONG*, TONY. STRONGER THAN YOU *KNOW*.
SHE'S *GOING* TO GET THROUGH THIS. SHE'S GOING TO BE FINE.
CHU, OLIVE
FACE HAS OWIE.

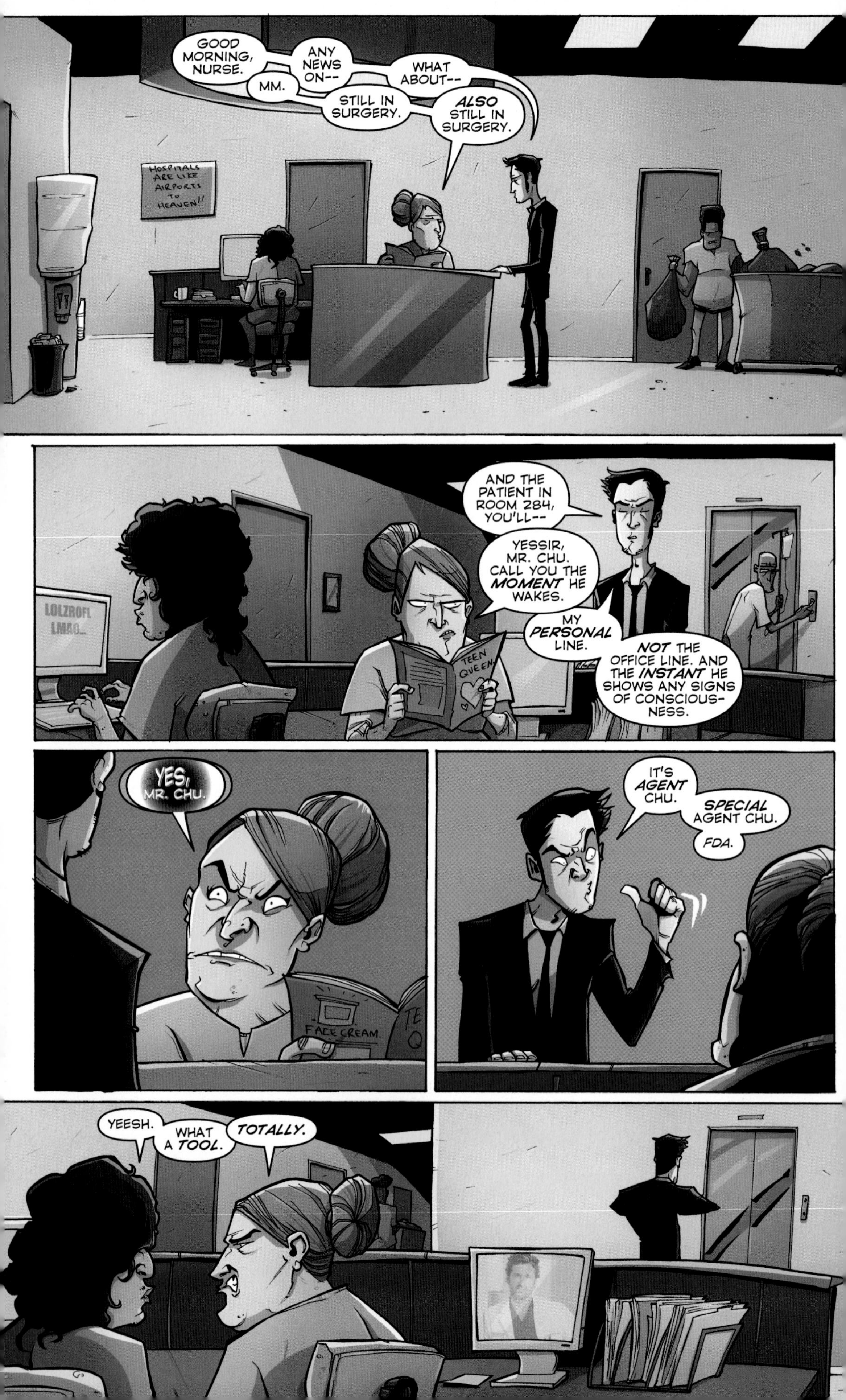
GOOD MORNING, NURSE.
MM.
ANY NEWS ON--
STILL IN SURGERY.
WHAT ABOUT--
ALSO STILL IN SURGERY.
HOSPITALS ARE LIKE AIRPORTS TO HEAVEN!!
AND THE PATIENT IN ROOM 284, YOU'LL--
YESSIR, MR. CHU. CALL YOU THE MOMENT HE WAKES.
MY PERSONAL LINE.
NOT THE OFFICE LINE. AND THE INSTANT HE SHOWS ANY SIGNS OF CONSCIOUS-NESS.
LOLZROFL LMAO...
TEEN QUEEN
YES, MR. CHU.
FACE CREAM.
IT'S AGENT CHU.
SPECIAL AGENT CHU.
FDA.
YEESH.
WHAT A TOOL.
TOTALLY.

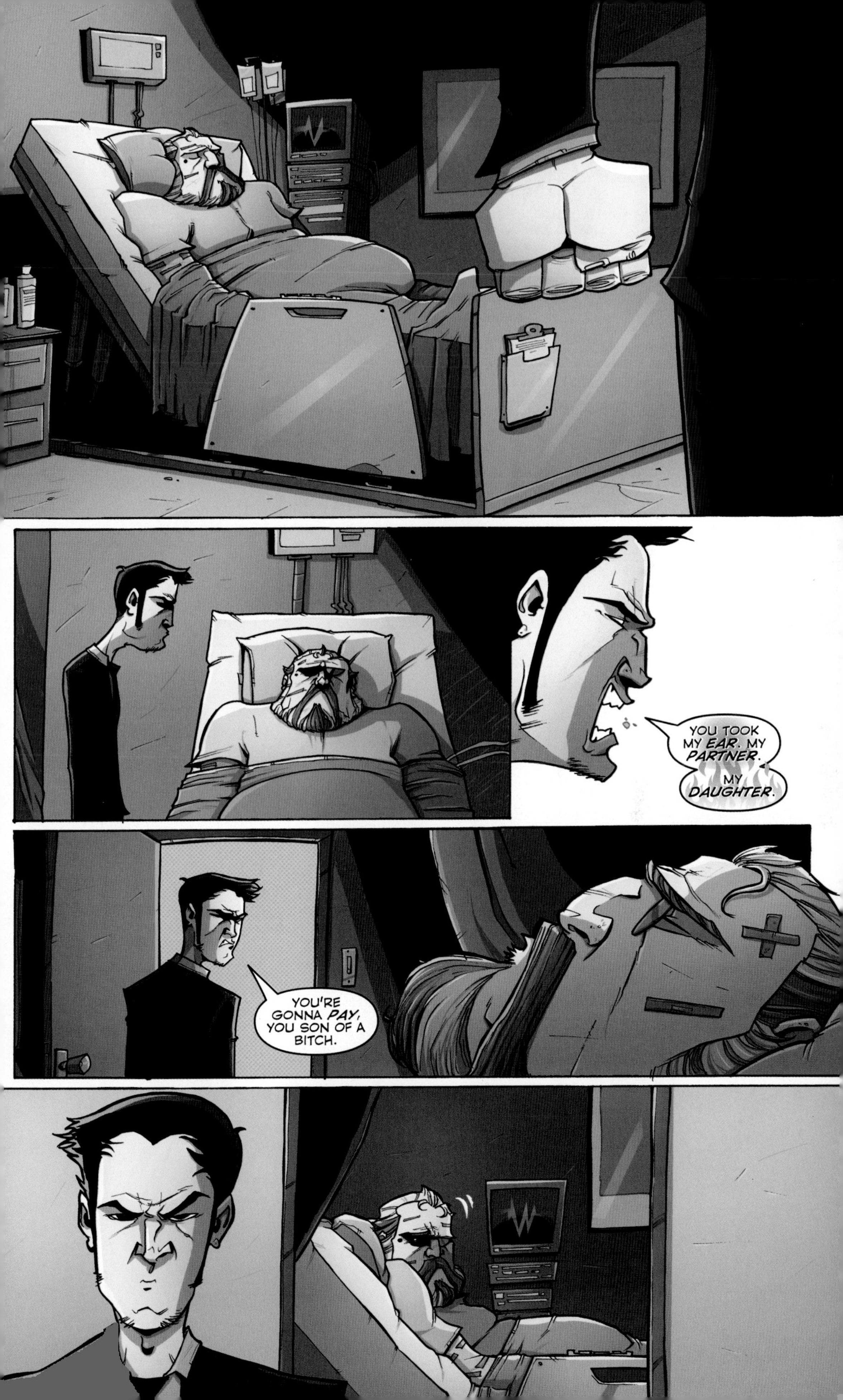
YOU TOOK MY EAR. MY PARTNER.
MY DAUGHTER.
YOU'RE GONNA PAY, YOU SON OF A BITCH.

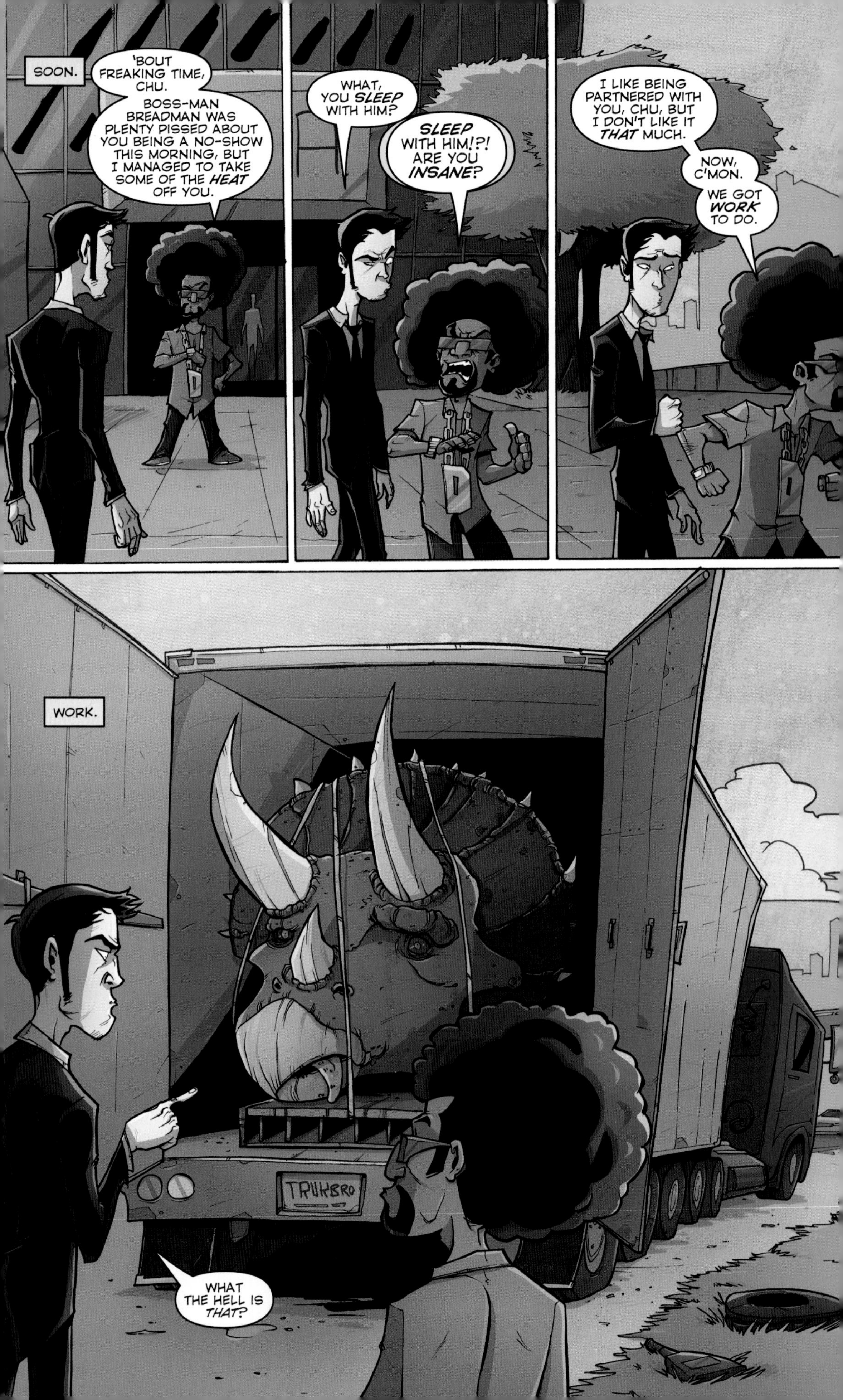
SOON.
'BOUT FREAKING TIME, CHU.
BOSS-MAN BREADMAN WAS PLENTY PISSED ABOUT YOU BEING A NO-SHOW THIS MORNING, BUT I MANAGED TO TAKE SOME OF THE *HEAT* OFF YOU.
WHAT, YOU *SLEEP* WITH HIM?
SLEEP WITH HIM!?! ARE YOU *INSANE*?
I LIKE BEING PARTNERED WITH YOU, CHU, BUT I DON'T LIKE IT *THAT* MUCH.
NOW, C'MON.
WE GOT *WORK* TO DO.
WORK.
TRUKBRO
WHAT THE HELL IS *THAT*?

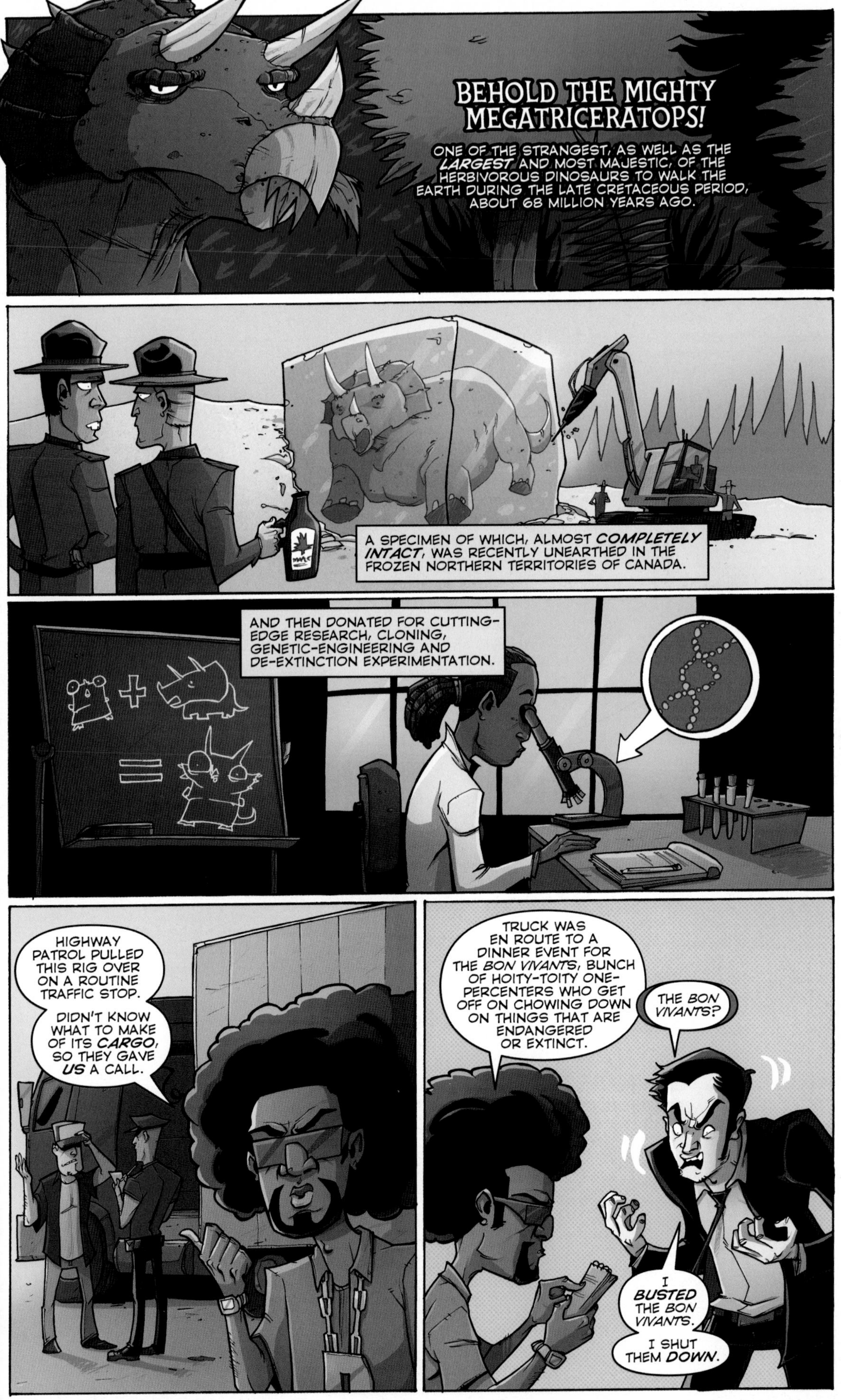
BEHOLD THE MIGHTY MEGATRICERATOPS!
ONE OF THE STRANGEST, AS WELL AS THE LARGEST AND MOST MAJESTIC, OF THE HERBIVOROUS DINOSAURS TO WALK THE EARTH DURING THE LATE CRETACEOUS PERIOD, ABOUT 68 MILLION YEARS AGO.
A SPECIMEN OF WHICH, ALMOST COMPLETELY INTACT, WAS RECENTLY UNEARTHED IN THE FROZEN NORTHERN TERRITORIES OF CANADA.
AND THEN DONATED FOR CUTTING-EDGE RESEARCH, CLONING, GENETIC-ENGINEERING AND DE-EXTINCTION EXPERIMENTATION.
HIGHWAY PATROL PULLED THIS RIG OVER ON A ROUTINE TRAFFIC STOP.
DIDN'T KNOW WHAT TO MAKE OF ITS CARGO, SO THEY GAVE US A CALL.
TRUCK WAS EN ROUTE TO A DINNER EVENT FOR THE BON VIVANTS, BUNCH OF HOITY-TOITY ONE-PERCENTERS WHO GET OFF ON CHOWING DOWN ON THINGS THAT ARE ENDANGERED OR EXTINCT.
THE BON VIVANTS?
I BUSTED THE BON VIVANTS.
I SHUT THEM DOWN.

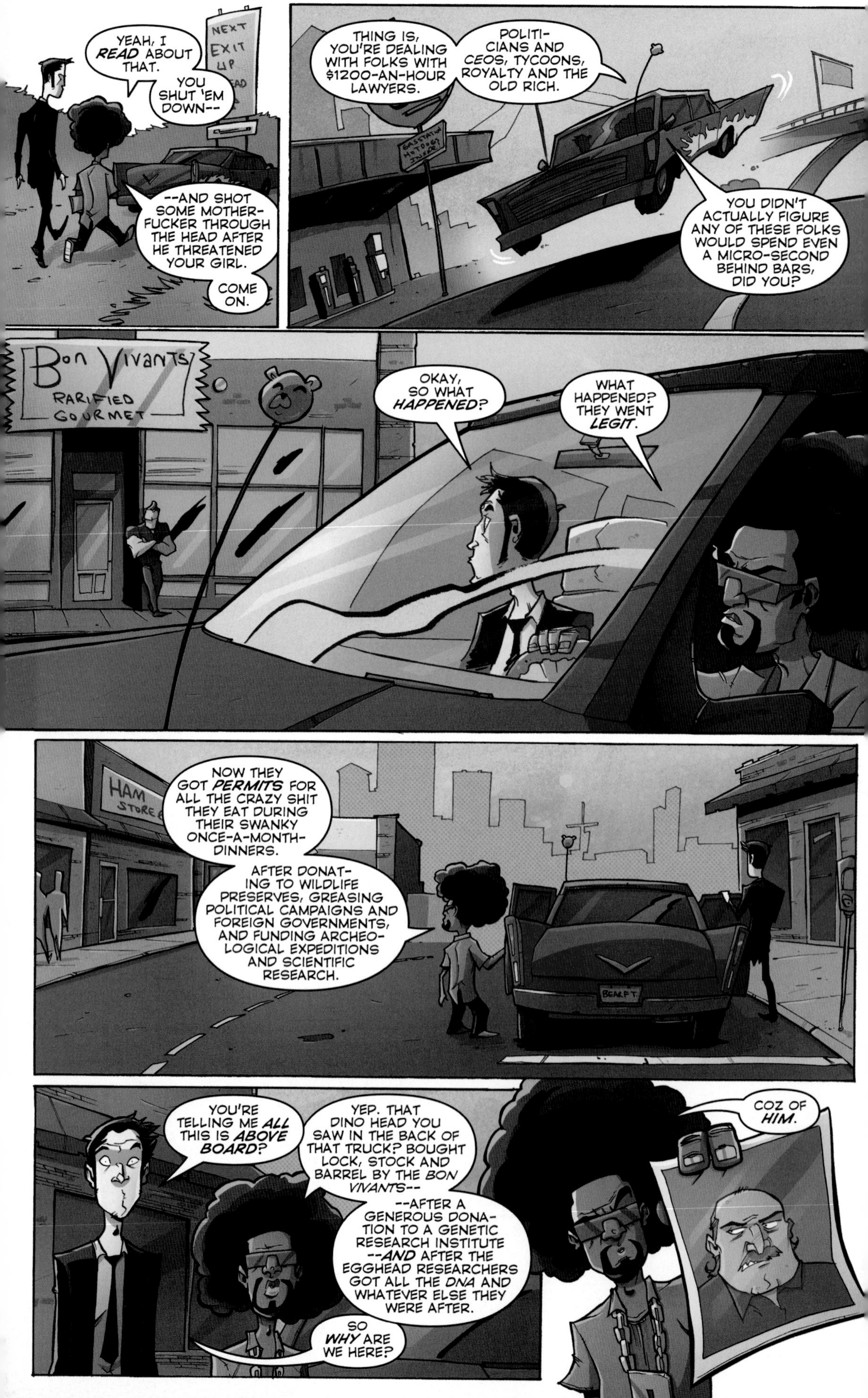

YEAH, I READ ABOUT THAT.
YOU SHUT 'EM DOWN--
--AND SHOT SOME MOTHER-FUCKER THROUGH THE HEAD AFTER HE THREATENED YOUR GIRL.
COME ON.
NEXT EXIT UP
THING IS, YOU'RE DEALING WITH FOLKS WITH $1200-AN-HOUR LAWYERS.
POLITI-CIANS AND CEOS, TYCOONS, ROYALTY AND THE OLD RICH.
YOU DIDN'T ACTUALLY FIGURE ANY OF THESE FOLKS WOULD SPEND EVEN A MICRO-SECOND BEHIND BARS, DID YOU?
Bon Vivants RARIFIED GOURMET
OKAY, SO WHAT HAPPENED?
WHAT HAPPENED? THEY WENT LEGIT.
HAM STORE
NOW THEY GOT PERMITS FOR ALL THE CRAZY SHIT THEY EAT DURING THEIR SWANKY ONCE-A-MONTH-DINNERS.
AFTER DONAT-ING TO WILDLIFE PRESERVES, GREASING POLITICAL CAMPAIGNS AND FOREIGN GOVERNMENTS, AND FUNDING ARCHEO-LOGICAL EXPEDITIONS AND SCIENTIFIC RESEARCH.
YOU'RE TELLING ME ALL THIS IS ABOVE BOARD?
YEP. THAT DINO HEAD YOU SAW IN THE BACK OF THAT TRUCK? BOUGHT LOCK, STOCK AND BARREL BY THE BON VIVANTS--
--AFTER A GENEROUS DONA-TION TO A GENETIC RESEARCH INSTITUTE --AND AFTER THE EGGHEAD RESEARCHERS GOT ALL THE DNA AND WHATEVER ELSE THEY WERE AFTER.
SO WHY ARE WE HERE?
COZ OF HIM.

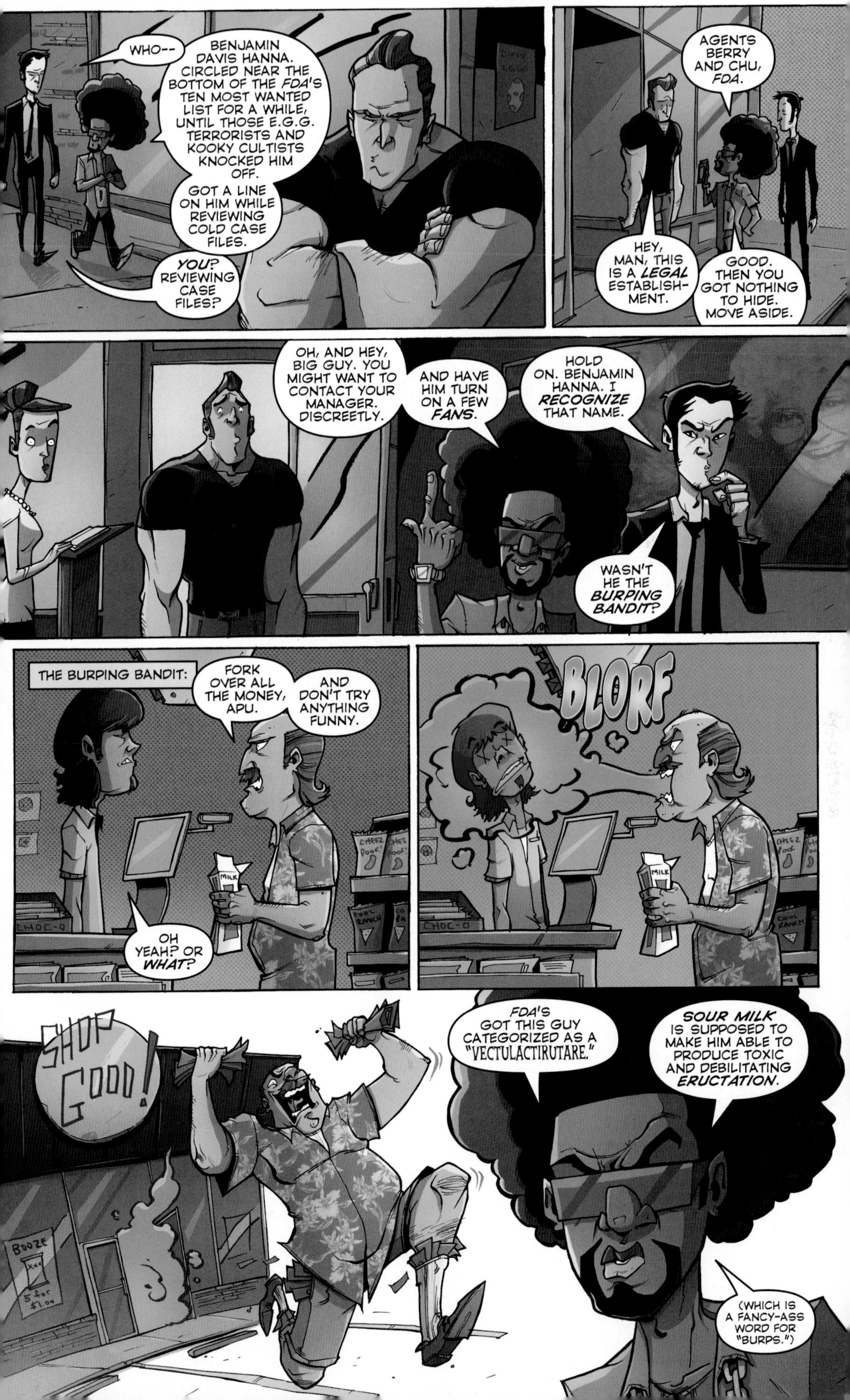
WHO--
BENJAMIN DAVIS HANNA. CIRCLED NEAR THE BOTTOM OF THE FDA'S TEN MOST WANTED LIST FOR A WHILE, UNTIL THOSE E.G.G. TERRORISTS AND KOOKY CULTISTS KNOCKED HIM OFF.
GOT A LINE ON HIM WHILE REVIEWING COLD CASE FILES.
YOU? REVIEWING CASE FILES?
AGENTS BERRY AND CHU, FDA.
HEY, MAN, THIS IS A LEGAL ESTABLISHMENT.
GOOD. THEN YOU GOT NOTHING TO HIDE. MOVE ASIDE.
OH, AND HEY, BIG GUY. YOU MIGHT WANT TO CONTACT YOUR MANAGER. DISCREETLY.
AND HAVE HIM TURN ON A FEW FANS.
HOLD ON. BENJAMIN HANNA. I RECOGNIZE THAT NAME.
WASN'T HE THE BURPING BANDIT?
THE BURPING BANDIT:
FORK OVER ALL THE MONEY, APU.
AND DON'T TRY ANYTHING FUNNY.
OH YEAH? OR WHAT?
BLORF
SHOP GOOD!
BOOZE
5 for $1.00
FDA'S GOT THIS GUY CATEGORIZED AS A "VECTULACTIRUTARE."
SOUR MILK IS SUPPOSED TO MAKE HIM ABLE TO PRODUCE TOXIC AND DEBILITATING ERUCTATION.
(WHICH IS A FANCY-ASS WORD FOR "BURPS.")

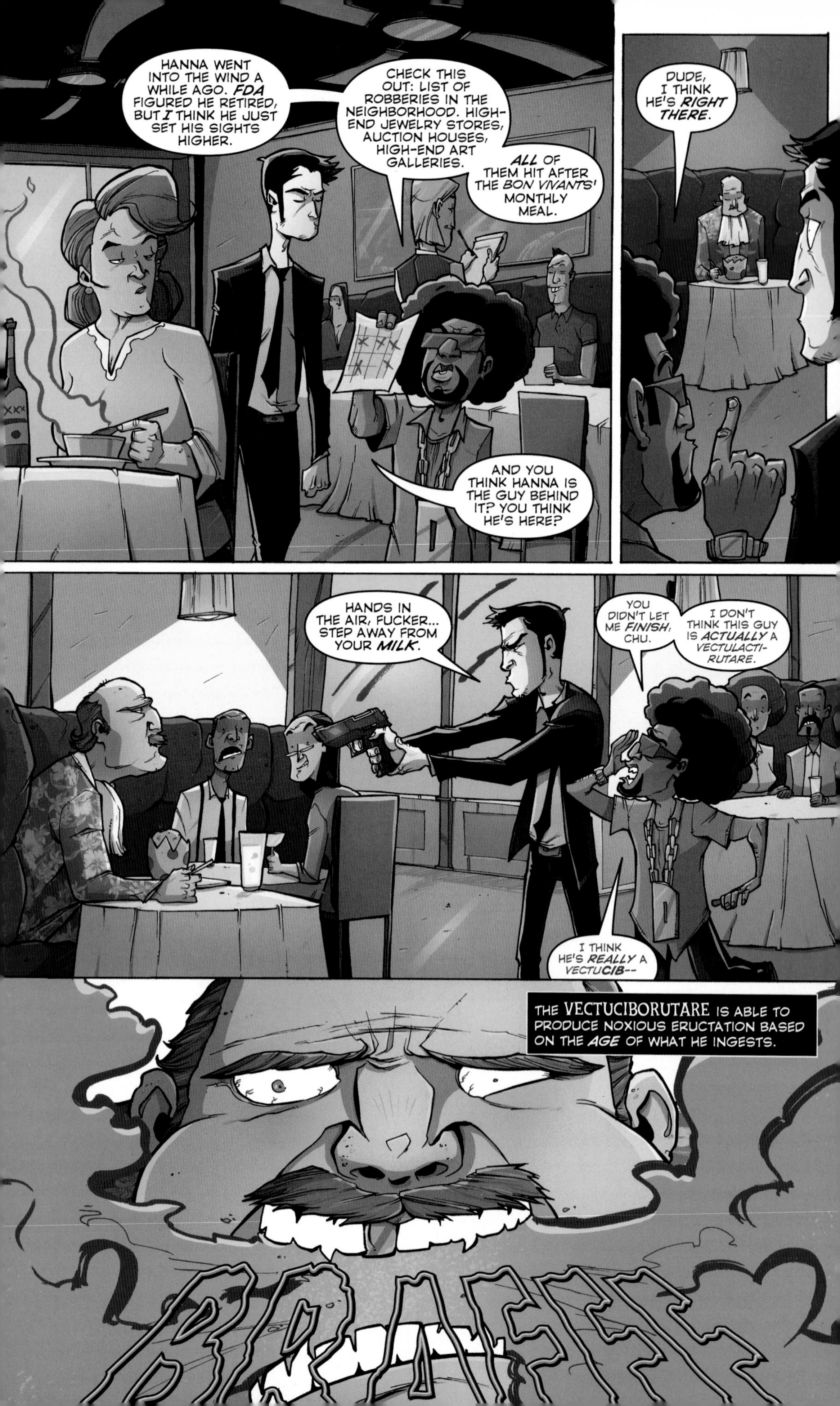

HANNA WENT INTO THE WIND A WHILE AGO. FDA FIGURED HE RETIRED, BUT I THINK HE JUST SET HIS SIGHTS HIGHER.
CHECK THIS OUT: LIST OF ROBBERIES IN THE NEIGHBORHOOD. HIGH-END JEWELRY STORES, AUCTION HOUSES, HIGH-END ART GALLERIES.
ALL OF THEM HIT AFTER THE BON VIVANTS' MONTHLY MEAL.
AND YOU THINK HANNA IS THE GUY BEHIND IT? YOU THINK HE'S HERE?
DUDE, I THINK HE'S RIGHT THERE.
HANDS IN THE AIR, FUCKER... STEP AWAY FROM YOUR MILK.
YOU DIDN'T LET ME FINISH, CHU.
I DON'T THINK THIS GUY IS ACTUALLY A VECTULACTI-RUTARE.
I THINK HE'S REALLY A VECTUCIB--
THE VECTUCIBORUTARE IS ABLE TO PRODUCE NOXIOUS ERUCTATION BASED ON THE AGE OF WHAT HE INGESTS.

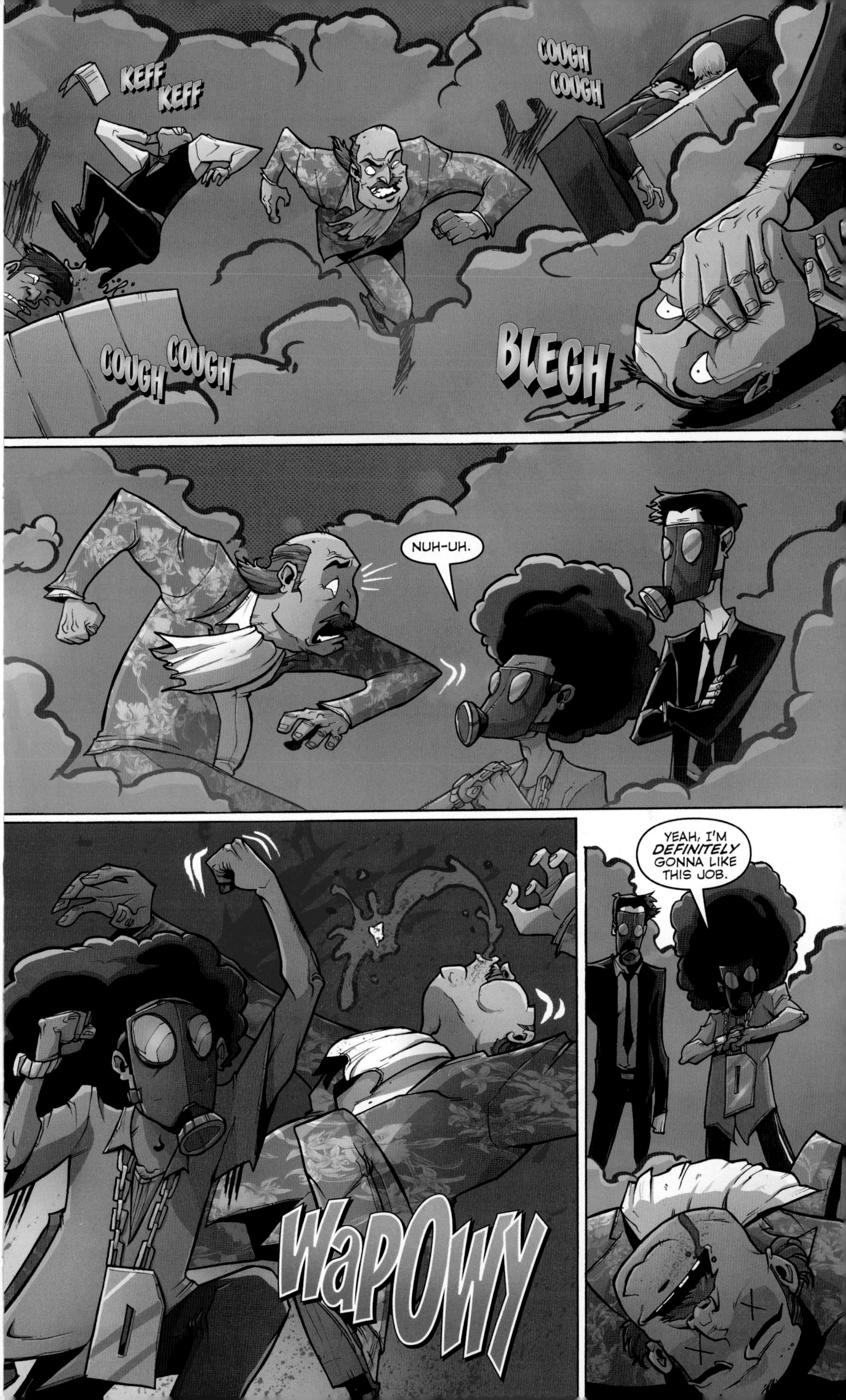
KEFF
KEFF
COUGH
COUGH
COUGH
COUGH
BLEGH
NUH-UH.
WAPOWY
YEAH, I'M *DEFINITELY* GONNA LIKE THIS JOB.

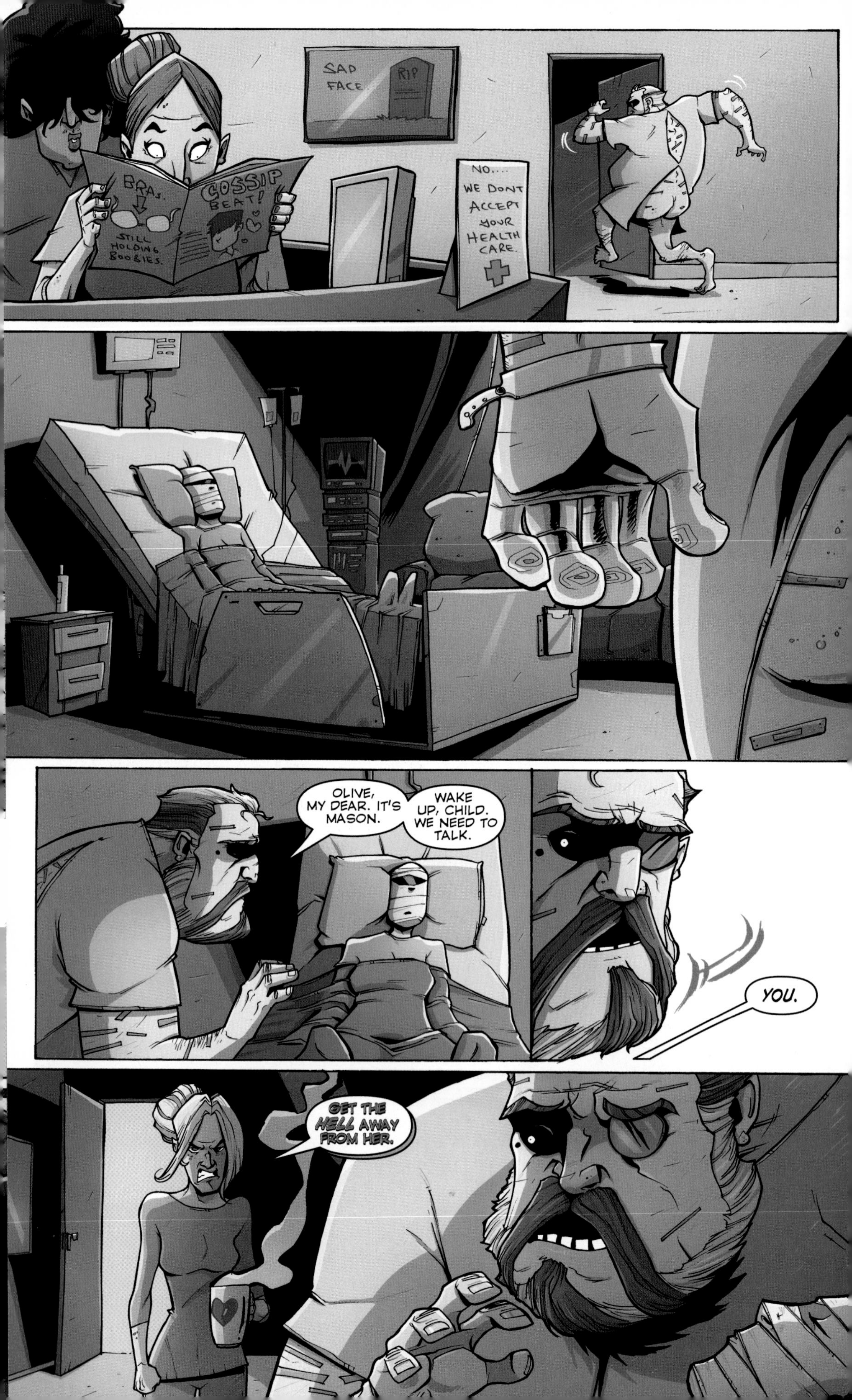
SAD FACE.
RIP
BRAS.
STILL HOLDING BOOBIES.
GOSSIP BEAT!
NO... WE DONT ACCEPT YOUR HEALTH CARE.
OLIVE, MY DEAR. IT'S MASON.
WAKE UP, CHILD. WE NEED TO TALK.
YOU.
GET THE HELL AWAY FROM HER.

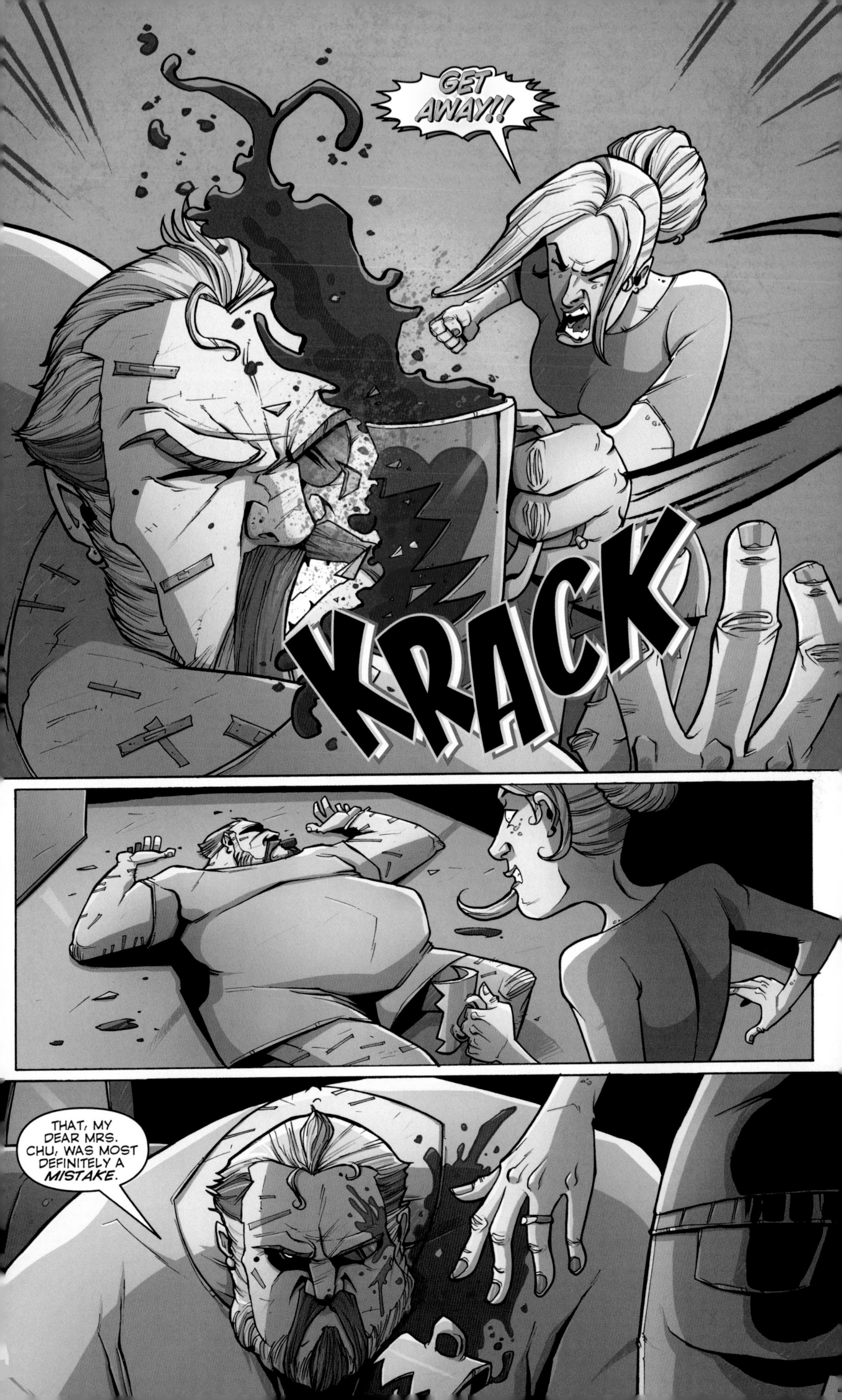
GET AWAY!!
KRACK
THAT, MY DEAR MRS. CHU, WAS MOST DEFINITELY A *MISTAKE*.

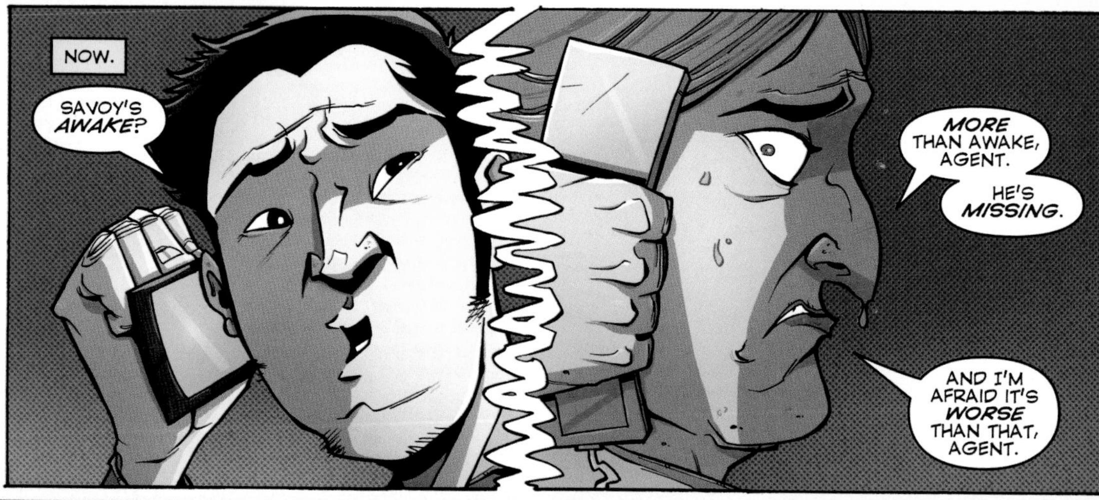
NOW.
SAVOY'S AWAKE?
MORE THAN AWAKE, AGENT.
HE'S MISSING.
AND I'M AFRAID IT'S WORSE THAN THAT, AGENT.

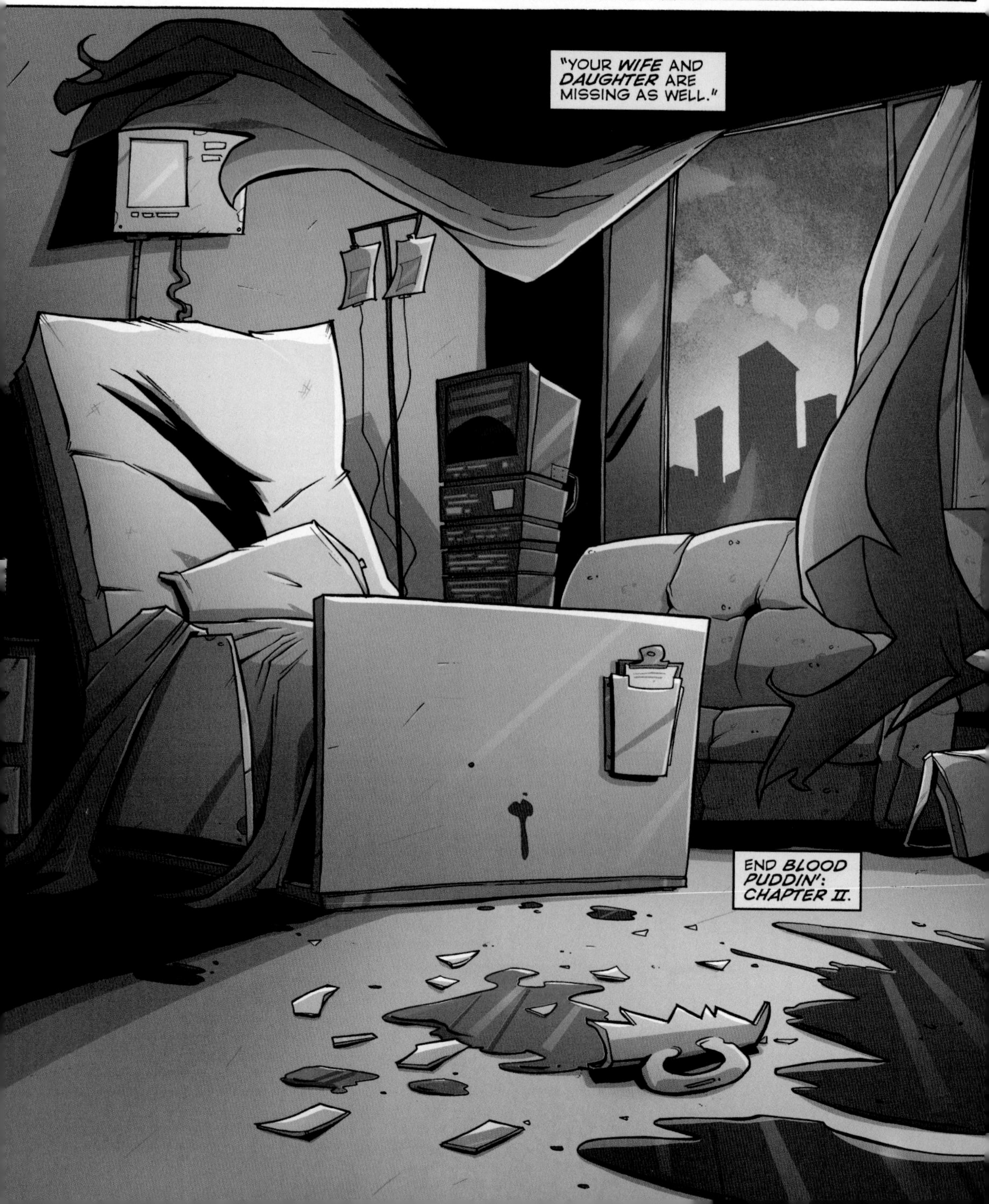
"YOUR WIFE AND DAUGHTER ARE MISSING AS WELL."
END BLOOD PUDDIN': CHAPTER II.

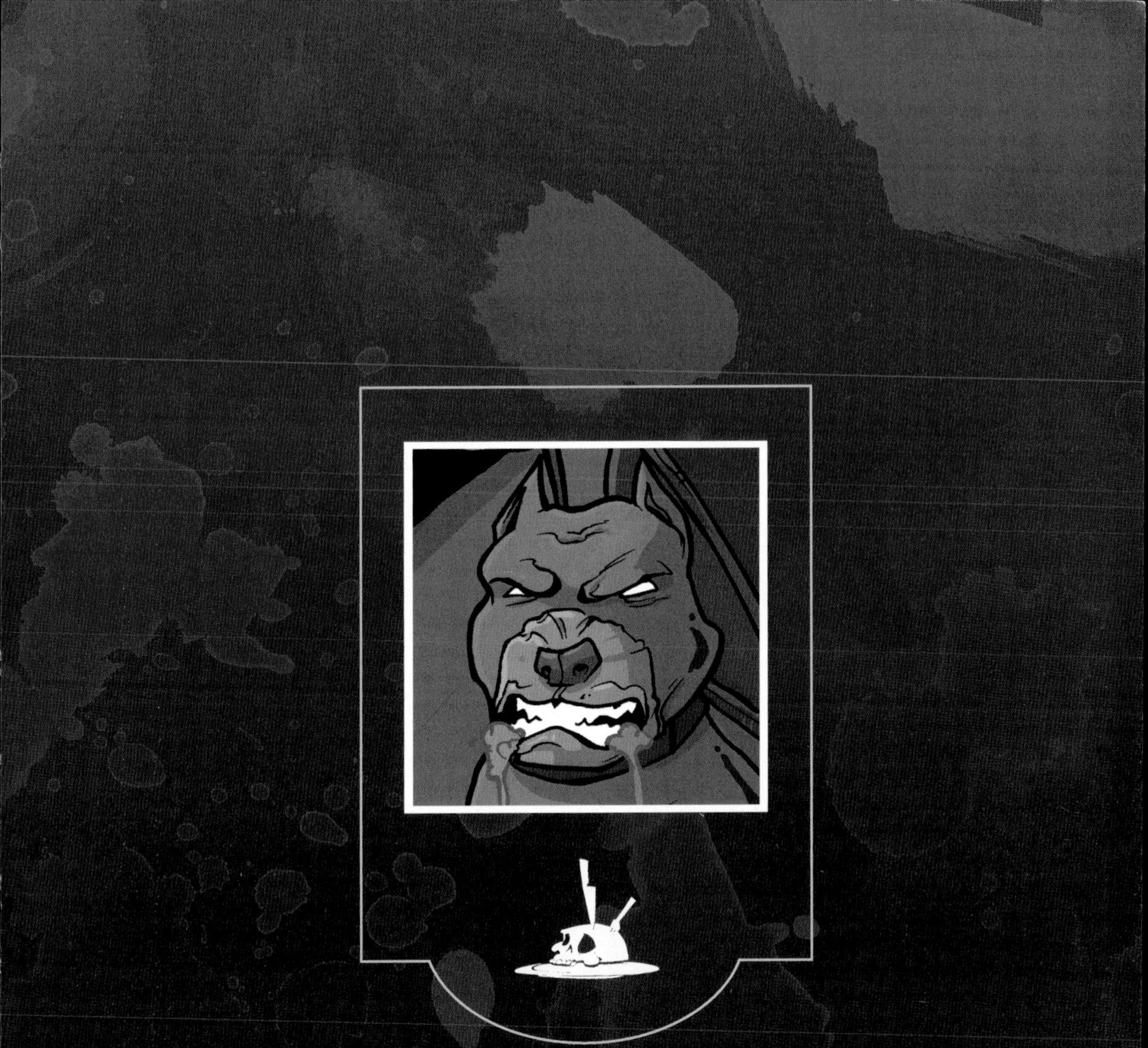

Chapter 3

AWFUL
SWEAT PITS
TITANIUM SPINE
ACCESS
PANEL
HYDRAULIC
TENDONS
HYDRAULIC CLAW
ARSENAL
COMPARTMENTS
PATENT
USDA
PENDING
SOPHISTICATED
POWER ADAPTER

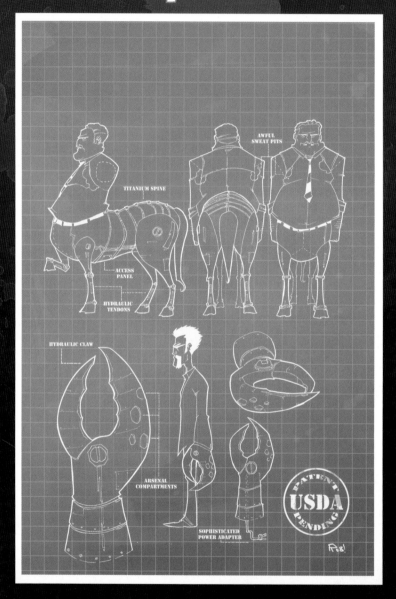

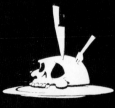

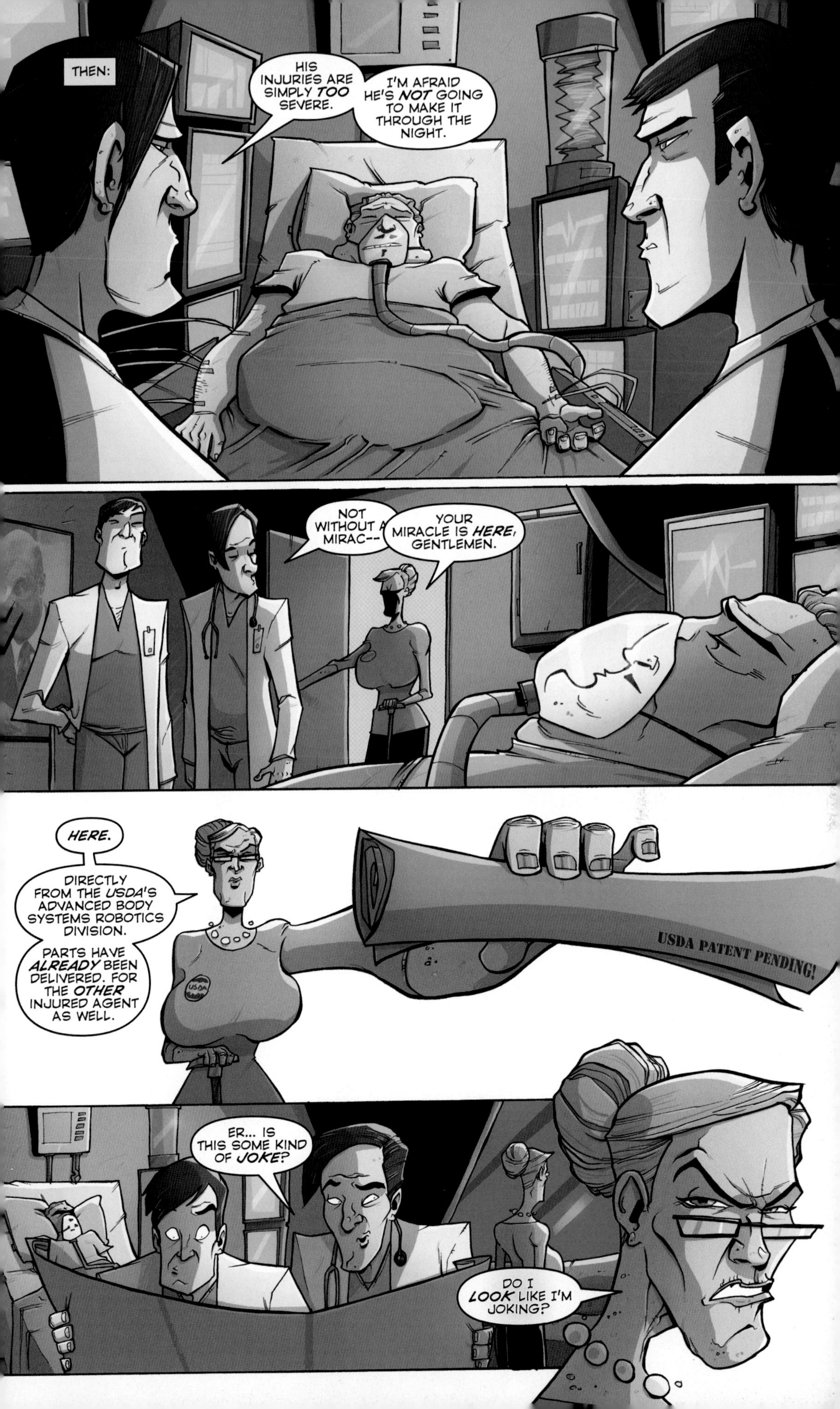

THEN:
HIS INJURIES ARE SIMPLY TOO SEVERE.
I'M AFRAID HE'S NOT GOING TO MAKE IT THROUGH THE NIGHT.
NOT WITHOUT A MIRAC--
YOUR MIRACLE IS HERE, GENTLEMEN.
HERE.
DIRECTLY FROM THE USDA'S ADVANCED BODY SYSTEMS ROBOTICS DIVISION.
PARTS HAVE ALREADY BEEN DELIVERED. FOR THE OTHER INJURED AGENT AS WELL.
USDA PATENT PENDING!
USDA
ER... IS THIS SOME KIND OF JOKE?
DO I LOOK LIKE I'M JOKING?

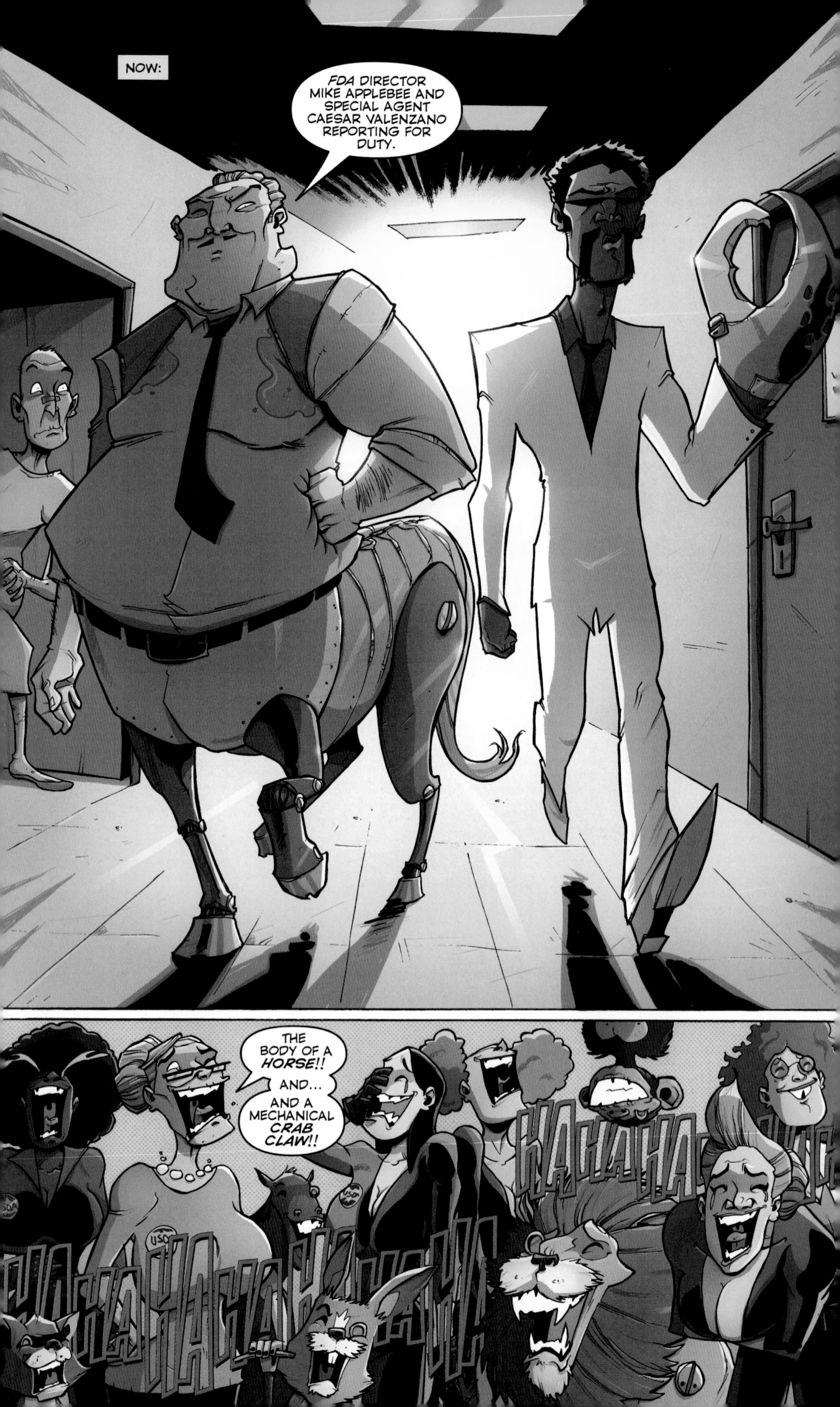
NOW:
FDA DIRECTOR MIKE APPLEBEE AND SPECIAL AGENT CAESAR VALENZANO REPORTING FOR DUTY.
THE BODY OF A HORSE!!
AND...
AND A MECHANICAL CRAB CLAW!!

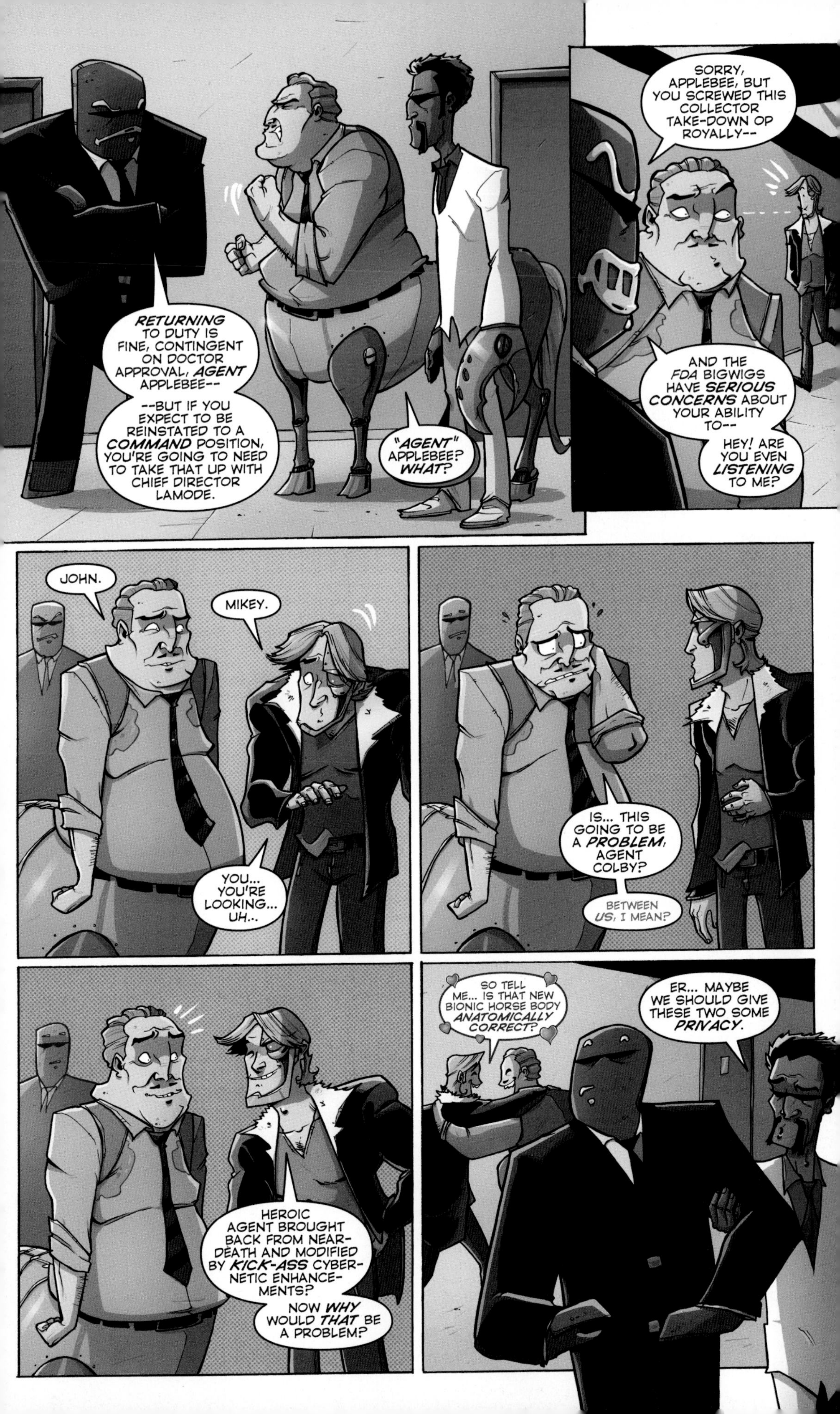

RETURNING TO DUTY IS FINE, CONTINGENT ON DOCTOR APPROVAL, AGENT APPLEBEE--
--BUT IF YOU EXPECT TO BE REINSTATED TO A COMMAND POSITION, YOU'RE GOING TO NEED TO TAKE THAT UP WITH CHIEF DIRECTOR LAMODE.
"AGENT" APPLEBEE? WHAT?
SORRY, APPLEBEE, BUT YOU SCREWED THIS COLLECTOR TAKE-DOWN OP ROYALLY--
AND THE FDA BIGWIGS HAVE SERIOUS CONCERNS ABOUT YOUR ABILITY TO--
HEY! ARE YOU EVEN LISTENING TO ME?
JOHN.
MIKEY.
YOU... YOU'RE LOOKING... UH...
IS... THIS GOING TO BE A PROBLEM, AGENT COLBY?
BETWEEN US, I MEAN?
HEROIC AGENT BROUGHT BACK FROM NEAR-DEATH AND MODIFIED BY KICK-ASS CYBERNETIC ENHANCEMENTS?
NOW WHY WOULD THAT BE A PROBLEM?
SO TELL ME... IS THAT NEW BIONIC HORSE BODY ANATOMICALLY CORRECT?
ER... MAYBE WE SHOULD GIVE THESE TWO SOME PRIVACY.

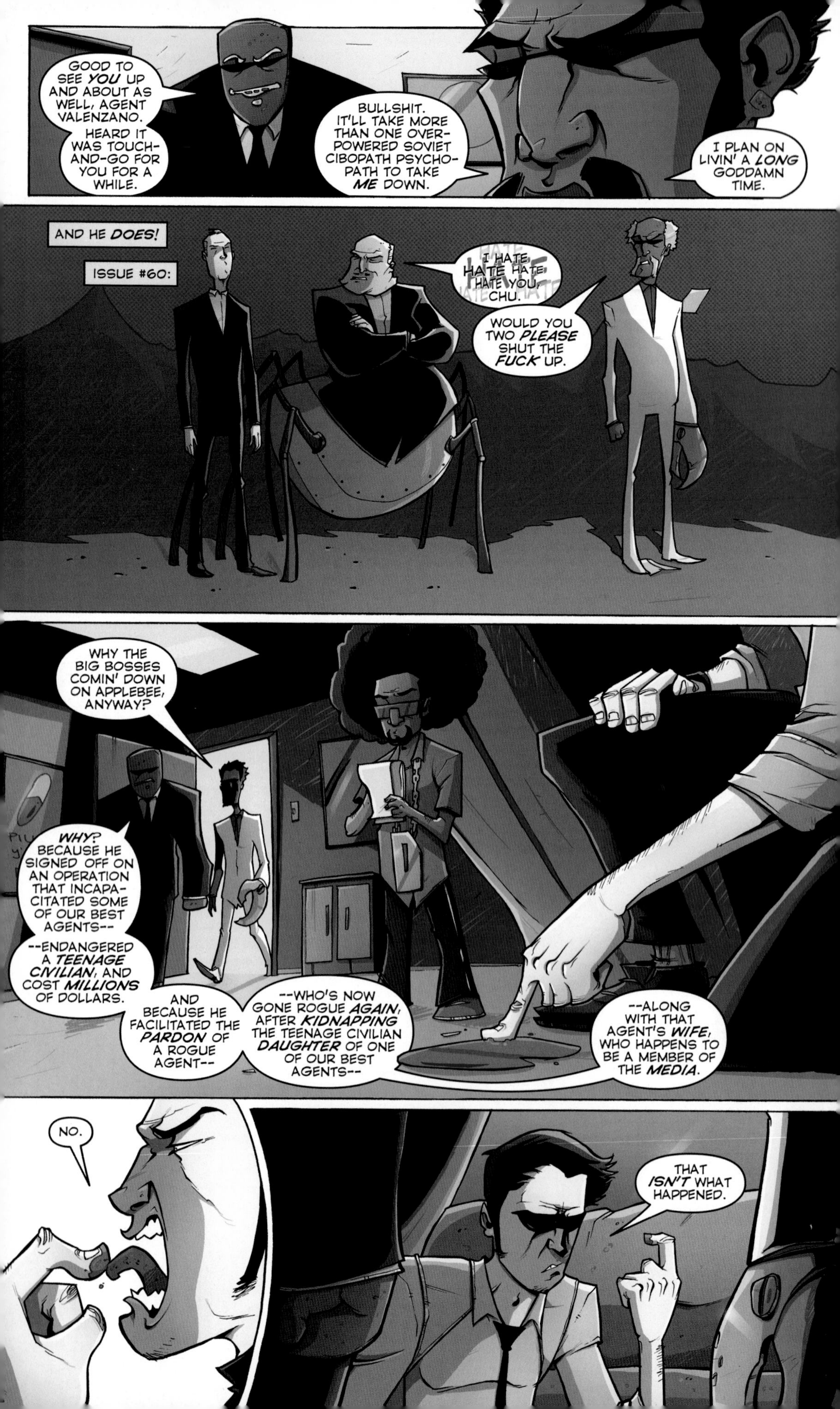
GOOD TO SEE *YOU* UP AND ABOUT AS WELL, AGENT VALENZANO.
HEARD IT WAS TOUCH-AND-GO FOR YOU FOR A WHILE.
BULLSHIT. IT'LL TAKE MORE THAN ONE OVER-POWERED SOVIET CIBOPATH PSYCHO-PATH TO TAKE *ME* DOWN.
I PLAN ON LIVIN' A *LONG* GODDAMN TIME.
AND HE *DOES!*
ISSUE #60:
I HATE HATE HATE HATE YOU, CHU.
WOULD YOU TWO *PLEASE* SHUT THE *FUCK* UP.
WHY THE BIG BOSSES COMIN' DOWN ON APPLEBEE, ANYWAY?
WHY? BECAUSE HE SIGNED OFF ON AN OPERATION THAT INCAPA-CITATED SOME OF OUR BEST AGENTS--
--ENDANGERED A *TEENAGE CIVILIAN*, AND COST *MILLIONS* OF DOLLARS.
AND BECAUSE HE FACILITATED THE *PARDON* OF A ROGUE AGENT--
--WHO'S NOW GONE ROGUE *AGAIN*, AFTER *KIDNAPPING* THE TEENAGE CIVILIAN *DAUGHTER* OF ONE OF OUR BEST AGENTS--
--ALONG WITH THAT AGENT'S *WIFE*, WHO HAPPENS TO BE A MEMBER OF THE *MEDIA*.
NO.
THAT *ISN'T* WHAT HAPPENED.

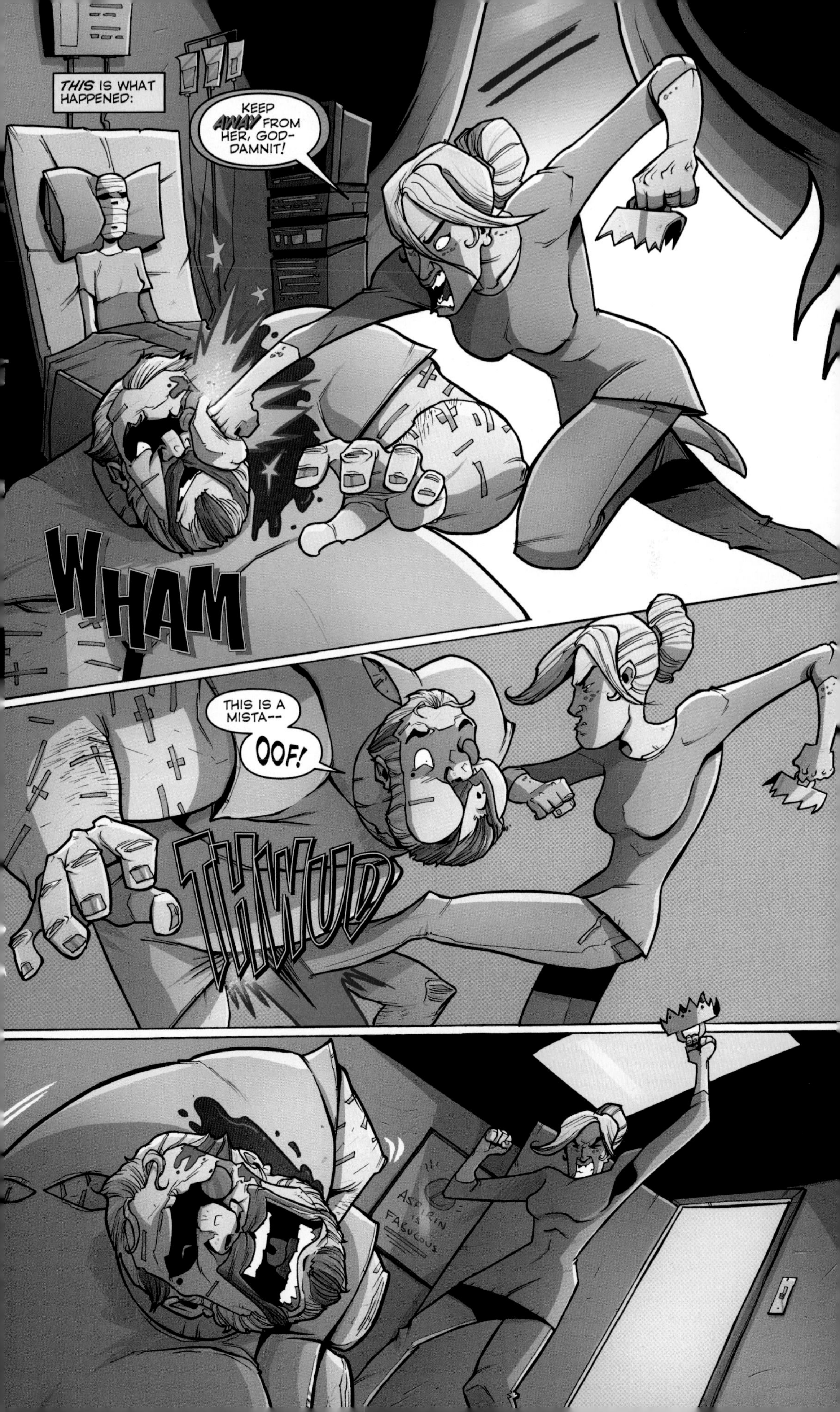
THIS IS WHAT HAPPENED:
KEEP AWAY FROM HER, GOD-DAMNIT!
WHAM
THIS IS A MISTA--
OOF!
THWUD
ASPIRIN IS FABULOUS.

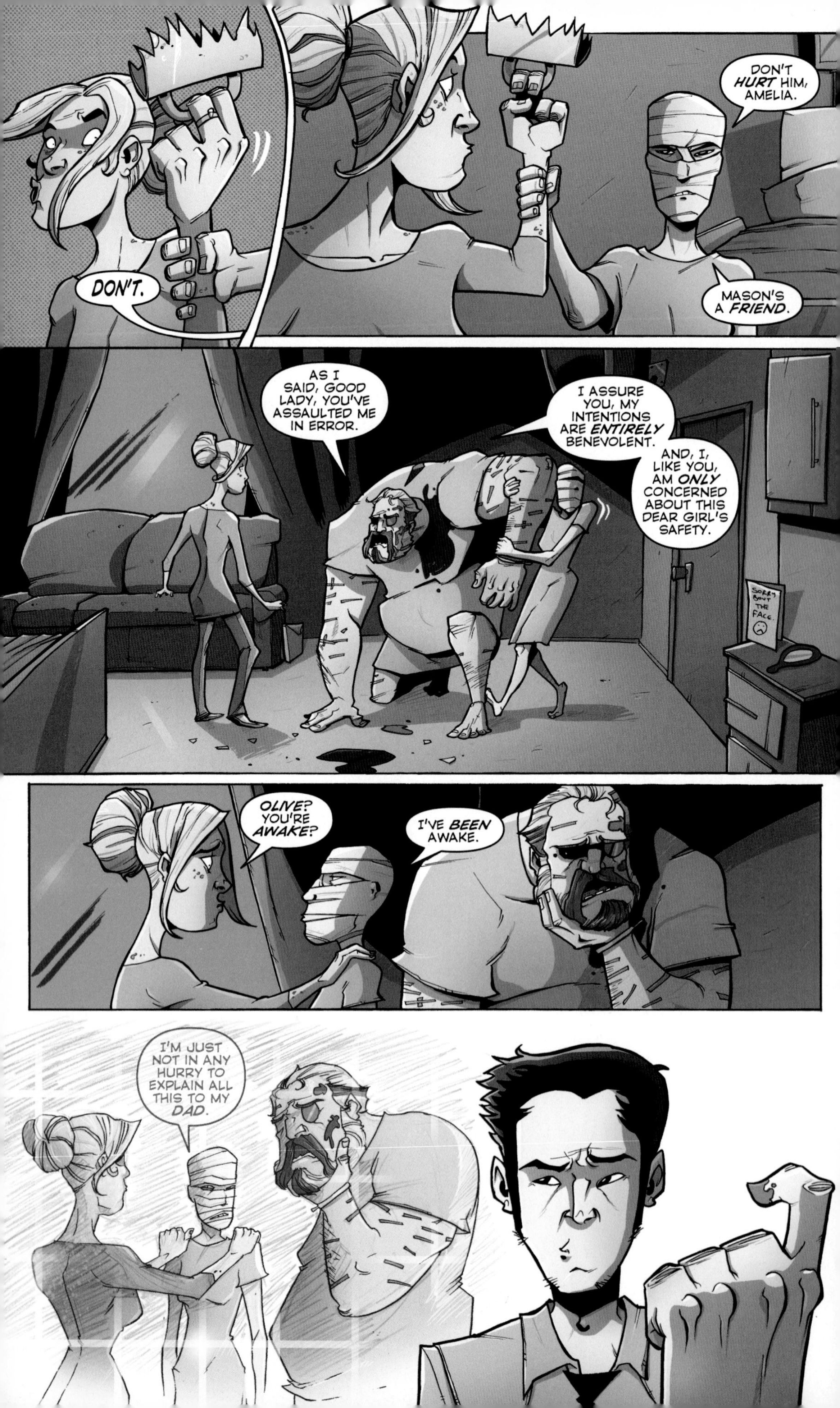
DON'T.
DON'T HURT HIM, AMELIA.
MASON'S A FRIEND.
AS I SAID, GOOD LADY, YOU'VE ASSAULTED ME IN ERROR.
I ASSURE YOU, MY INTENTIONS ARE ENTIRELY BENEVOLENT.
AND, I, LIKE YOU, AM ONLY CONCERNED ABOUT THIS DEAR GIRL'S SAFETY.
SORRY BOUT THE FACE.
OLIVE? YOU'RE AWAKE?
I'VE BEEN AWAKE.
I'M JUST NOT IN ANY HURRY TO EXPLAIN ALL THIS TO MY DAD.

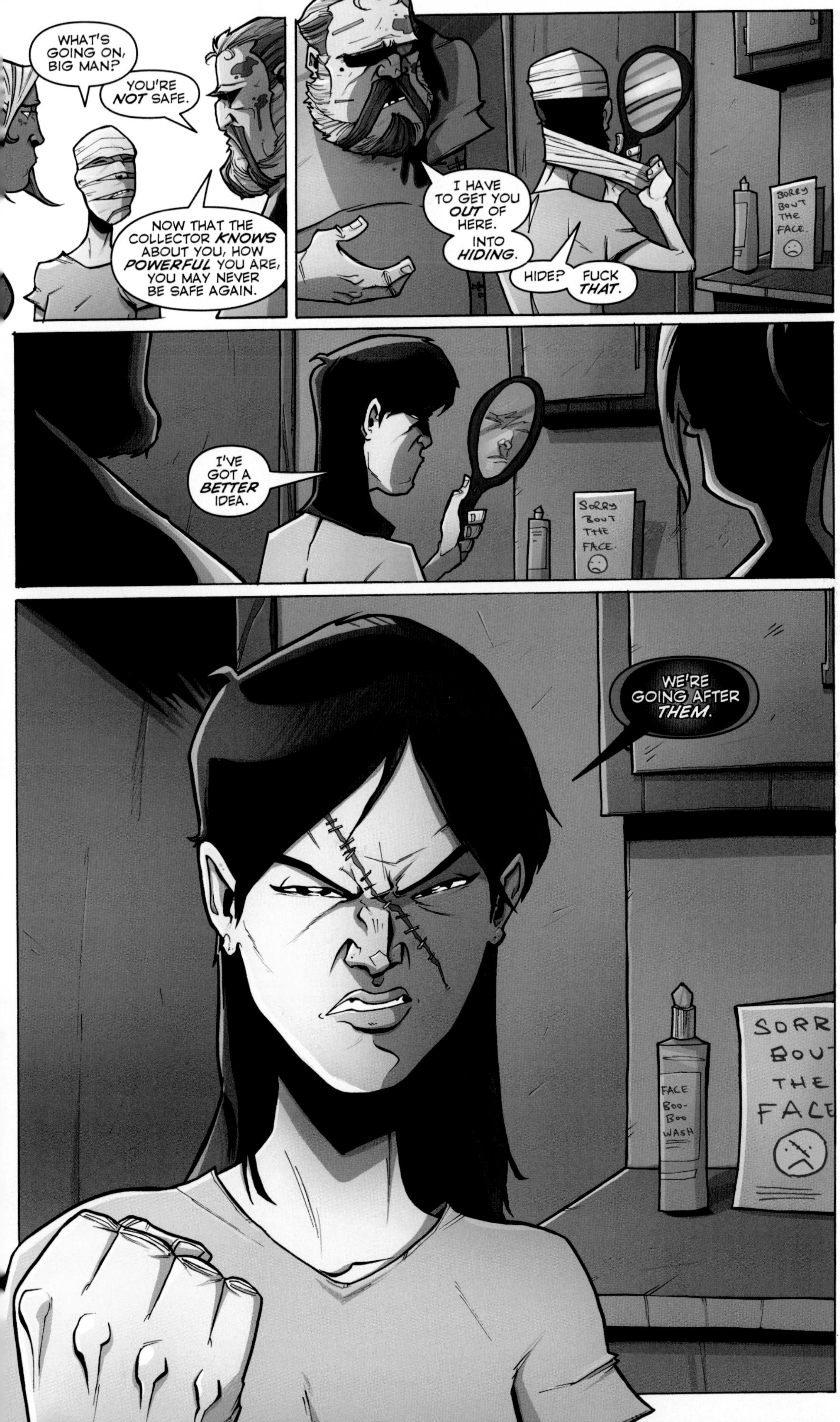
WHAT'S GOING ON, BIG MAN?
YOU'RE NOT SAFE.
NOW THAT THE COLLECTOR KNOWS ABOUT YOU, HOW POWERFUL YOU ARE, YOU MAY NEVER BE SAFE AGAIN.
I HAVE TO GET YOU OUT OF HERE.
INTO HIDING.
HIDE? FUCK THAT.
SORRY BOUT THE FACE.
I'VE GOT A BETTER IDEA.
SORRY BOUT THE FACE.
WE'RE GOING AFTER THEM.
FACE BOO-BOO WASH

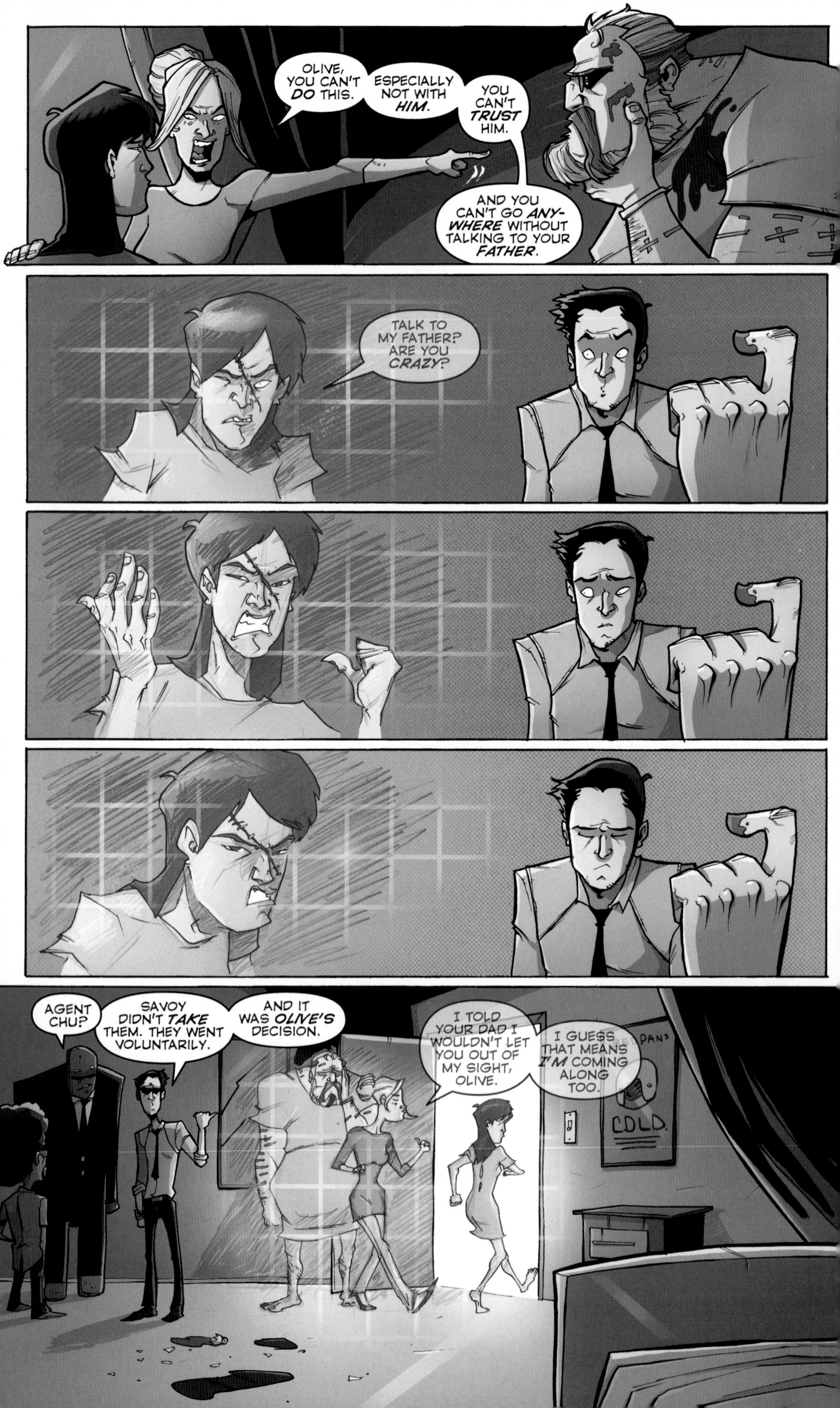
OLIVE, YOU CAN'T *DO* THIS.
ESPECIALLY NOT WITH *HIM*.
YOU CAN'T *TRUST* HIM.
AND YOU CAN'T GO *ANY-WHERE* WITHOUT TALKING TO YOUR *FATHER*.
TALK TO MY FATHER? ARE YOU *CRAZY*?
AGENT CHU?
SAVOY DIDN'T *TAKE* THEM. THEY WENT VOLUNTARILY.
AND IT WAS *OLIVE'S* DECISION.
I TOLD YOUR DAD I WOULDN'T LET YOU OUT OF MY SIGHT, OLIVE.
I GUESS THAT MEANS *I'M* COMING ALONG TOO.
C.D.L.D.

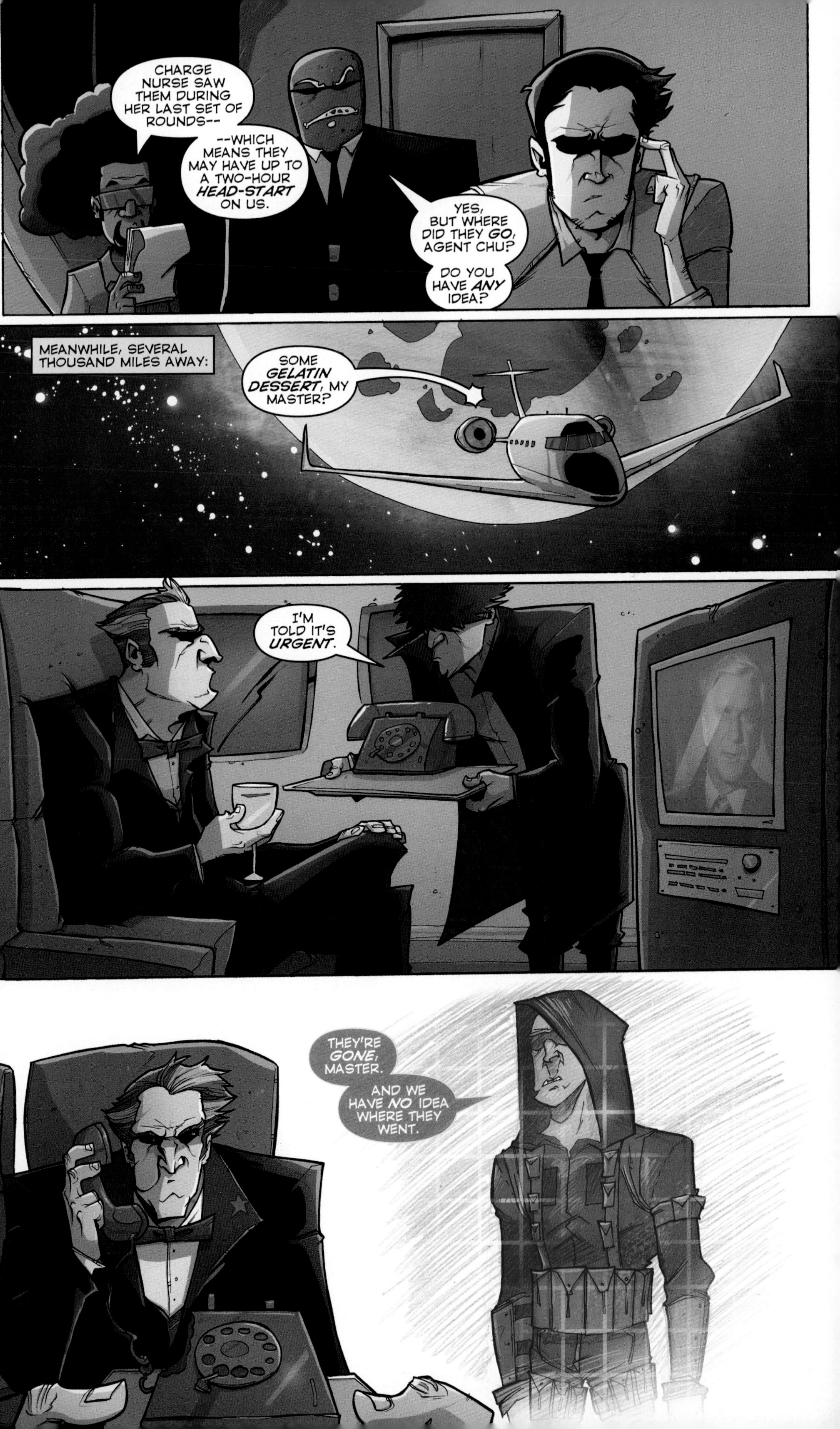

CHARGE NURSE SAW THEM DURING HER LAST SET OF ROUNDS--
--WHICH MEANS THEY MAY HAVE UP TO A TWO-HOUR HEAD-START ON US.
YES, BUT WHERE DID THEY GO, AGENT CHU?
DO YOU HAVE ANY IDEA?
MEANWHILE, SEVERAL THOUSAND MILES AWAY:
SOME GELATIN DESSERT, MY MASTER?
I'M TOLD IT'S URGENT.
THEY'RE GONE, MASTER.
AND WE HAVE NO IDEA WHERE THEY WENT.

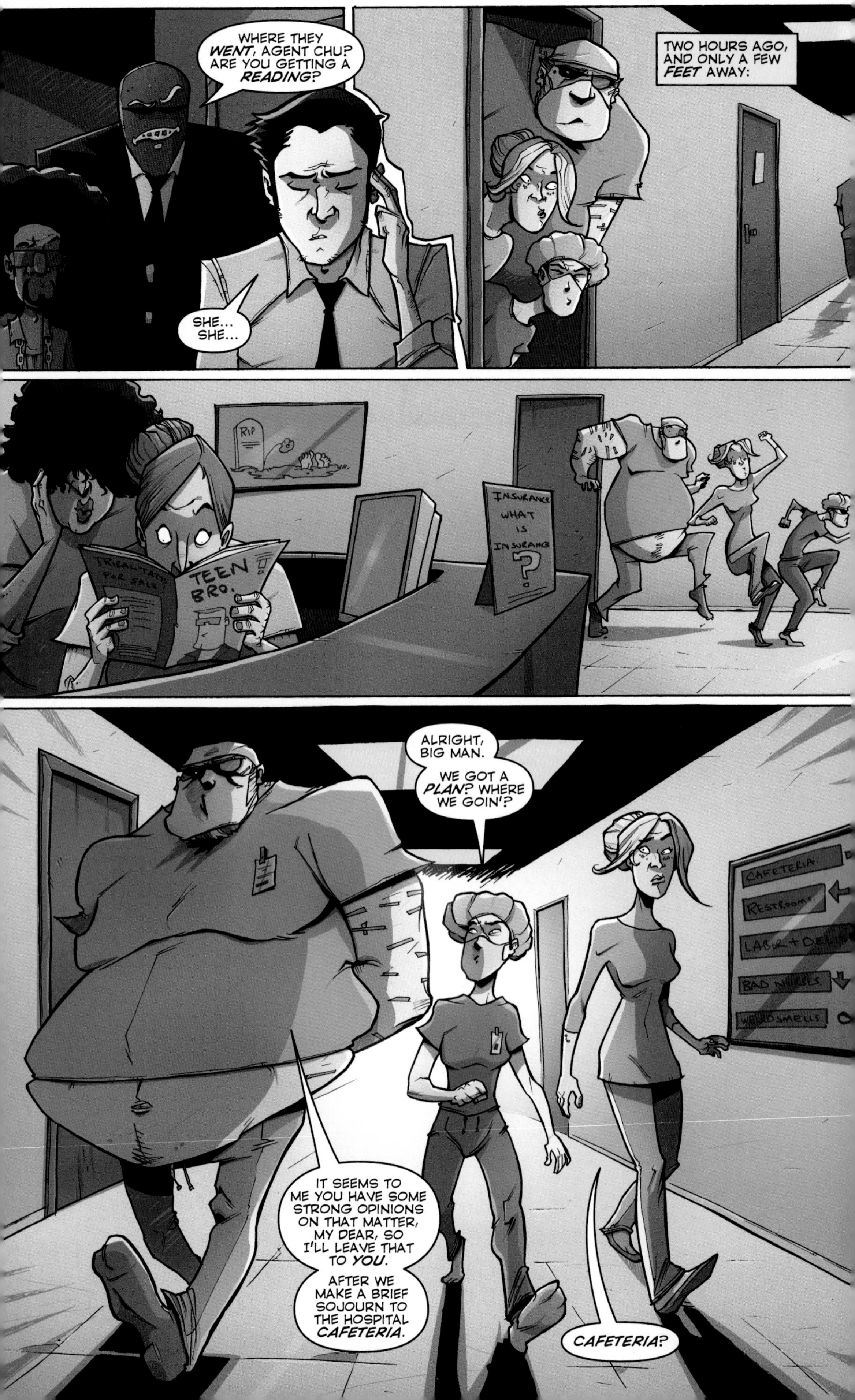
WHERE THEY *WENT*, AGENT CHU? ARE YOU GETTING A *READING*?
SHE... SHE...
TWO HOURS AGO, AND ONLY A FEW *FEET* AWAY:
RIP
TRIBAL TATS FOR SALE!
TEEN BRO.
INSURANCE WHAT IS INSURANCE ?
ALRIGHT, BIG MAN.
WE GOT A *PLAN*? WHERE WE GOIN'?
CAFETERIA
RESTROOMS
BAD NURSES
IT SEEMS TO ME YOU HAVE SOME STRONG OPINIONS ON THAT MATTER, MY DEAR, SO I'LL LEAVE THAT TO *YOU*.
AFTER WE MAKE A BRIEF SOJOURN TO THE HOSPITAL *CAFETERIA*.
CAFETERIA?

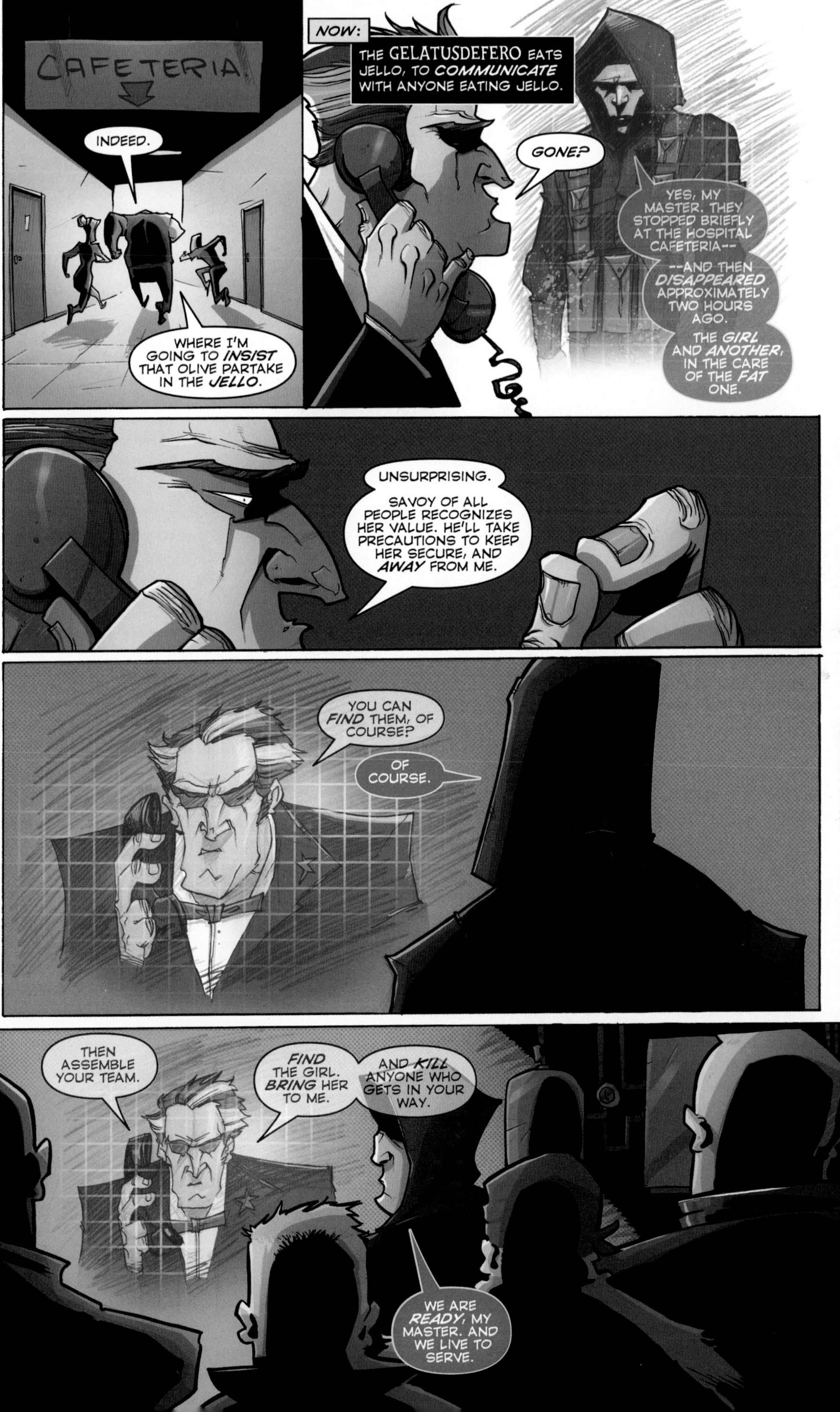
CAFETERIA
INDEED.
WHERE I'M GOING TO INSIST THAT OLIVE PARTAKE IN THE JELLO.
NOW:
THE GELATUSDEFERO EATS JELLO, TO COMMUNICATE WITH ANYONE EATING JELLO.
GONE?
YES, MY MASTER. THEY STOPPED BRIEFLY AT THE HOSPITAL CAFETERIA--
--AND THEN DISAPPEARED APPROXIMATELY TWO HOURS AGO.
THE GIRL AND ANOTHER, IN THE CARE OF THE FAT ONE.
UNSURPRISING.
SAVOY OF ALL PEOPLE RECOGNIZES HER VALUE. HE'LL TAKE PRECAUTIONS TO KEEP HER SECURE, AND AWAY FROM ME.
YOU CAN FIND THEM, OF COURSE?
OF COURSE.
THEN ASSEMBLE YOUR TEAM.
FIND THE GIRL. BRING HER TO ME.
AND KILL ANYONE WHO GETS IN YOUR WAY.
WE ARE READY, MY MASTER. AND WE LIVE TO SERVE.

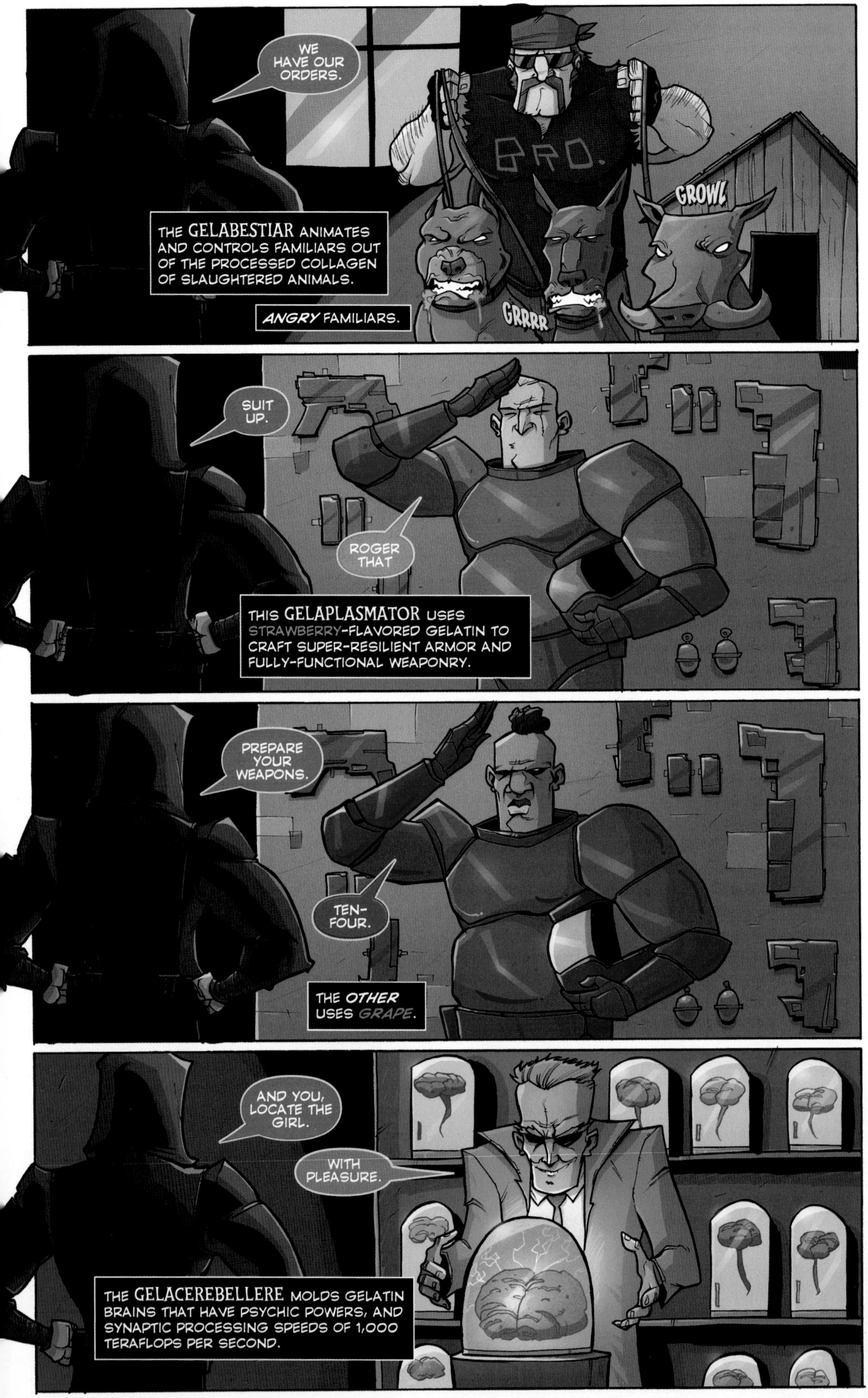

WE HAVE OUR ORDERS.
GROWL
THE GELABESTIAR ANIMATES AND CONTROLS FAMILIARS OUT OF THE PROCESSED COLLAGEN OF SLAUGHTERED ANIMALS.
ANGRY FAMILIARS.
GRRRR
SUIT UP.
ROGER THAT
THIS GELAPLASMATOR USES STRAWBERRY-FLAVORED GELATIN TO CRAFT SUPER-RESILIENT ARMOR AND FULLY-FUNCTIONAL WEAPONRY.
PREPARE YOUR WEAPONS.
TEN-FOUR.
THE OTHER USES GRAPE.
AND YOU, LOCATE THE GIRL.
WITH PLEASURE.
THE GELACEREBELLERE MOLDS GELATIN BRAINS THAT HAVE PSYCHIC POWERS, AND SYNAPTIC PROCESSING SPEEDS OF 1,000 TERAFLOPS PER SECOND.

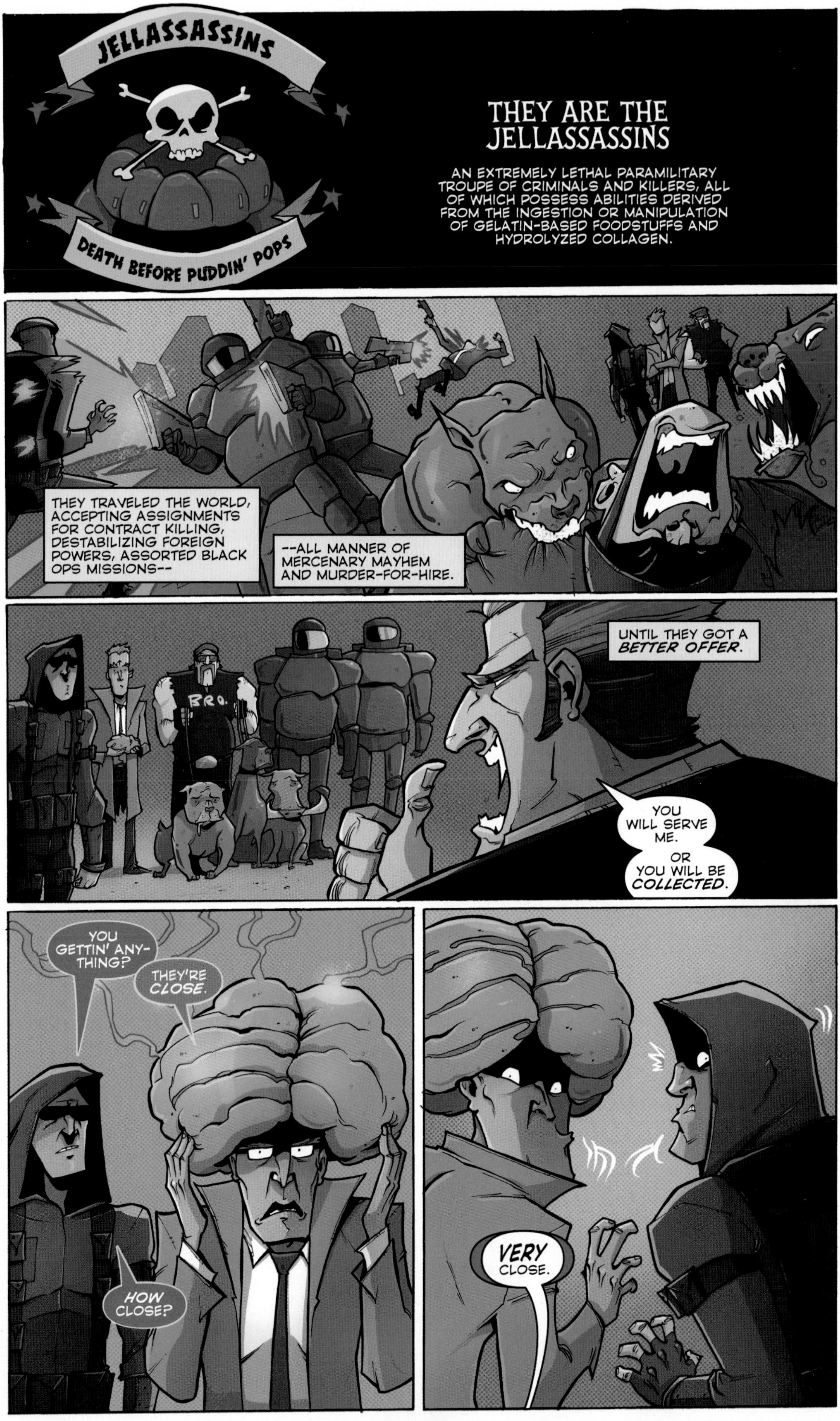
JELLASSASSINS
DEATH BEFORE PUDDIN' POPS
THEY ARE THE JELLASSASSINS
AN EXTREMELY LETHAL PARAMILITARY TROUPE OF CRIMINALS AND KILLERS, ALL OF WHICH POSSESS ABILITIES DERIVED FROM THE INGESTION OR MANIPULATION OF GELATIN-BASED FOODSTUFFS AND HYDROLYZED COLLAGEN.
THEY TRAVELED THE WORLD, ACCEPTING ASSIGNMENTS FOR CONTRACT KILLING, DESTABILIZING FOREIGN POWERS, ASSORTED BLACK OPS MISSIONS--
--ALL MANNER OF MERCENARY MAYHEM AND MURDER-FOR-HIRE.
BRO.
UNTIL THEY GOT A BETTER OFFER.
YOU WILL SERVE ME.
OR YOU WILL BE COLLECTED.
YOU GETTIN' ANYTHING?
THEY'RE CLOSE.
HOW CLOSE?
VERY CLOSE.

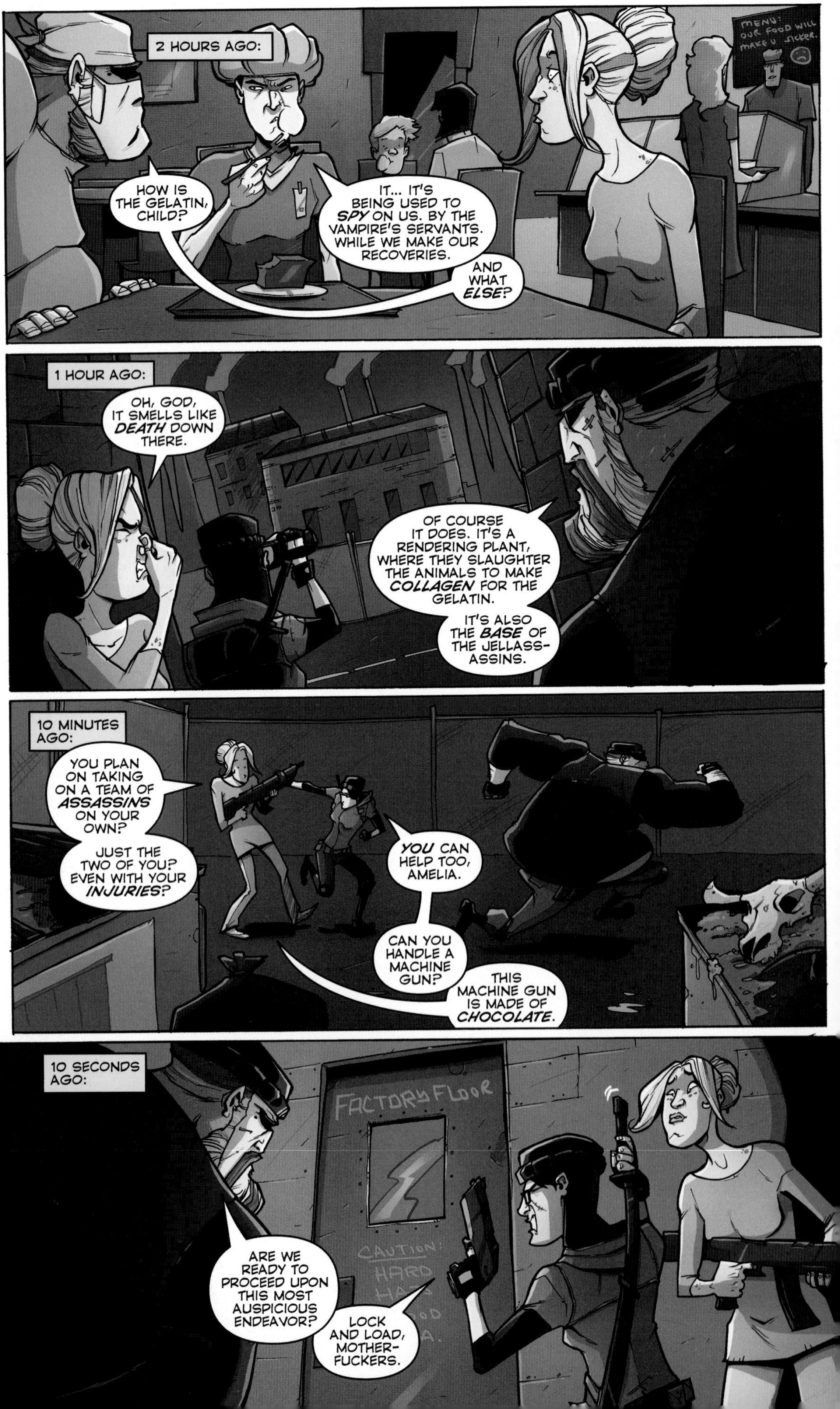
2 HOURS AGO:
MENU: OUR FOOD WILL MAKE U SICKER.
HOW IS THE GELATIN, CHILD?
IT... IT'S BEING USED TO SPY ON US. BY THE VAMPIRE'S SERVANTS. WHILE WE MAKE OUR RECOVERIES.
AND WHAT ELSE?
1 HOUR AGO:
OH, GOD, IT SMELLS LIKE DEATH DOWN THERE.
OF COURSE IT DOES. IT'S A RENDERING PLANT, WHERE THEY SLAUGHTER THE ANIMALS TO MAKE COLLAGEN FOR THE GELATIN.
IT'S ALSO THE BASE OF THE JELLASS-ASSINS.
10 MINUTES AGO:
YOU PLAN ON TAKING ON A TEAM OF ASSASSINS ON YOUR OWN?
JUST THE TWO OF YOU? EVEN WITH YOUR INJURIES?
YOU CAN HELP TOO, AMELIA.
CAN YOU HANDLE A MACHINE GUN?
THIS MACHINE GUN IS MADE OF CHOCOLATE.
10 SECONDS AGO:
FACTORY FLOOR
ARE WE READY TO PROCEED UPON THIS MOST AUSPICIOUS ENDEAVOR?
LOCK AND LOAD, MOTHER-FUCKERS.

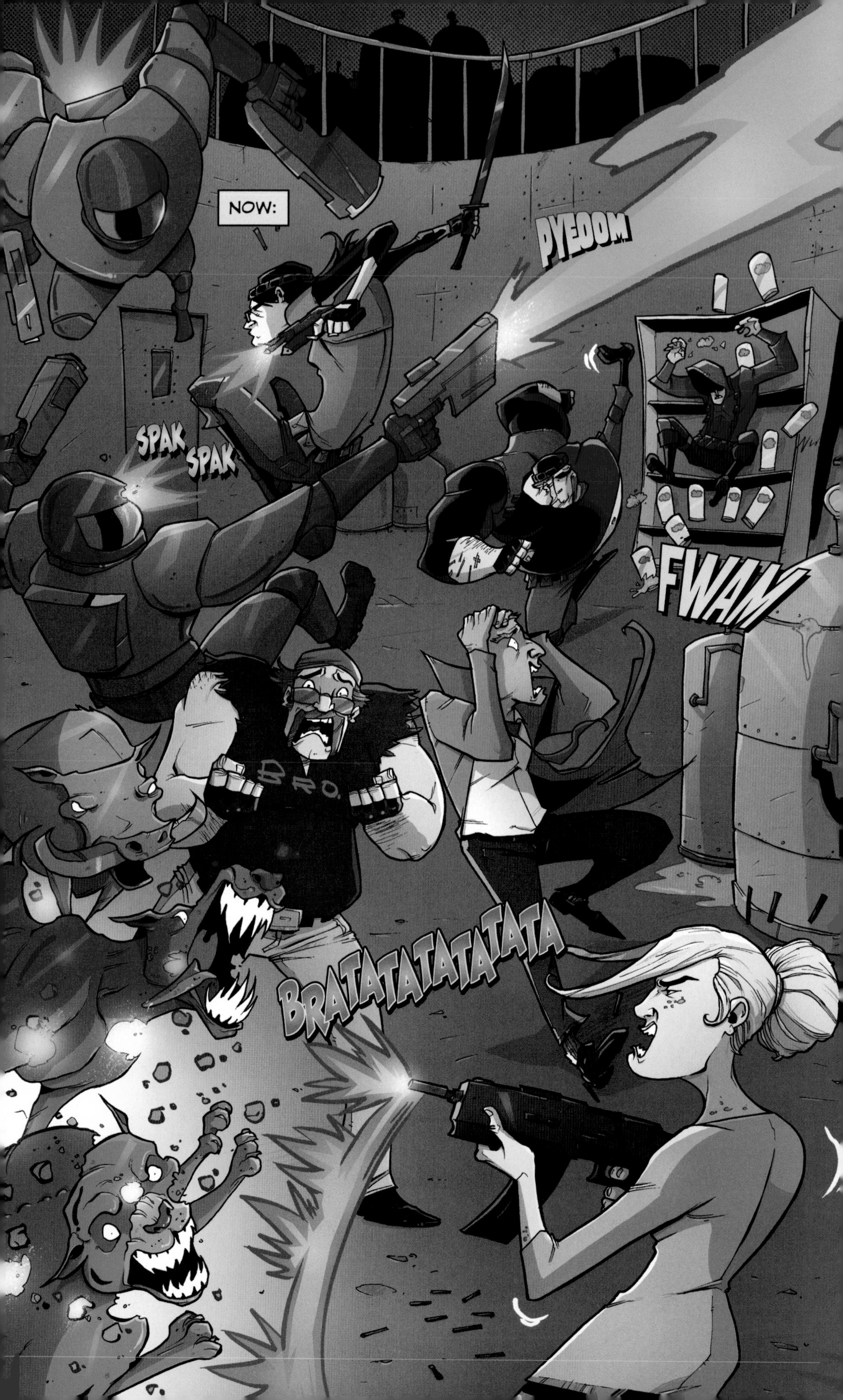
NOW:
PYEOOM
SPAK
SPAK
FWAM
BRATATATATATATA

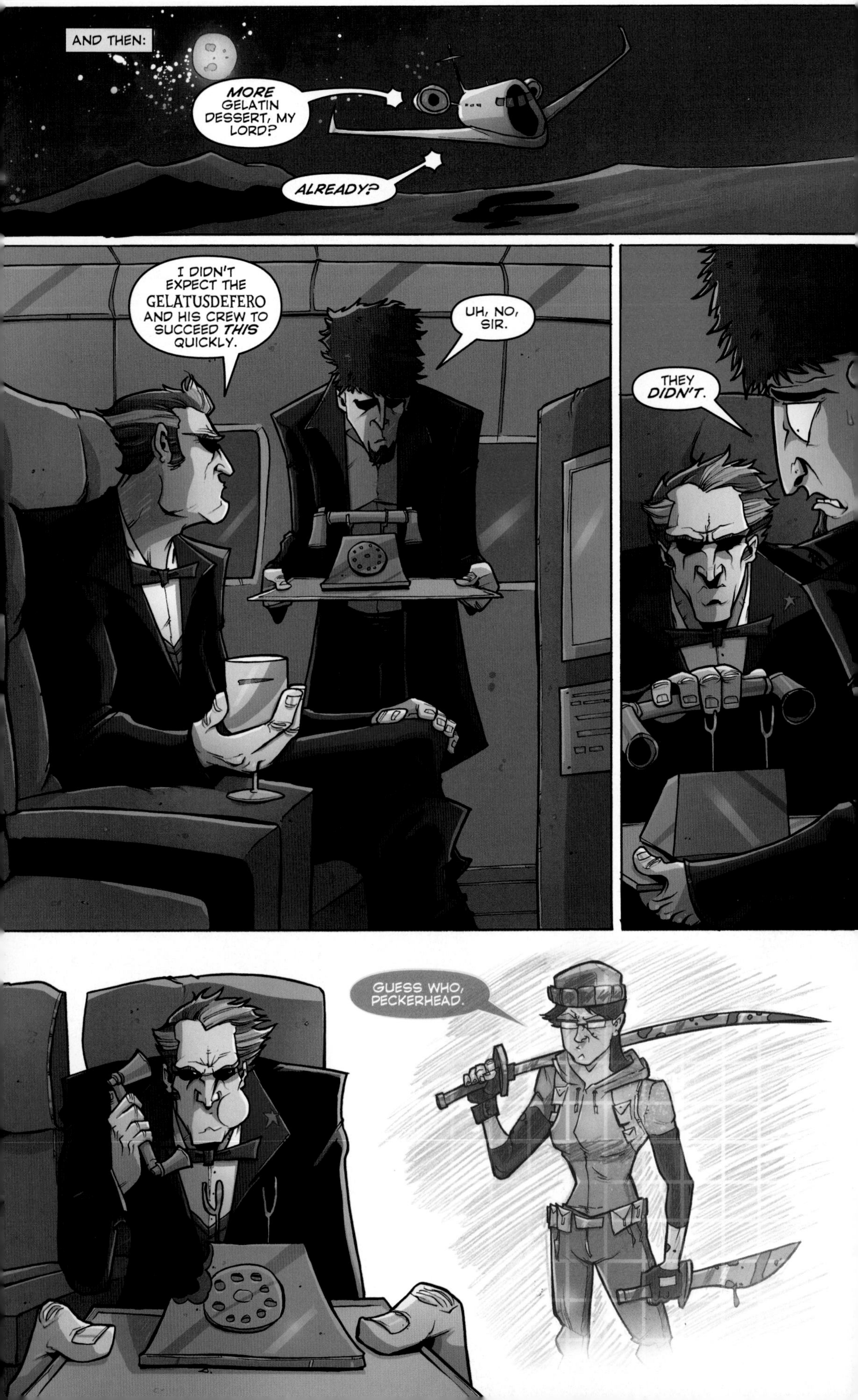
AND THEN:
MORE GELATIN DESSERT, MY LORD?
ALREADY?
I DIDN'T EXPECT THE GELATUSDEFERO AND HIS CREW TO SUCCEED THIS QUICKLY.
UH, NO, SIR.
THEY DIDN'T.
GUESS WHO, PECKERHEAD.

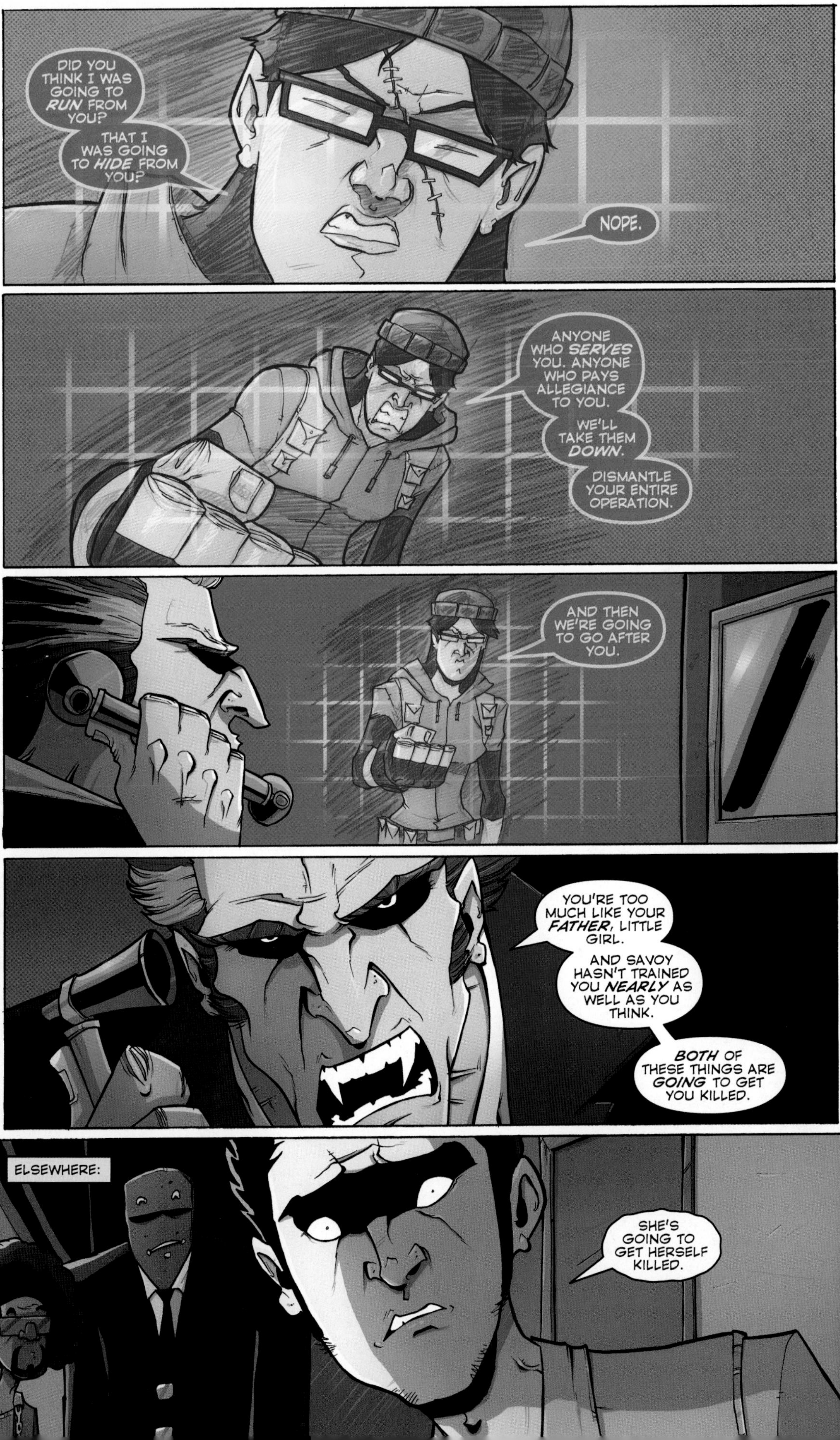

DID YOU THINK I WAS GOING TO RUN FROM YOU?
THAT I WAS GOING TO HIDE FROM YOU?
NOPE.
ANYONE WHO SERVES YOU. ANYONE WHO PAYS ALLEGIANCE TO YOU.
WE'LL TAKE THEM DOWN.
DISMANTLE YOUR ENTIRE OPERATION.
AND THEN WE'RE GOING TO GO AFTER YOU.
YOU'RE TOO MUCH LIKE YOUR FATHER, LITTLE GIRL.
AND SAVOY HASN'T TRAINED YOU NEARLY AS WELL AS YOU THINK.
BOTH OF THESE THINGS ARE GOING TO GET YOU KILLED.
ELSEWHERE:
SHE'S GOING TO GET HERSELF KILLED.

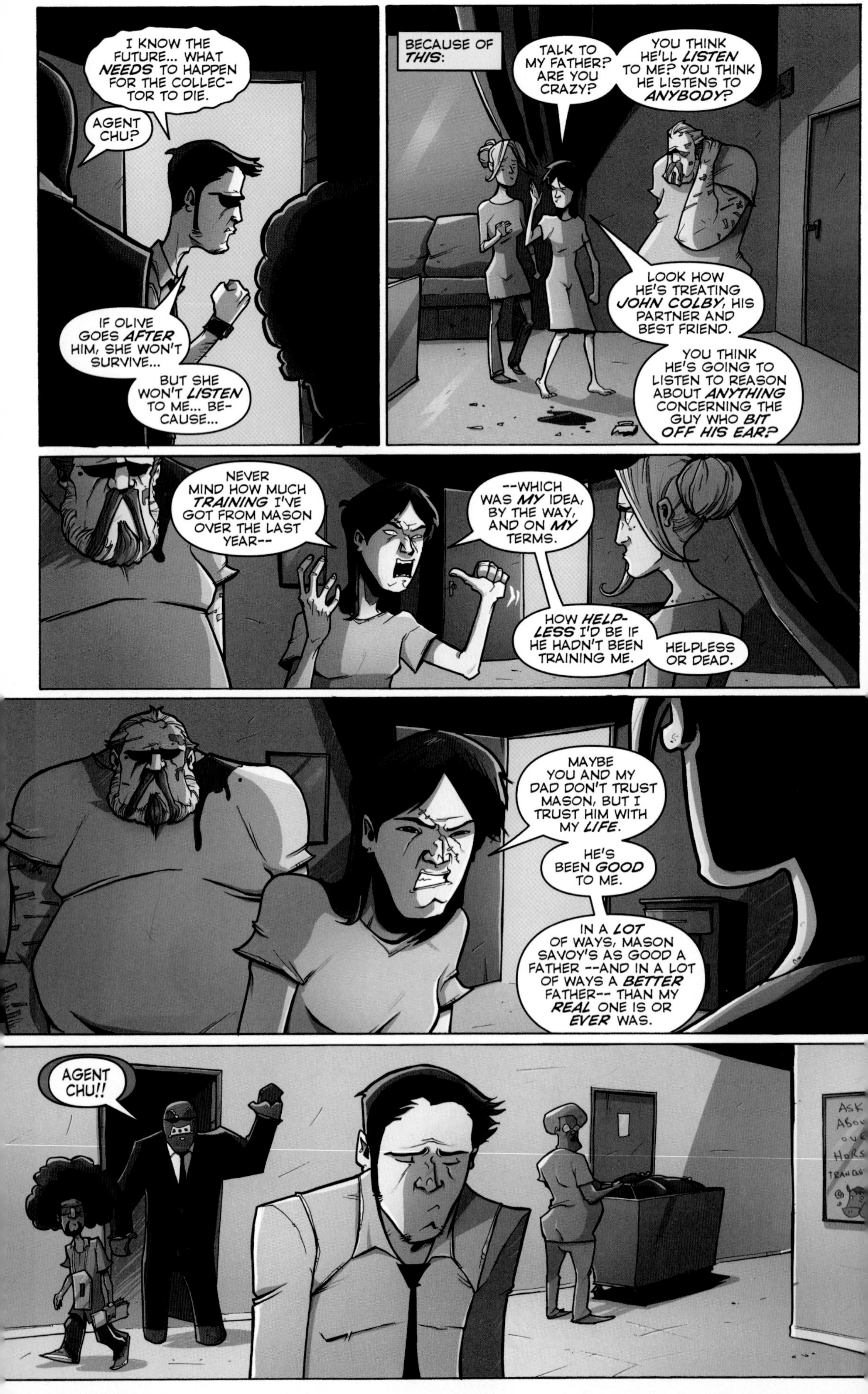
I KNOW THE FUTURE... WHAT NEEDS TO HAPPEN FOR THE COLLECTOR TO DIE.
AGENT CHU?
IF OLIVE GOES AFTER HIM, SHE WON'T SURVIVE...
BUT SHE WON'T LISTEN TO ME... BECAUSE...
BECAUSE OF THIS:
TALK TO MY FATHER? ARE YOU CRAZY?
YOU THINK HE'LL LISTEN TO ME? YOU THINK HE LISTENS TO ANYBODY?
LOOK HOW HE'S TREATING JOHN COLBY, HIS PARTNER AND BEST FRIEND.
YOU THINK HE'S GOING TO LISTEN TO REASON ABOUT ANYTHING CONCERNING THE GUY WHO BIT OFF HIS EAR?
NEVER MIND HOW MUCH TRAINING I'VE GOT FROM MASON OVER THE LAST YEAR--
--WHICH WAS MY IDEA, BY THE WAY, AND ON MY TERMS.
HOW HELPLESS I'D BE IF HE HADN'T BEEN TRAINING ME.
HELPLESS OR DEAD.
MAYBE YOU AND MY DAD DON'T TRUST MASON, BUT I TRUST HIM WITH MY LIFE.
HE'S BEEN GOOD TO ME.
IN A LOT OF WAYS, MASON SAVOY'S AS GOOD A FATHER --AND IN A LOT OF WAYS A BETTER FATHER-- THAN MY REAL ONE IS OR EVER WAS.
AGENT CHU!!
ASK

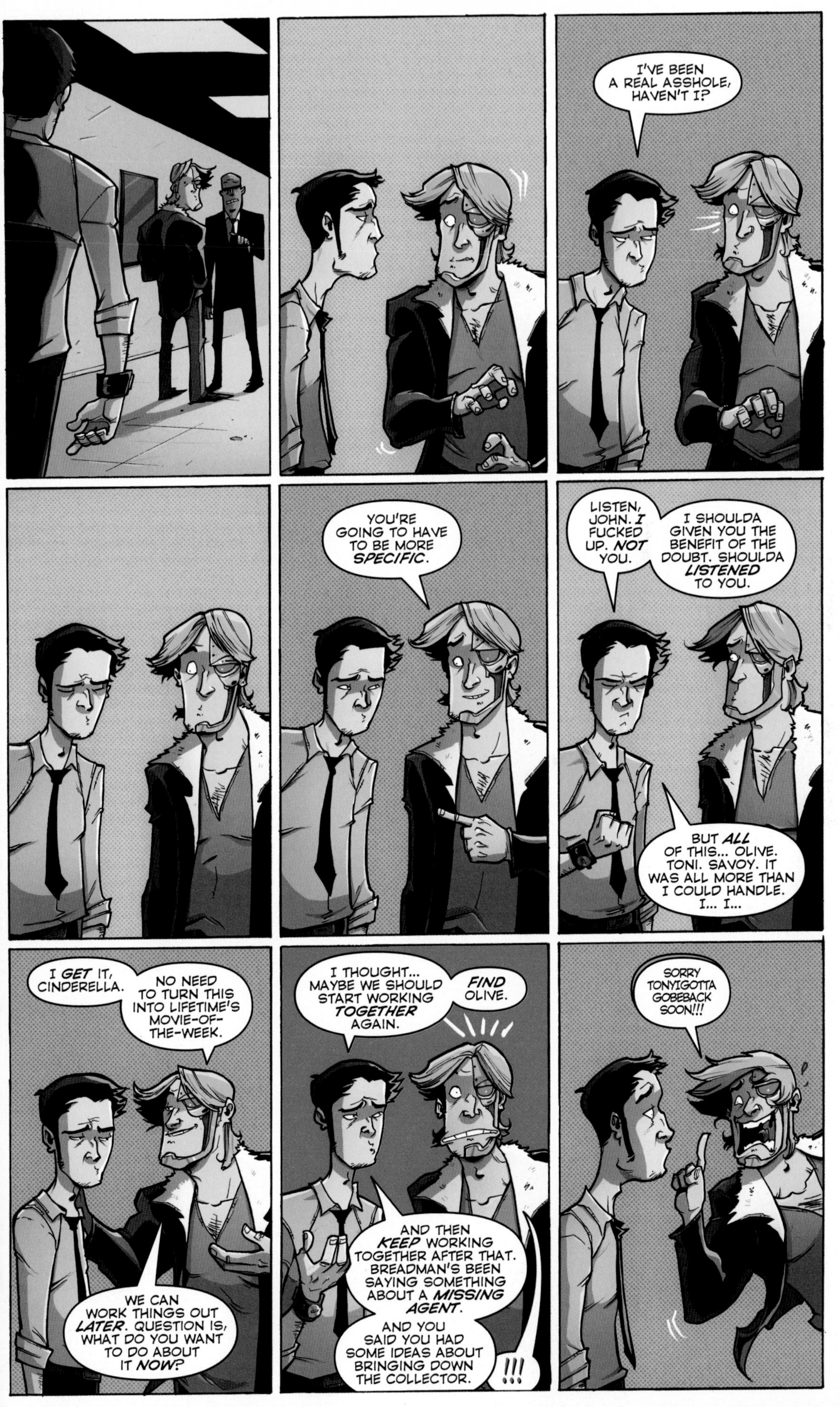
I'VE BEEN A REAL ASSHOLE, HAVEN'T I?
YOU'RE GOING TO HAVE TO BE MORE *SPECIFIC*.
LISTEN, JOHN. *I* FUCKED UP. *NOT* YOU.
I SHOULDA GIVEN YOU THE BENEFIT OF THE DOUBT. SHOULDA *LISTENED* TO YOU.
BUT *ALL* OF THIS... OLIVE. TONI. SAVOY. IT WAS ALL MORE THAN I COULD HANDLE. I... I...
I *GET* IT, CINDERELLA.
NO NEED TO TURN THIS INTO LIFETIME'S MOVIE-OF-THE-WEEK.
WE CAN WORK THINGS OUT *LATER*. QUESTION IS, WHAT DO YOU WANT TO DO ABOUT IT *NOW*?
I THOUGHT... MAYBE WE SHOULD START WORKING *TOGETHER* AGAIN.
FIND OLIVE.
AND THEN *KEEP* WORKING TOGETHER AFTER THAT. BREADMAN'S BEEN SAYING SOMETHING ABOUT A *MISSING AGENT*.
AND YOU SAID YOU HAD SOME IDEAS ABOUT BRINGING DOWN THE COLLECTOR.
!!!
SORRY TONYIGOTTA GOBEBACK SOON!!!

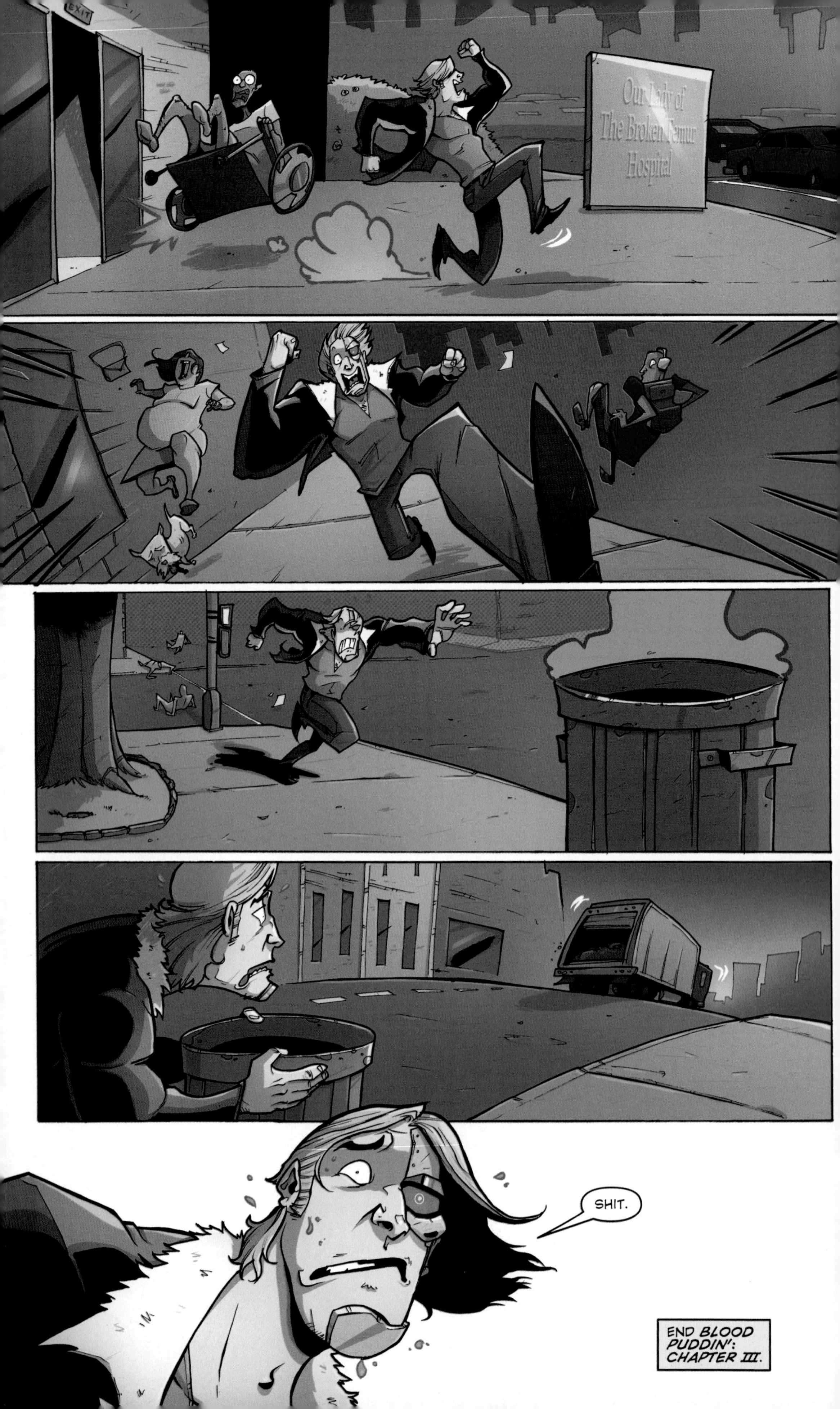
EXIT
Our Lady of The Broken Femur Hospital
SHIT.
END BLOOD PUDDIN': CHAPTER III.

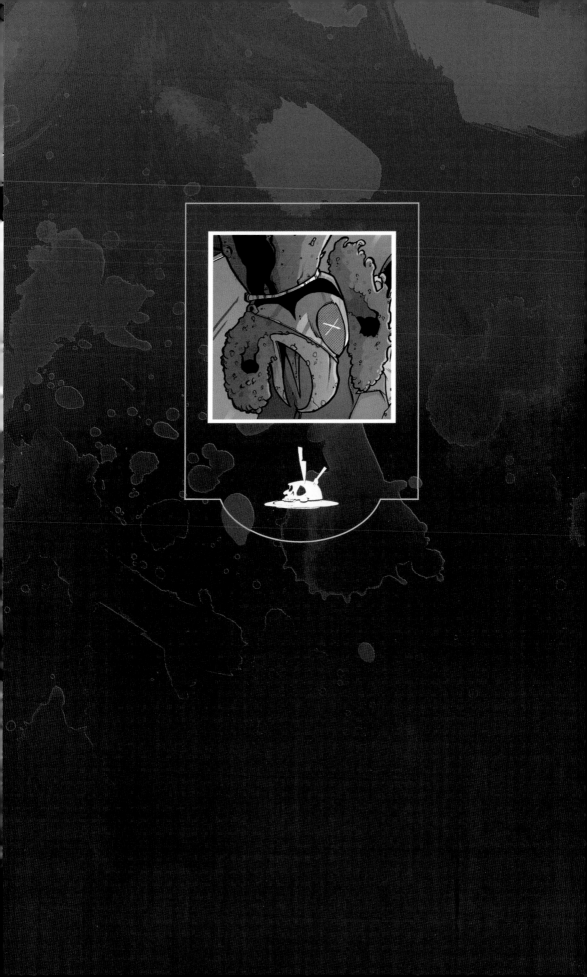

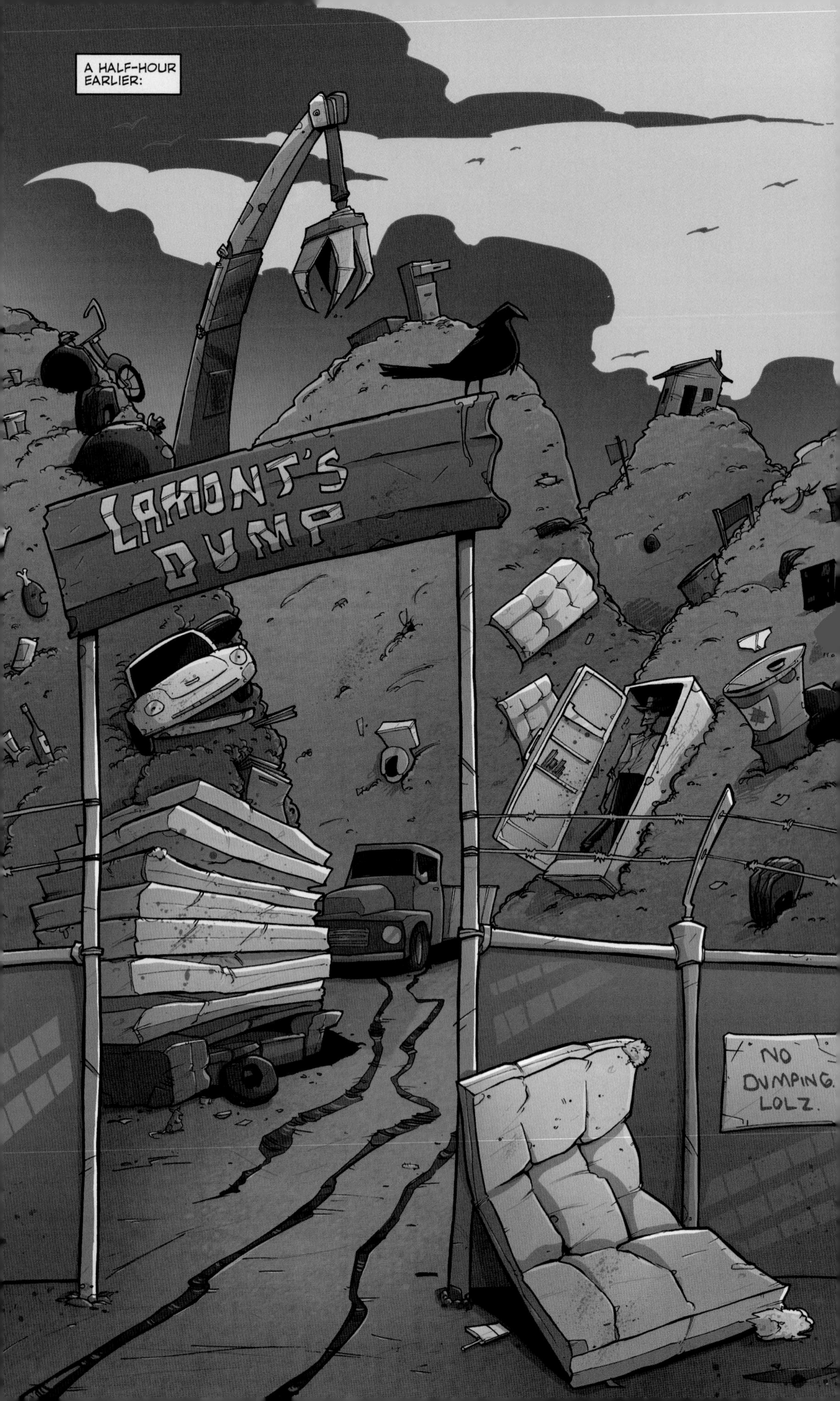

A HALF-HOUR EARLIER:
LAMONT'S DUMP
NO DUMPING. LOLZ.

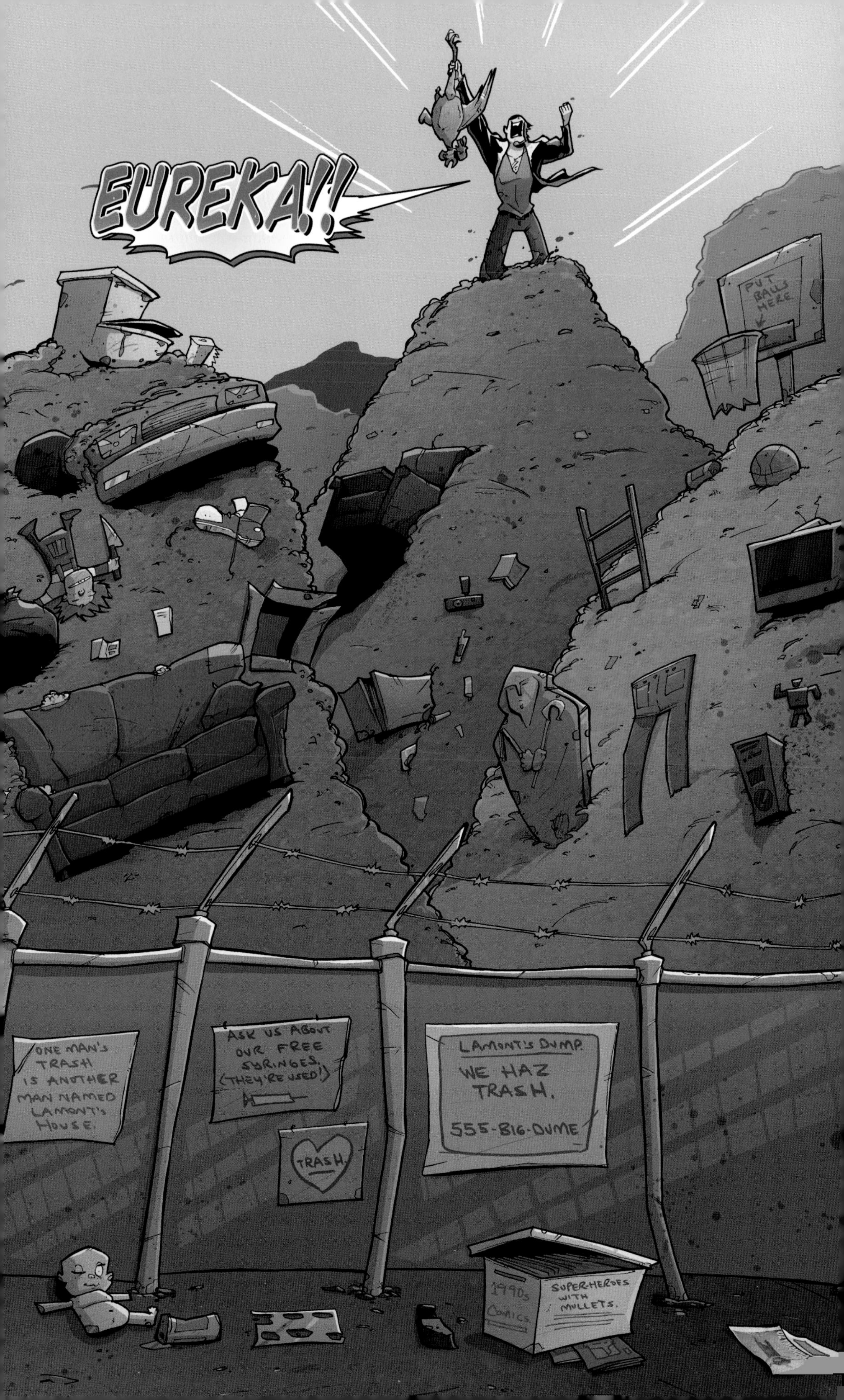
EUREKA!!
PUT BALLS HERE
ONE MAN'S TRASH IS ANOTHER MAN NAMED LAMONT'S HOUSE.
ASK US ABOUT OUR FREE SYRINGES. (THEY'RE USED!)
TRASH
LAMONT'S DUMP.
WE HAZ TRASH.
555-816-DUMP
1990s Comics.
SUPER-HEROES WITH MULLETS.

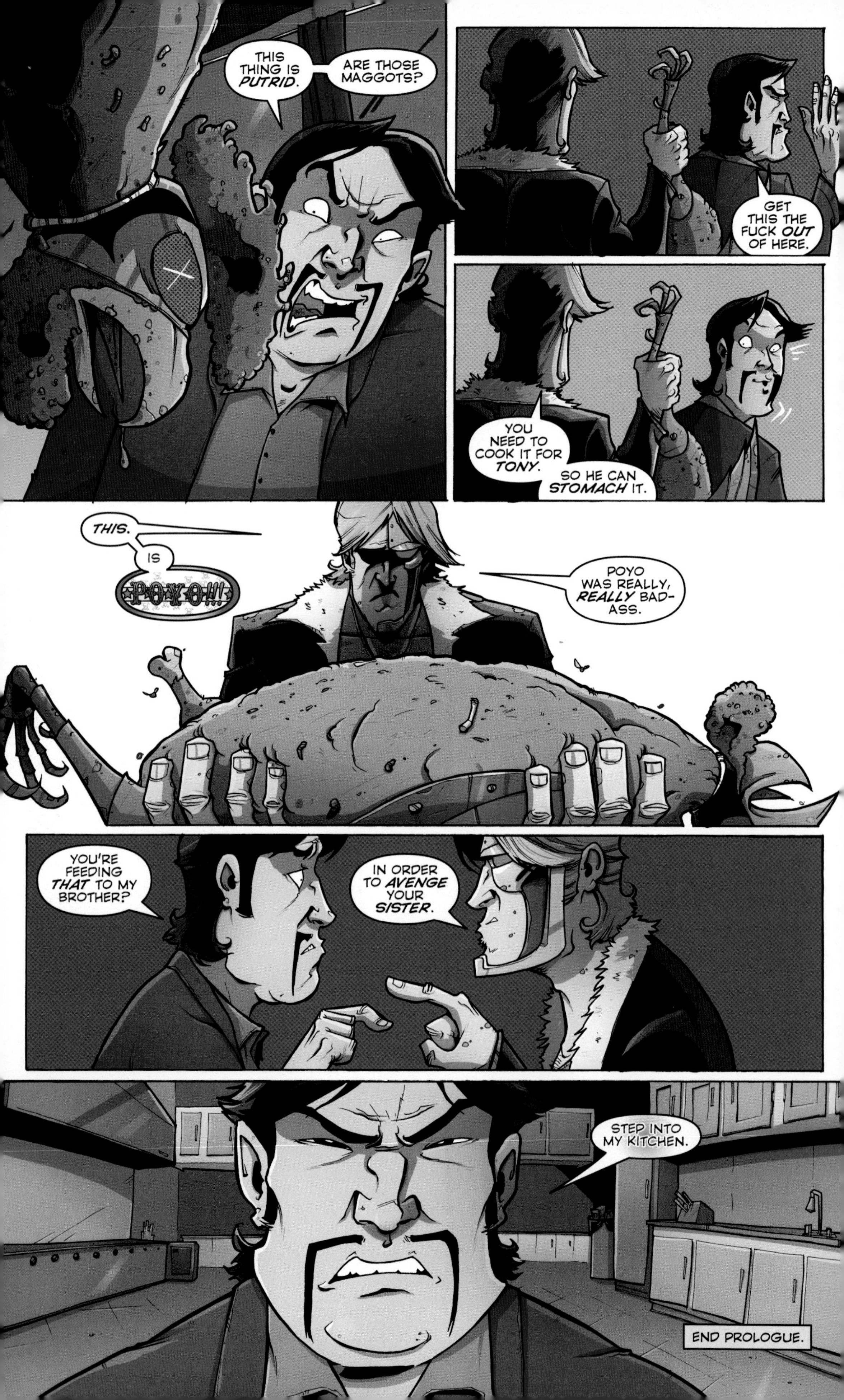

THIS THING IS PUTRID.
ARE THOSE MAGGOTS?
GET THIS THE FUCK OUT OF HERE.
YOU NEED TO COOK IT FOR TONY.
SO HE CAN STOMACH IT.
THIS.
IS
POYO!!!
POYO WAS REALLY, REALLY BAD-ASS.
YOU'RE FEEDING THAT TO MY BROTHER?
IN ORDER TO AVENGE YOUR SISTER.
STEP INTO MY KITCHEN.
END PROLOGUE.

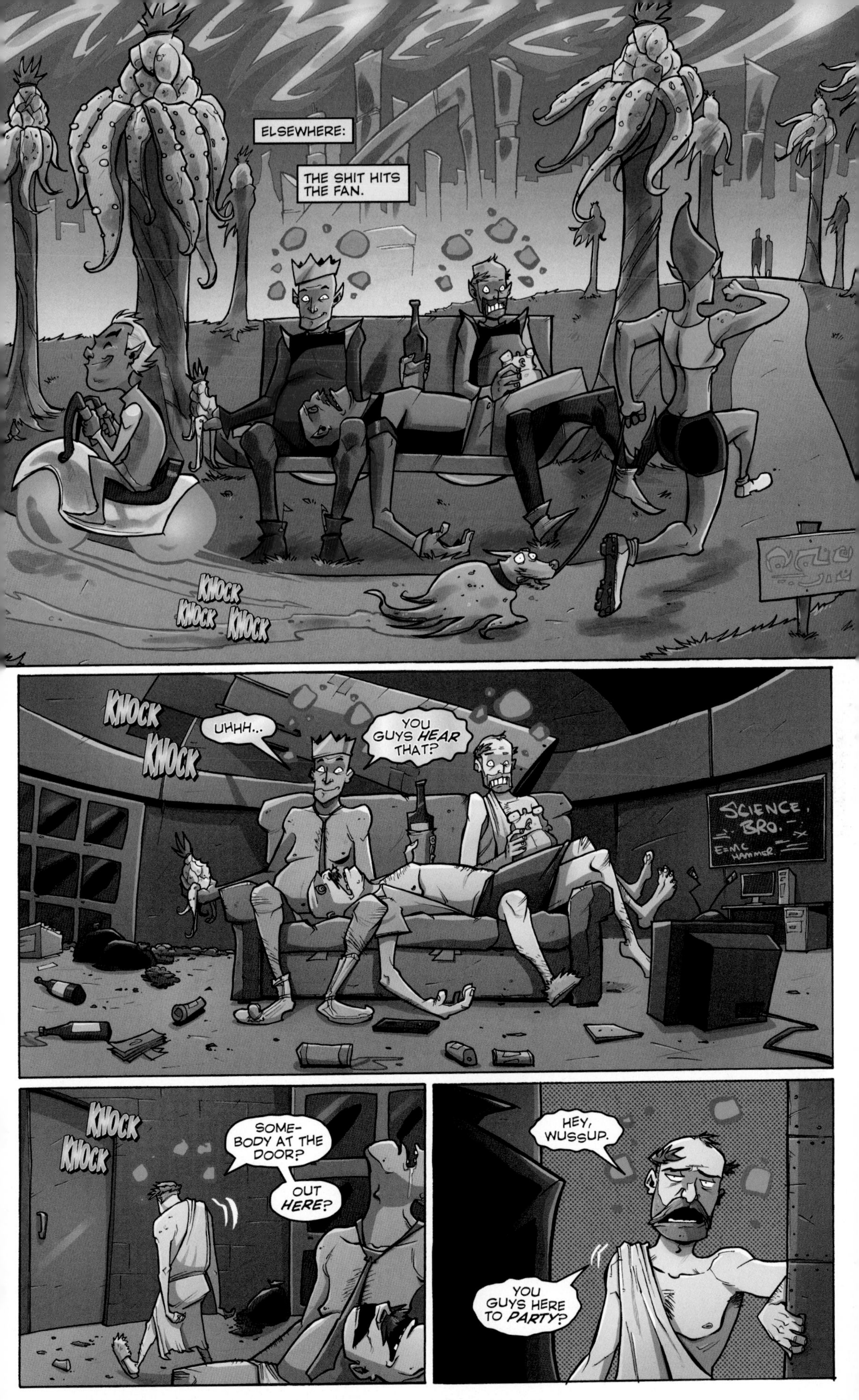

ELSEWHERE:
THE SHIT HITS THE FAN.
KNOCK KNOCK KNOCK
KNOCK KNOCK
UHHH...
YOU GUYS HEAR THAT?
SCIENCE. BRO.
E=MC HAMMER
KNOCK KNOCK
SOME-BODY AT THE DOOR?
OUT HERE?
HEY, WUSSUP.
YOU GUYS HERE TO PARTY?

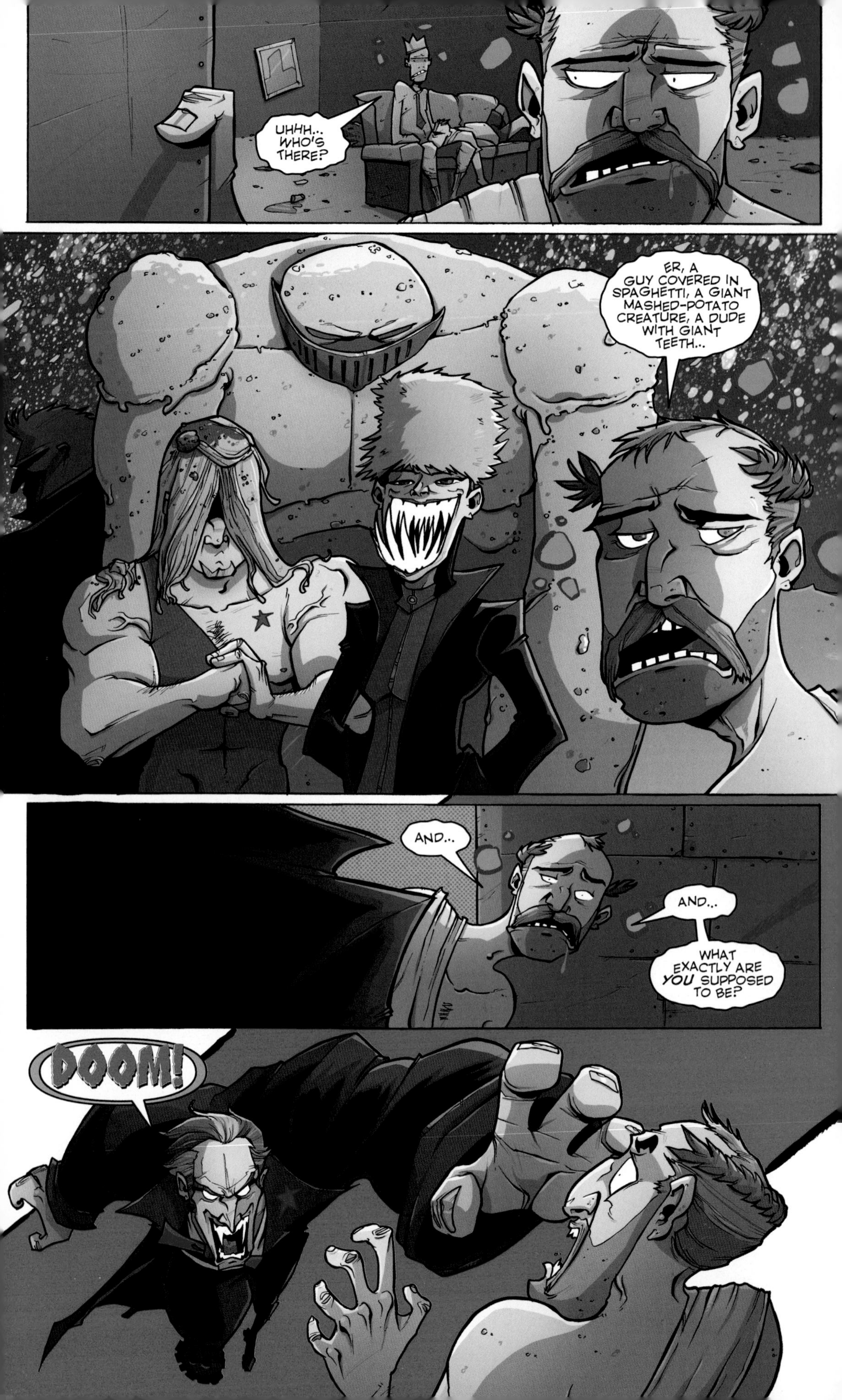
UHHH...
WHO'S
THERE?
ER, A GUY COVERED IN SPAGHETTI, A GIANT MASHED-POTATO CREATURE, A DUDE WITH GIANT TEETH...
AND...
AND...
WHAT EXACTLY ARE YOU SUPPOSED TO BE?
DOOM!

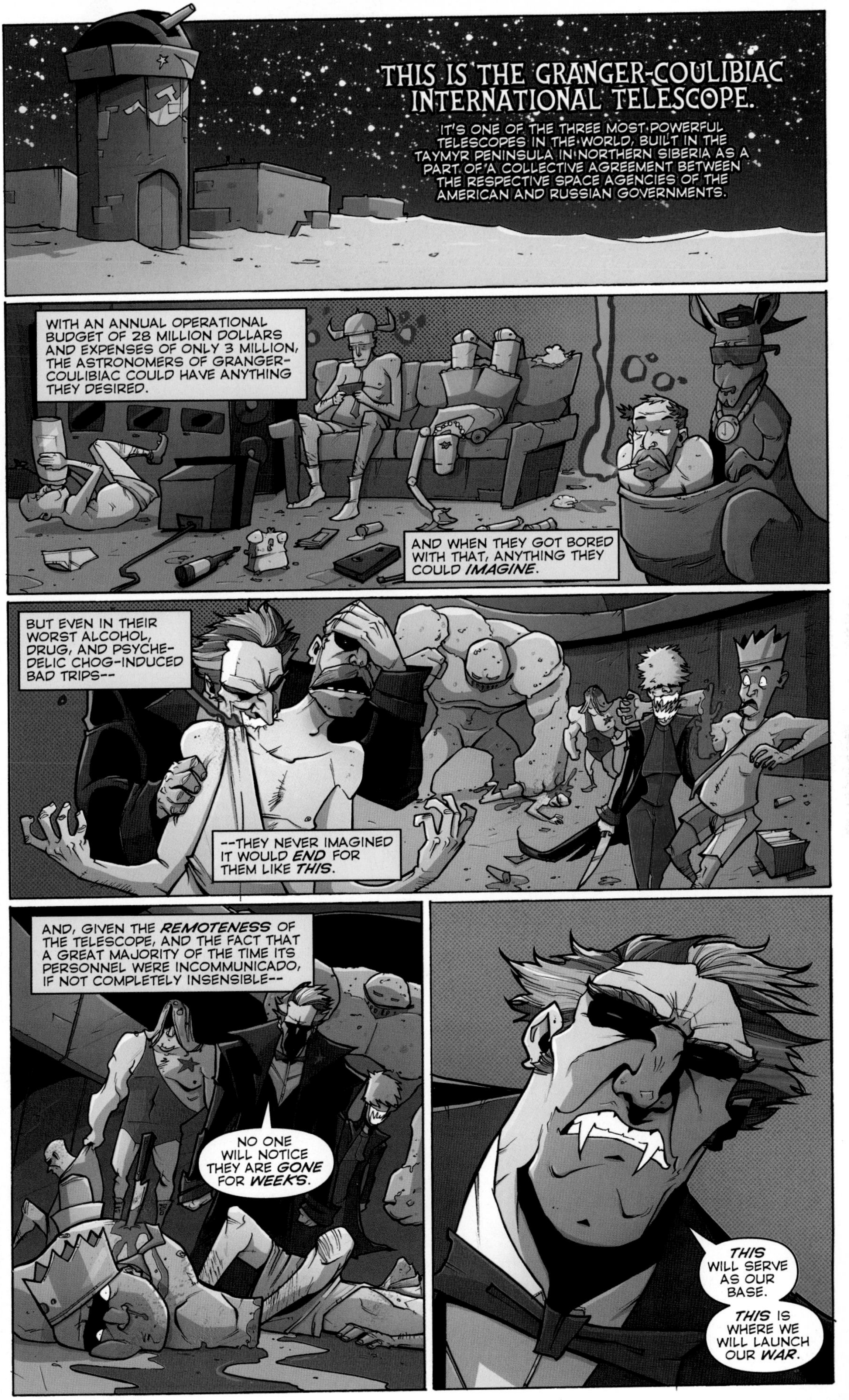
THIS IS THE GRANGER-COULIBIAC INTERNATIONAL TELESCOPE.
IT'S ONE OF THE THREE MOST POWERFUL TELESCOPES IN THE WORLD, BUILT IN THE TAYMYR PENINSULA IN NORTHERN SIBERIA AS A PART OF A COLLECTIVE AGREEMENT BETWEEN THE RESPECTIVE SPACE AGENCIES OF THE AMERICAN AND RUSSIAN GOVERNMENTS.
WITH AN ANNUAL OPERATIONAL BUDGET OF 28 MILLION DOLLARS AND EXPENSES OF ONLY 3 MILLION, THE ASTRONOMERS OF GRANGER-COULIBIAC COULD HAVE ANYTHING THEY DESIRED.
AND WHEN THEY GOT BORED WITH THAT, ANYTHING THEY COULD *IMAGINE*.
BUT EVEN IN THEIR WORST ALCOHOL, DRUG, AND PSYCHEDELIC CHOG-INDUCED BAD TRIPS--
--THEY NEVER IMAGINED IT WOULD *END* FOR THEM LIKE *THIS*.
AND, GIVEN THE *REMOTENESS* OF THE TELESCOPE, AND THE FACT THAT A GREAT MAJORITY OF THE TIME ITS PERSONNEL WERE INCOMMUNICADO, IF NOT COMPLETELY INSENSIBLE--
NO ONE WILL NOTICE THEY ARE *GONE* FOR *WEEKS*.
THIS WILL SERVE AS OUR BASE.
THIS IS WHERE WE WILL LAUNCH OUR *WAR*.

INDEED IT HAS. THIS COLLECTOR MONSTER IS OUT OF CONTROL. IT SEEMS HE'S DECLARED *WAR*.

ACCELERATING HIS COLLECTING, SENDING HIS SERVANTS TO FORCE EVERYBODY WITH FOOD POWERS INTO HIS SERVICE--

AND KILLING *ANY-BODY* WHO RESISTS.

HE'S GOING TO BE TOO POWERFUL TO STOP SOON, IF HE ISN'T ALREADY.

OF COURSE, TO *STOP* HIM, FIRST WE'RE GOING TO HAVE TO *FIND* HIM.

HE'S BEEN IN *HIDING* SINCE THE FDA'S DISASTROUS OFFENSIVE ON THE COLLECTOR'S CASTLE.

DAYS SINCE LAST TERRIBLE "ACCIDENT" -5

DIRECTOR *BREADMAN*, I GOT A *READING* ON THAT WHICH CAN HELP.

A LEAD ON THE COLLECTOR'S *LOCALE*.

GONNA NEED AGENT *VALENZANO* WITH ME ON THIS ASSIGN-MENT.

FINE. JUST GET ME *RESULTS*, AGENTS! AND DO IT *QUICKLY!*

YO. WHAT ABOUT *ME*, BOSS?

DOCTORS HAVE CLEARED AGENT *VORHEES* FOR RETURN TO DUTY.

YOU CAN BE TEAMED WITH *HIM*, AGENT BERRY.

THE CRIPPLED RETARDED GUY?

SHIT.

FUCK.

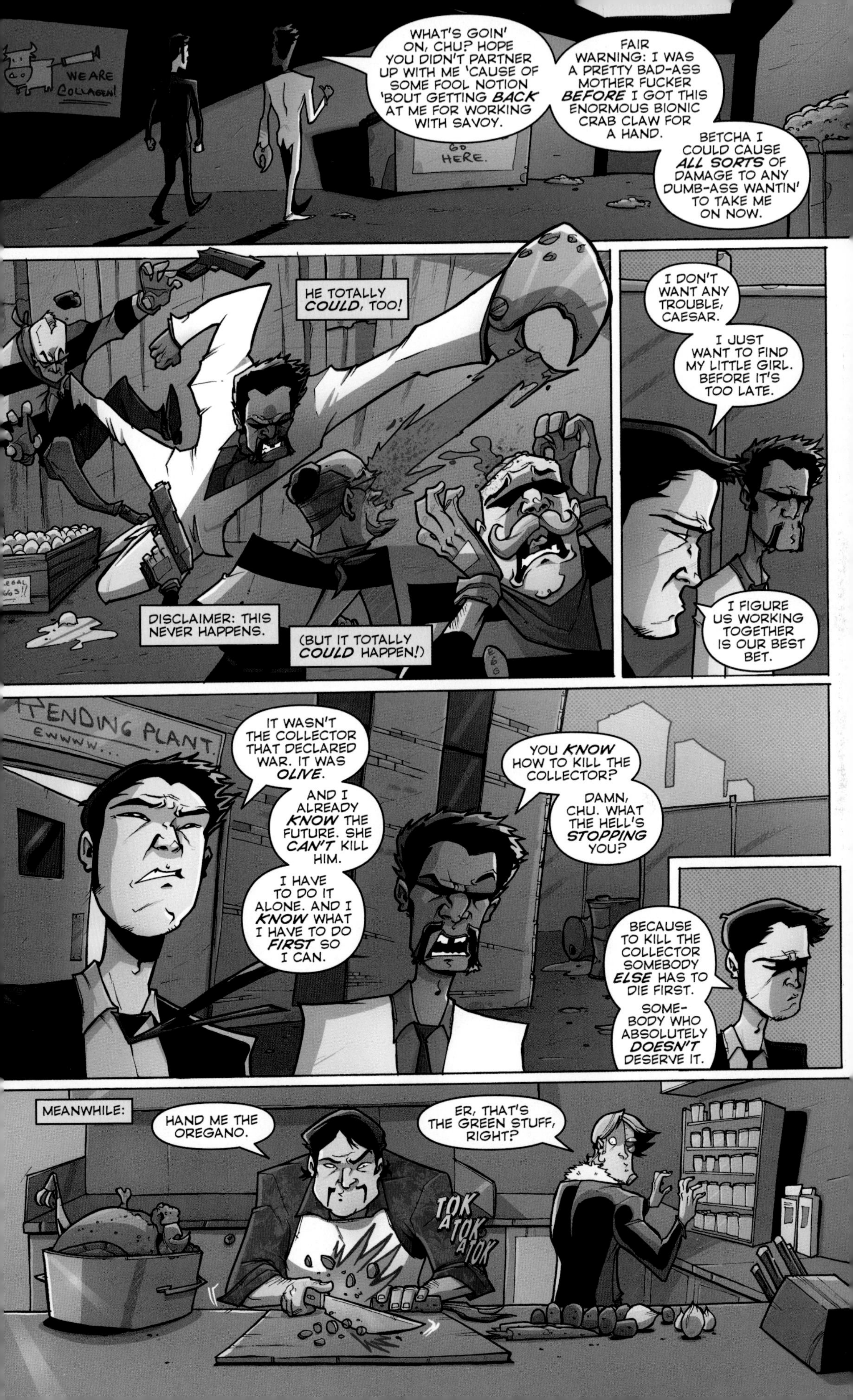
WE ARE COLLAGEN!
GO HERE.
WHAT'S GOIN' ON, CHU? HOPE YOU DIDN'T PARTNER UP WITH ME 'CAUSE OF SOME FOOL NOTION 'BOUT GETTING BACK AT ME FOR WORKING WITH SAVOY.
FAIR WARNING: I WAS A PRETTY BAD-ASS MOTHER FUCKER BEFORE I GOT THIS ENORMOUS BIONIC CRAB CLAW FOR A HAND.
BETCHA I COULD CAUSE ALL SORTS OF DAMAGE TO ANY DUMB-ASS WANTIN' TO TAKE ME ON NOW.
HE TOTALLY COULD, TOO!
DISCLAIMER: THIS NEVER HAPPENS.
(BUT IT TOTALLY COULD HAPPEN!)
I DON'T WANT ANY TROUBLE, CAESAR.
I JUST WANT TO FIND MY LITTLE GIRL. BEFORE IT'S TOO LATE.
I FIGURE US WORKING TOGETHER IS OUR BEST BET.
ENDING PLANT.
EWWWW...
IT WASN'T THE COLLECTOR THAT DECLARED WAR. IT WAS OLIVE.
AND I ALREADY KNOW THE FUTURE. SHE CAN'T KILL HIM.
I HAVE TO DO IT ALONE. AND I KNOW WHAT I HAVE TO DO FIRST SO I CAN.
YOU KNOW HOW TO KILL THE COLLECTOR?
DAMN, CHU. WHAT THE HELL'S STOPPING YOU?
BECAUSE TO KILL THE COLLECTOR SOMEBODY ELSE HAS TO DIE FIRST.
SOME-BODY WHO ABSOLUTELY DOESN'T DESERVE IT.
MEANWHILE:
HAND ME THE OREGANO.
ER, THAT'S THE GREEN STUFF, RIGHT?
TOK A TOK A TOK

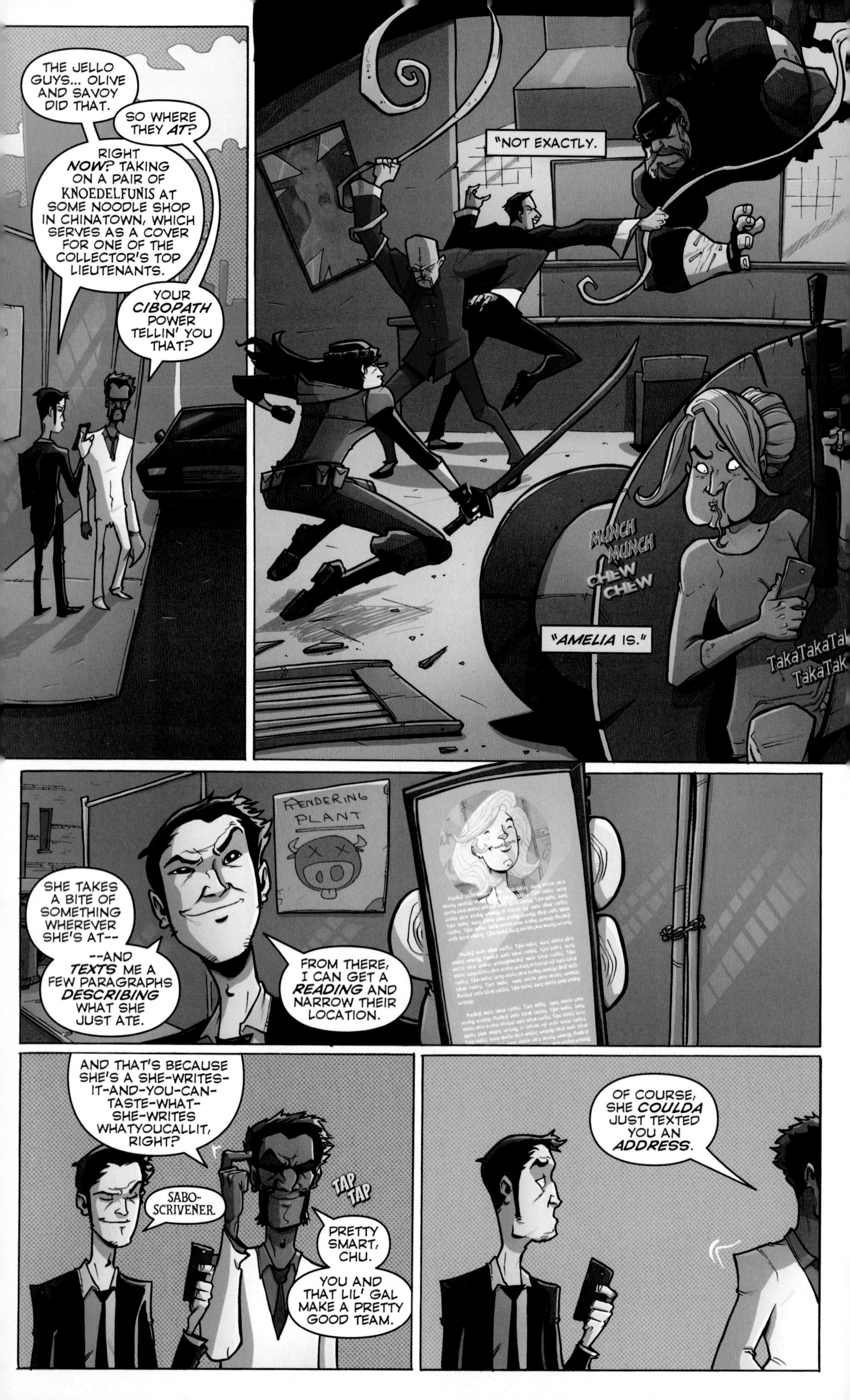
THE JELLO GUYS... OLIVE AND SAVOY DID THAT.
SO WHERE THEY *AT*?
RIGHT *NOW*? TAKING ON A PAIR OF KNOEDELFUNIS AT SOME NOODLE SHOP IN CHINATOWN, WHICH SERVES AS A COVER FOR ONE OF THE COLLECTOR'S TOP LIEUTENANTS.
YOUR *CIBOPATH* POWER TELLIN' YOU THAT?
"NOT EXACTLY.
MUNCH MUNCH
CHEW CHEW
"*AMELIA* IS."
TakaTakaTak
TakaTak
RENDERING PLANT
SHE TAKES A BITE OF SOMETHING WHEREVER SHE'S AT--
--AND *TEXTS* ME A FEW PARAGRAPHS *DESCRIBING* WHAT SHE JUST ATE.
FROM THERE, I CAN GET A *READING* AND NARROW THEIR LOCATION.
AND THAT'S BECAUSE SHE'S A SHE-WRITES-IT-AND-YOU-CAN-TASTE-WHAT-SHE-WRITES WHATYOUCALLIT, RIGHT?
SABO-SCRIVENER.
TAP TAP
PRETTY SMART, CHU.
YOU AND THAT LIL' GAL MAKE A PRETTY GOOD TEAM.
OF COURSE, SHE *COULDA* JUST TEXTED YOU AN *ADDRESS*.

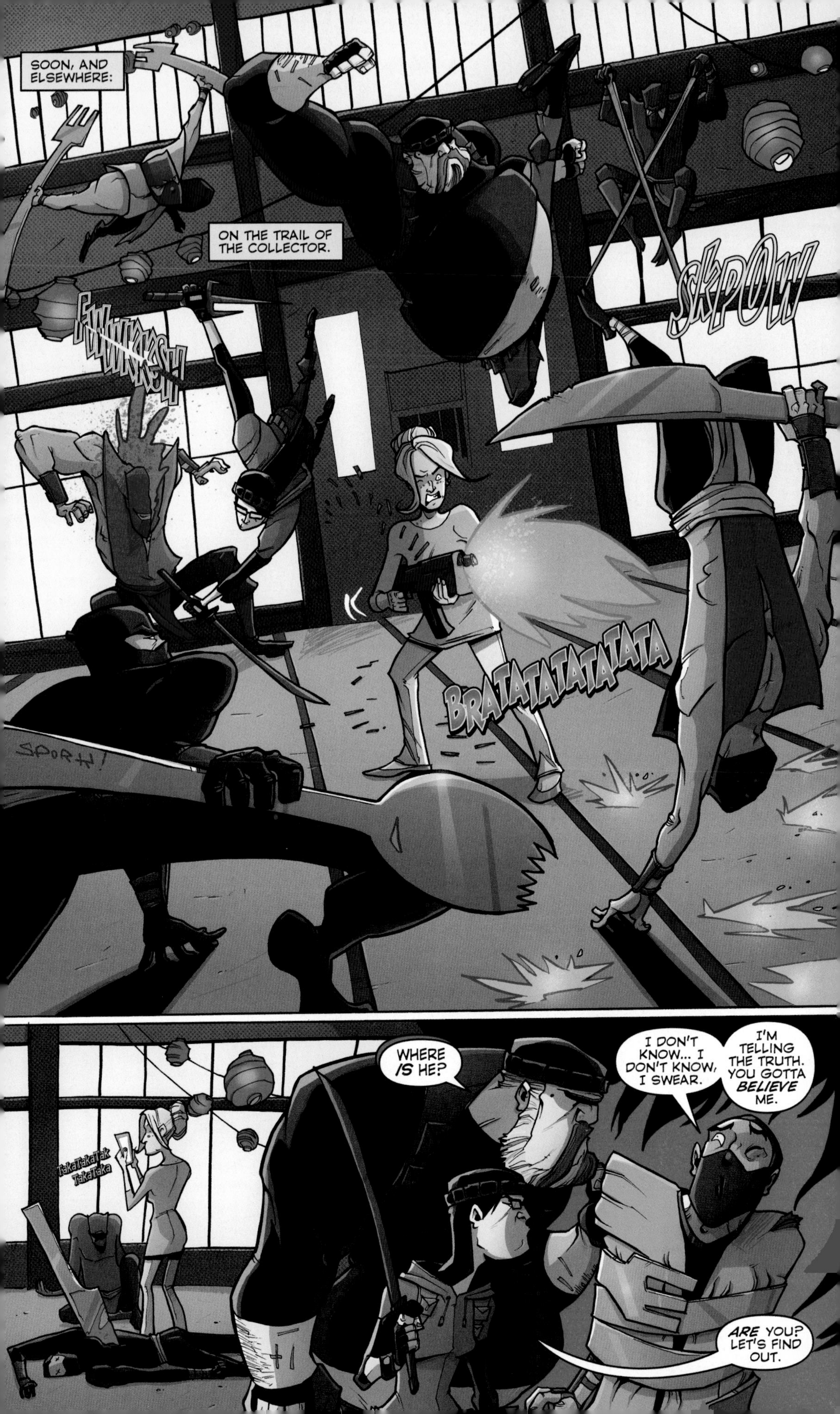
SOON, AND ELSEWHERE:
ON THE TRAIL OF THE COLLECTOR.
SKPOW
BRATATATATATA
SPORK!
TakaTakaTak TakaTaka
WHERE IS HE?
I DON'T KNOW... I DON'T KNOW, I SWEAR.
I'M TELLING THE TRUTH. YOU GOTTA BELIEVE ME.
ARE YOU? LET'S FIND OUT.

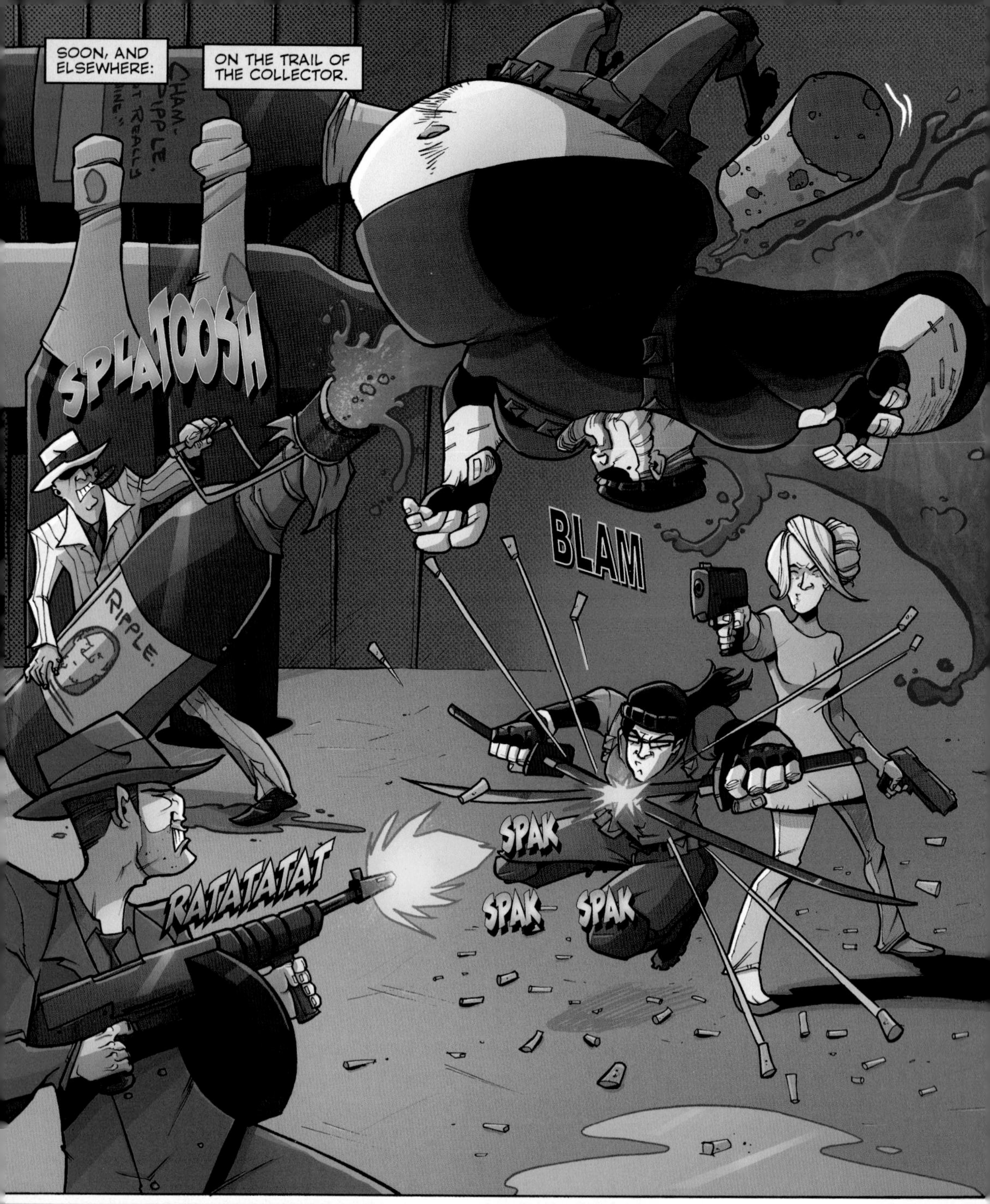
SOON, AND ELSEWHERE:
ON THE TRAIL OF THE COLLECTOR.
SPLATOOSH
RIPPLE.
BLAM
SPAK
RATATATAT
SPAK
SPAK

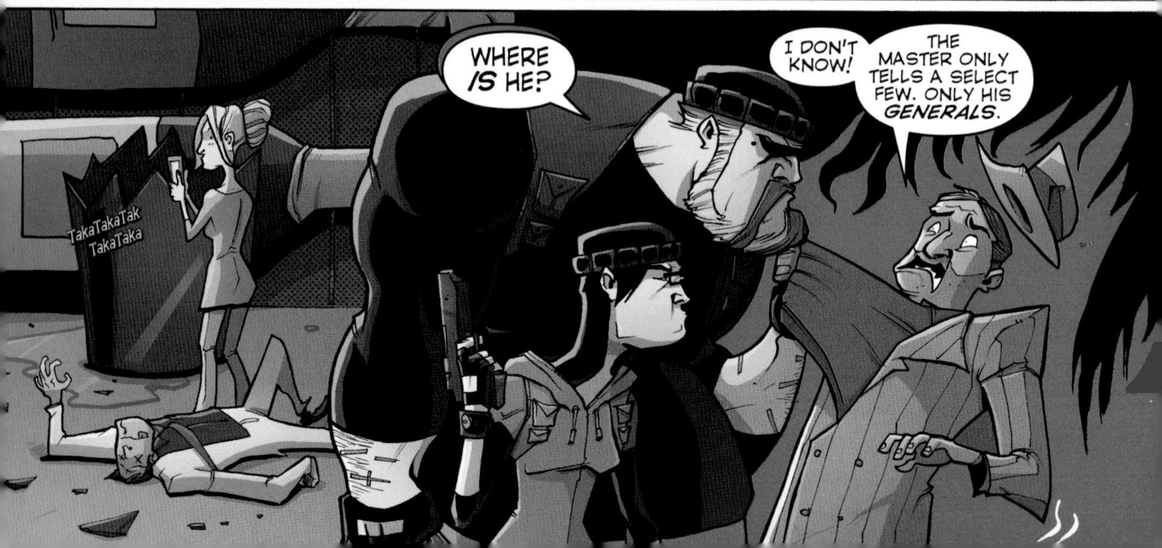
WHERE *IS* HE?
I DON'T KNOW!
THE MASTER ONLY TELLS A SELECT FEW. ONLY HIS *GENERALS*.
TakaTakaTak
TakaTaka

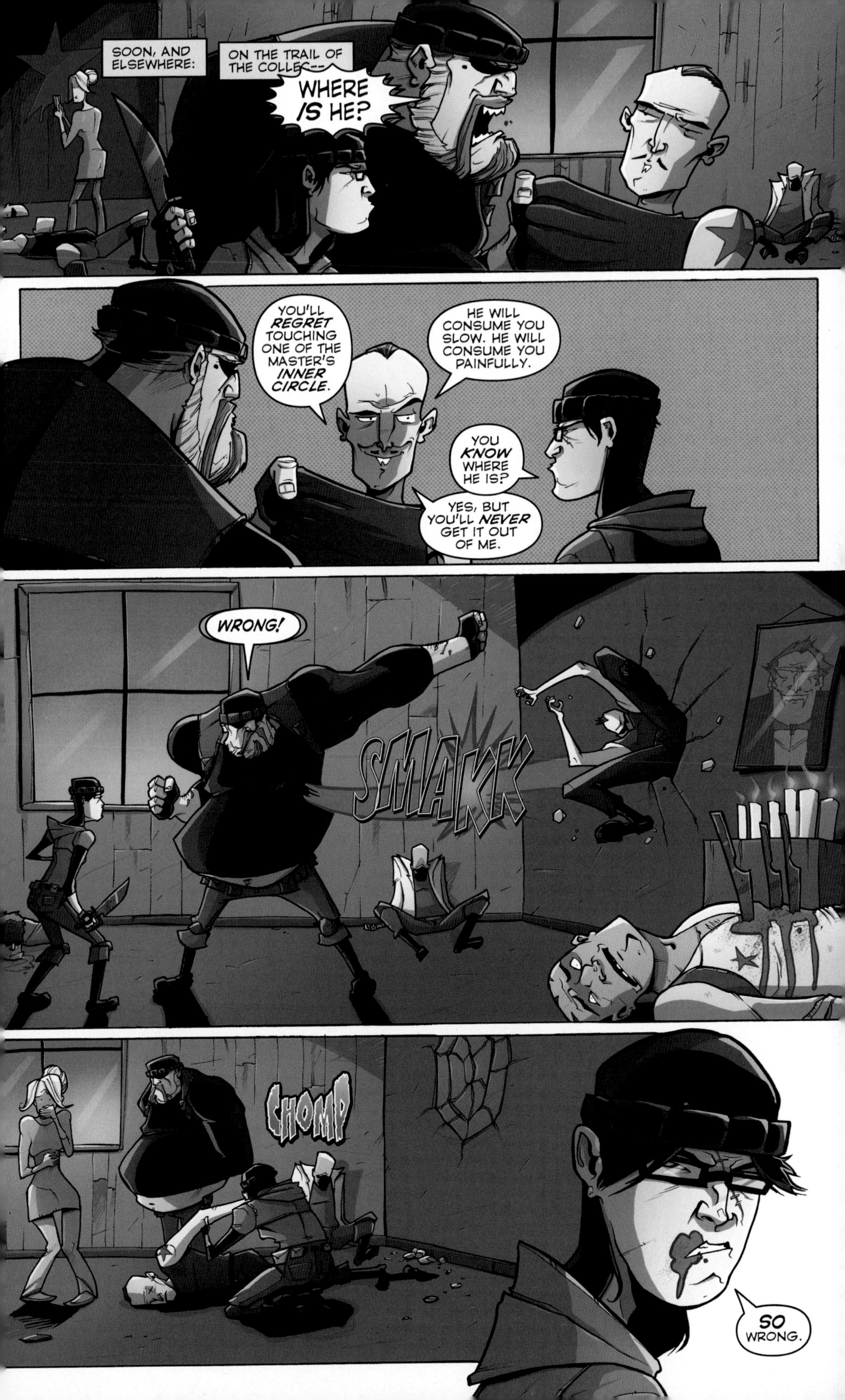
SOON, AND ELSEWHERE:
ON THE TRAIL OF THE COLLEC--
WHERE IS HE?
YOU'LL REGRET TOUCHING ONE OF THE MASTER'S INNER CIRCLE.
HE WILL CONSUME YOU SLOW. HE WILL CONSUME YOU PAINFULLY.
YOU KNOW WHERE HE IS?
YES, BUT YOU'LL NEVER GET IT OUT OF ME.
WRONG!
SMAKK
CHOMP
SO WRONG.

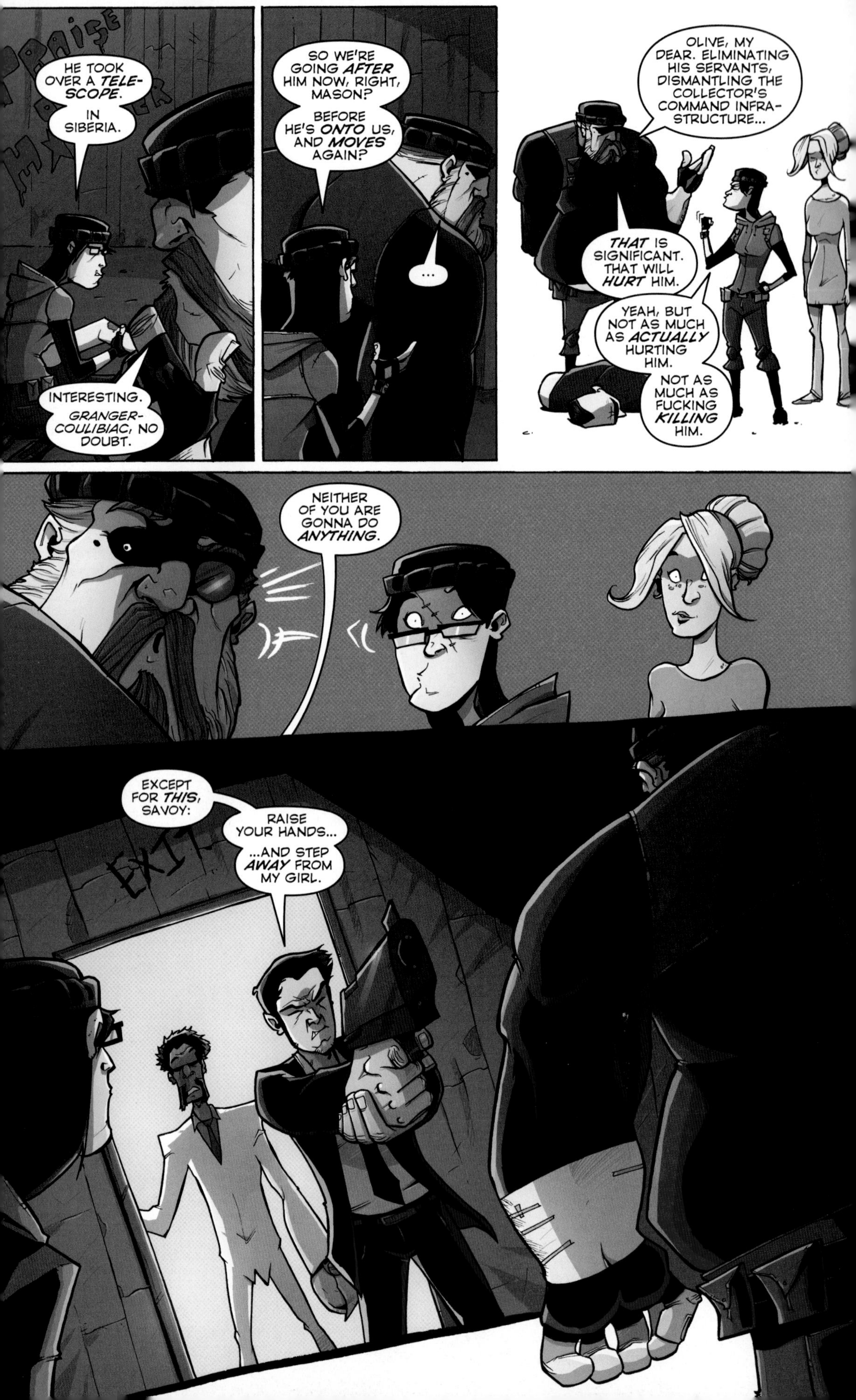

HE TOOK OVER A *TELESCOPE*.
IN SIBERIA.
INTERESTING. *GRANGER-COULIBIAC*, NO DOUBT.
SO WE'RE GOING *AFTER* HIM NOW, RIGHT, MASON?
BEFORE HE'S *ONTO* US, AND *MOVES* AGAIN?
...
OLIVE, MY DEAR. ELIMINATING HIS SERVANTS, DISMANTLING THE COLLECTOR'S COMMAND INFRASTRUCTURE...
THAT IS SIGNIFICANT. THAT WILL *HURT* HIM.
YEAH, BUT NOT AS MUCH AS *ACTUALLY* HURTING HIM.
NOT AS MUCH AS FUCKING *KILLING* HIM.
NEITHER OF YOU ARE GONNA DO *ANYTHING*.
EXCEPT FOR *THIS*, SAVOY:
RAISE YOUR HANDS...
...AND STEP *AWAY* FROM MY GIRL.

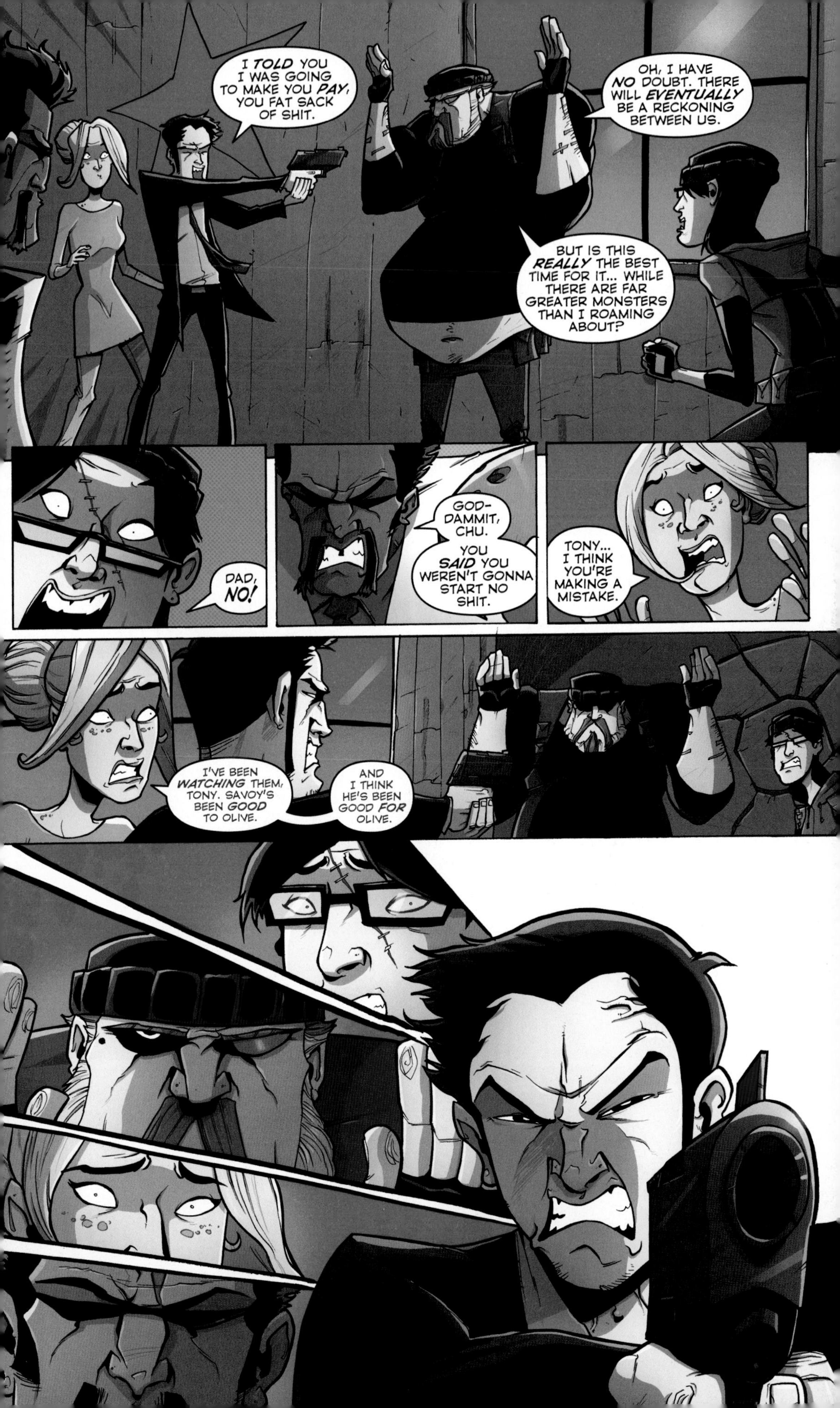
I TOLD YOU I WAS GOING TO MAKE YOU PAY, YOU FAT SACK OF SHIT.
OH, I HAVE NO DOUBT. THERE WILL EVENTUALLY BE A RECKONING BETWEEN US.
BUT IS THIS REALLY THE BEST TIME FOR IT... WHILE THERE ARE FAR GREATER MONSTERS THAN I ROAMING ABOUT?
DAD, NO!
GOD-DAMMIT, CHU.
YOU SAID YOU WEREN'T GONNA START NO SHIT.
TONY... I THINK YOU'RE MAKING A MISTAKE.
I'VE BEEN WATCHING THEM, TONY. SAVOY'S BEEN GOOD TO OLIVE.
AND I THINK HE'S BEEN GOOD FOR OLIVE.

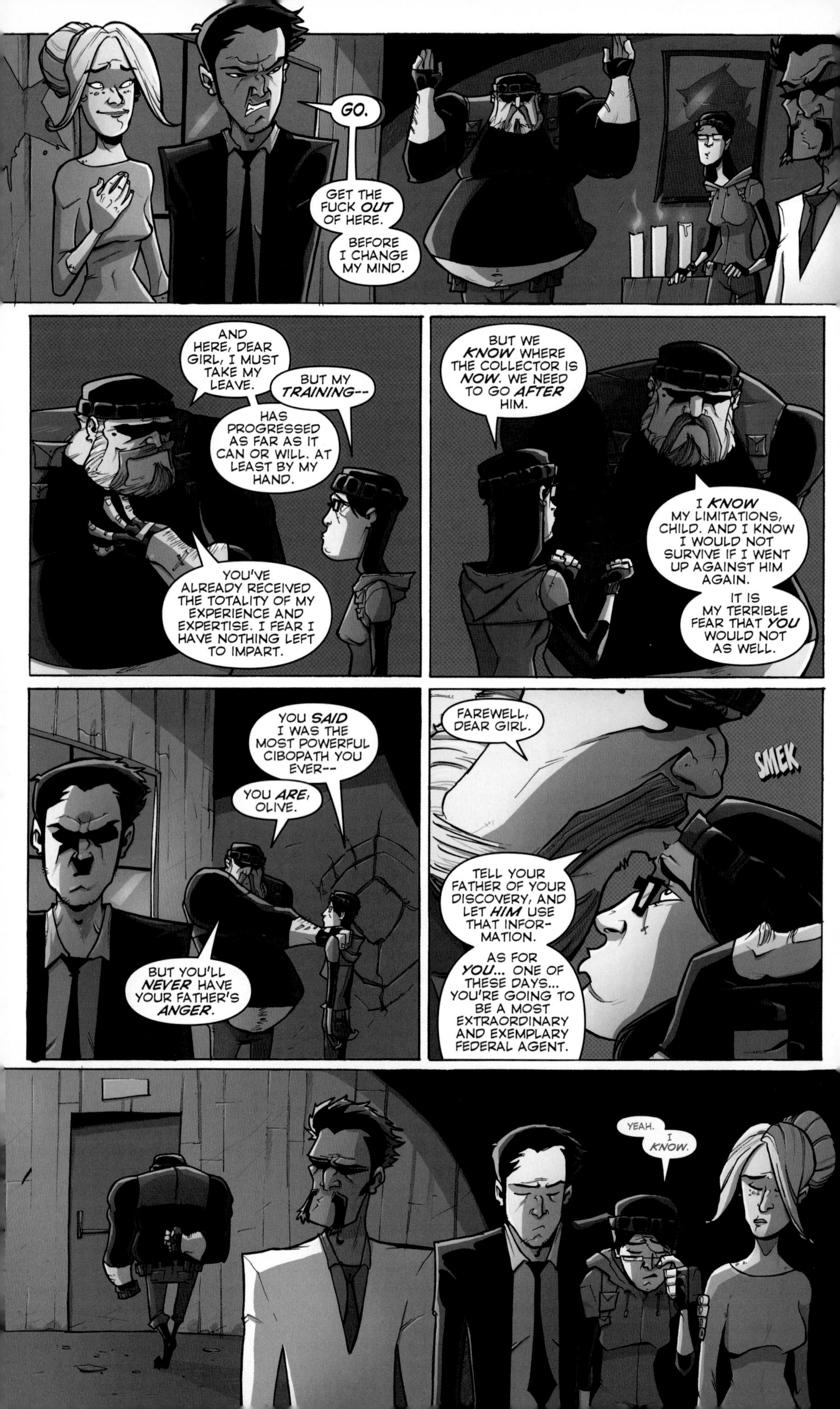
GO.
GET THE FUCK OUT OF HERE.
BEFORE I CHANGE MY MIND.
AND HERE, DEAR GIRL, I MUST TAKE MY LEAVE.
BUT MY TRAINING--
HAS PROGRESSED AS FAR AS IT CAN OR WILL. AT LEAST BY MY HAND.
YOU'VE ALREADY RECEIVED THE TOTALITY OF MY EXPERIENCE AND EXPERTISE. I FEAR I HAVE NOTHING LEFT TO IMPART.
BUT WE KNOW WHERE THE COLLECTOR IS NOW. WE NEED TO GO AFTER HIM.
I KNOW MY LIMITATIONS, CHILD. AND I KNOW I WOULD NOT SURVIVE IF I WENT UP AGAINST HIM AGAIN.
IT IS MY TERRIBLE FEAR THAT YOU WOULD NOT AS WELL.
YOU SAID I WAS THE MOST POWERFUL CIBOPATH YOU EVER--
YOU ARE, OLIVE.
BUT YOU'LL NEVER HAVE YOUR FATHER'S ANGER.
FAREWELL, DEAR GIRL.
SMEK
TELL YOUR FATHER OF YOUR DISCOVERY, AND LET HIM USE THAT INFORMATION.
AS FOR YOU... ONE OF THESE DAYS... YOU'RE GOING TO BE A MOST EXTRAORDINARY AND EXEMPLARY FEDERAL AGENT.
YEAH. I KNOW.

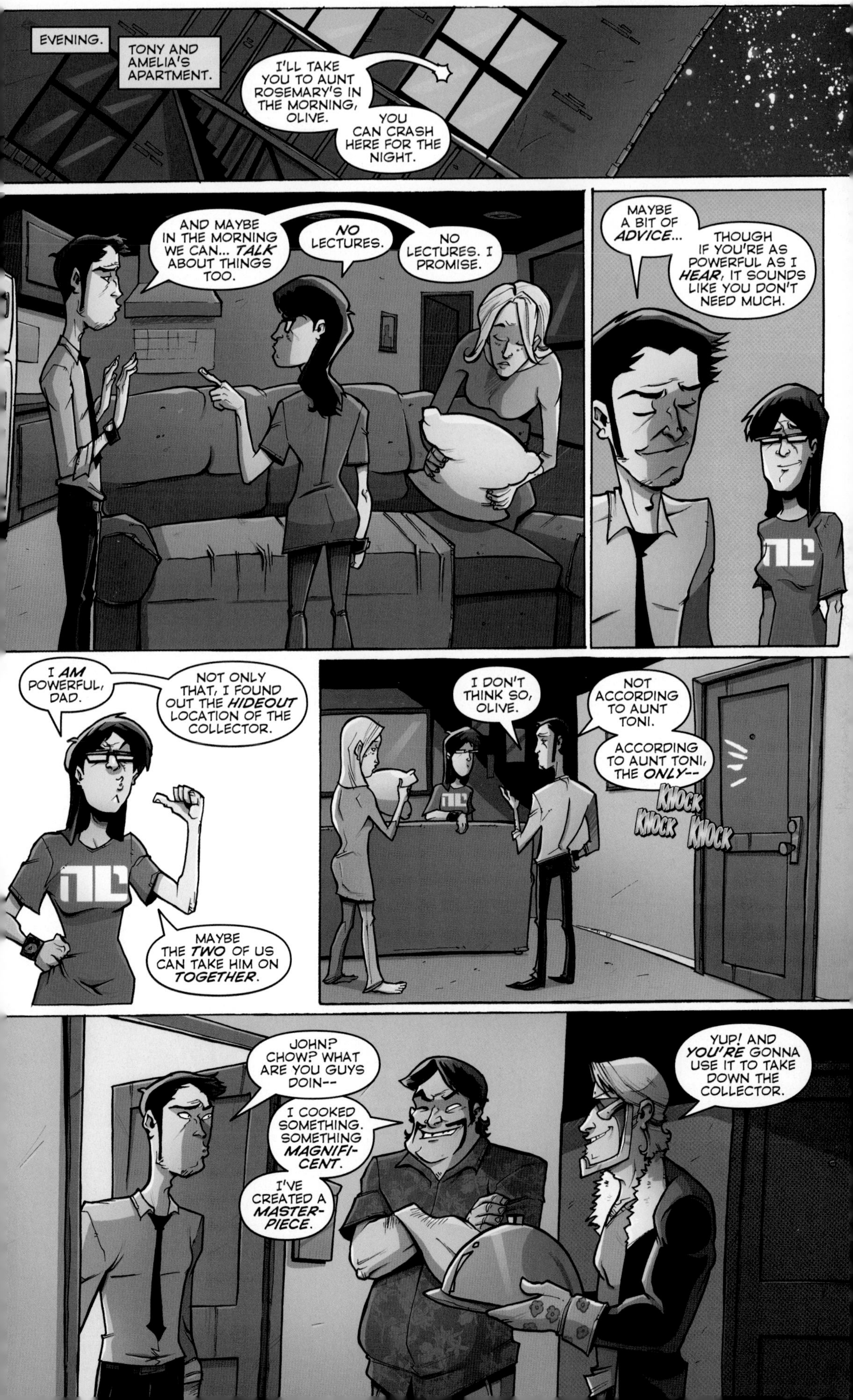

EVENING.
TONY AND AMELIA'S APARTMENT.
I'LL TAKE YOU TO AUNT ROSEMARY'S IN THE MORNING, OLIVE.
YOU CAN CRASH HERE FOR THE NIGHT.
AND MAYBE IN THE MORNING WE CAN... TALK ABOUT THINGS TOO.
NO LECTURES.
NO LECTURES. I PROMISE.
MAYBE A BIT OF ADVICE...
THOUGH IF YOU'RE AS POWERFUL AS I HEAR, IT SOUNDS LIKE YOU DON'T NEED MUCH.
I AM POWERFUL, DAD.
NOT ONLY THAT, I FOUND OUT THE HIDEOUT LOCATION OF THE COLLECTOR.
MAYBE THE TWO OF US CAN TAKE HIM ON TOGETHER.
I DON'T THINK SO, OLIVE.
NOT ACCORDING TO AUNT TONI.
ACCORDING TO AUNT TONI, THE ONLY--
KNOCK
KNOCK
KNOCK
JOHN? CHOW? WHAT ARE YOU GUYS DOIN--
I COOKED SOMETHING. SOMETHING MAGNIFI-CENT.
I'VE CREATED A MASTER-PIECE.
YUP! AND YOU'RE GONNA USE IT TO TAKE DOWN THE COLLECTOR.

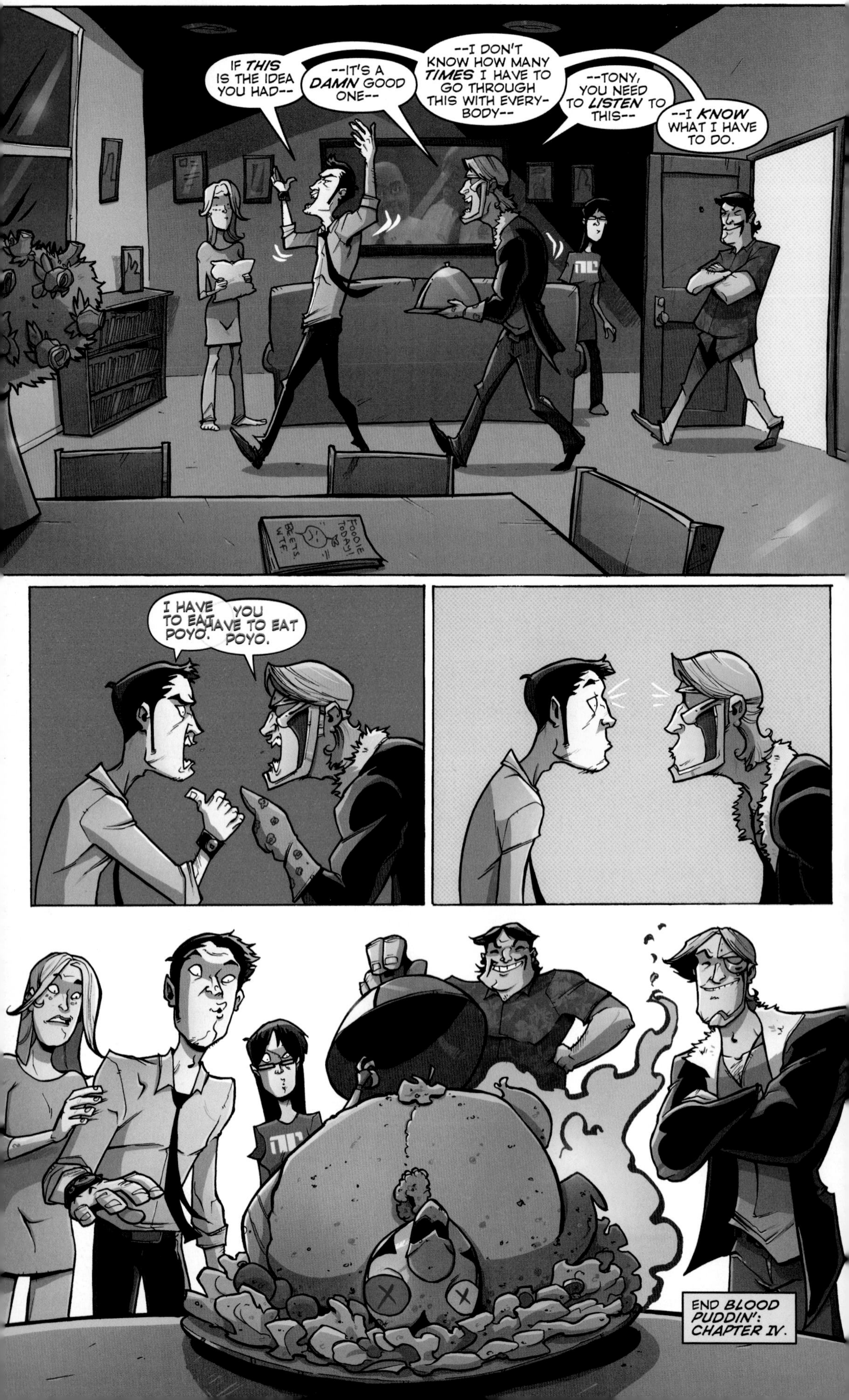

IF *THIS* IS THE IDEA YOU HAD--
--IT'S A *DAMN* GOOD ONE--
--I DON'T KNOW HOW MANY *TIMES* I HAVE TO GO THROUGH THIS WITH EVERY-BODY--
--TONY, YOU NEED TO *LISTEN* TO THIS--
--I *KNOW* WHAT I HAVE TO DO.
FOODIE TODAY!
BEETS. WTF
I HAVE TO EAT POYO.
YOU HAVE TO EAT POYO.
END *BLOOD PUDDIN'*: *CHAPTER IV.*

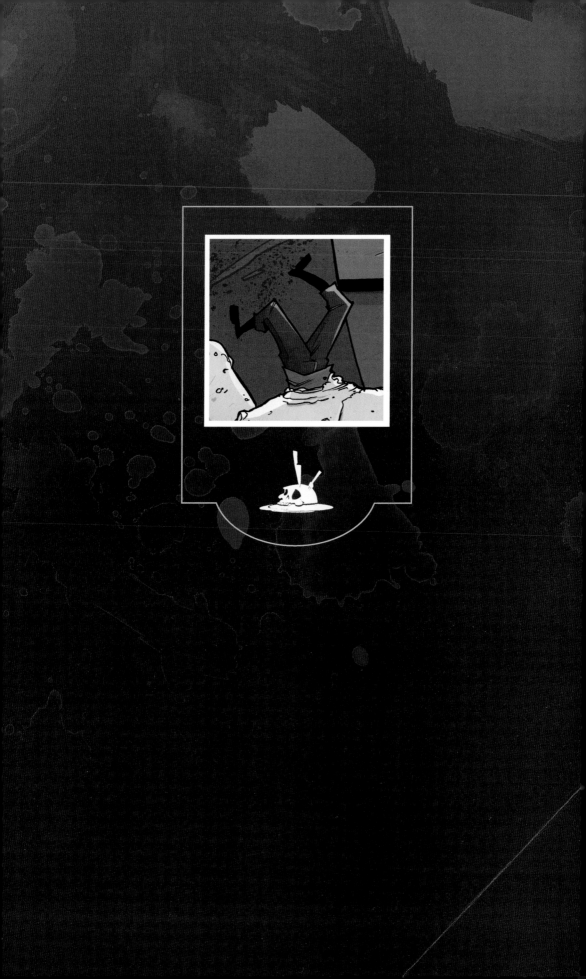

Chapter 5

ROB!

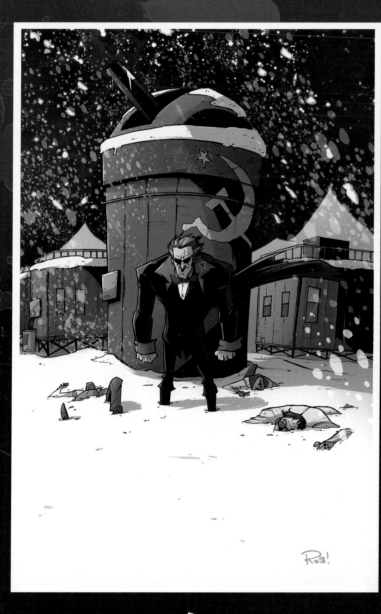

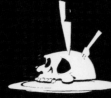

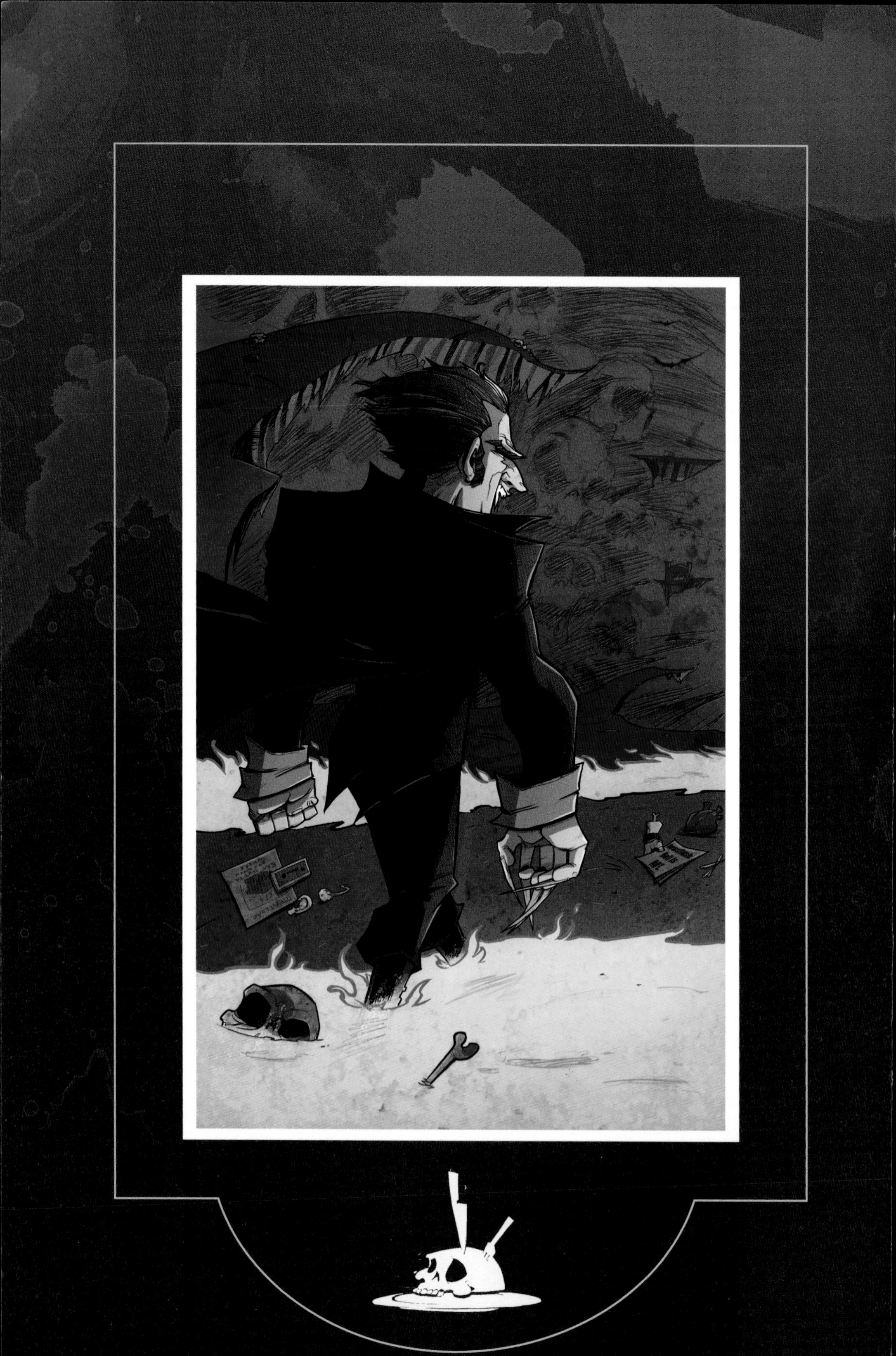

ROB!

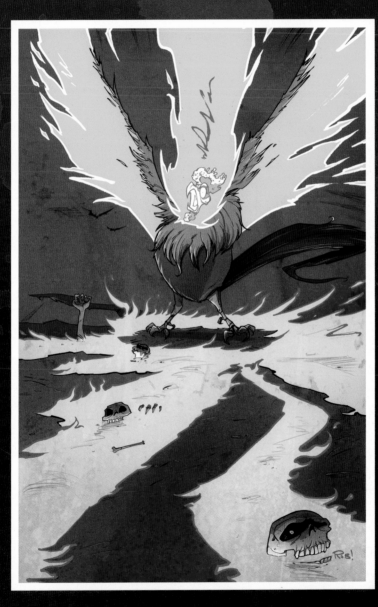

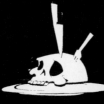

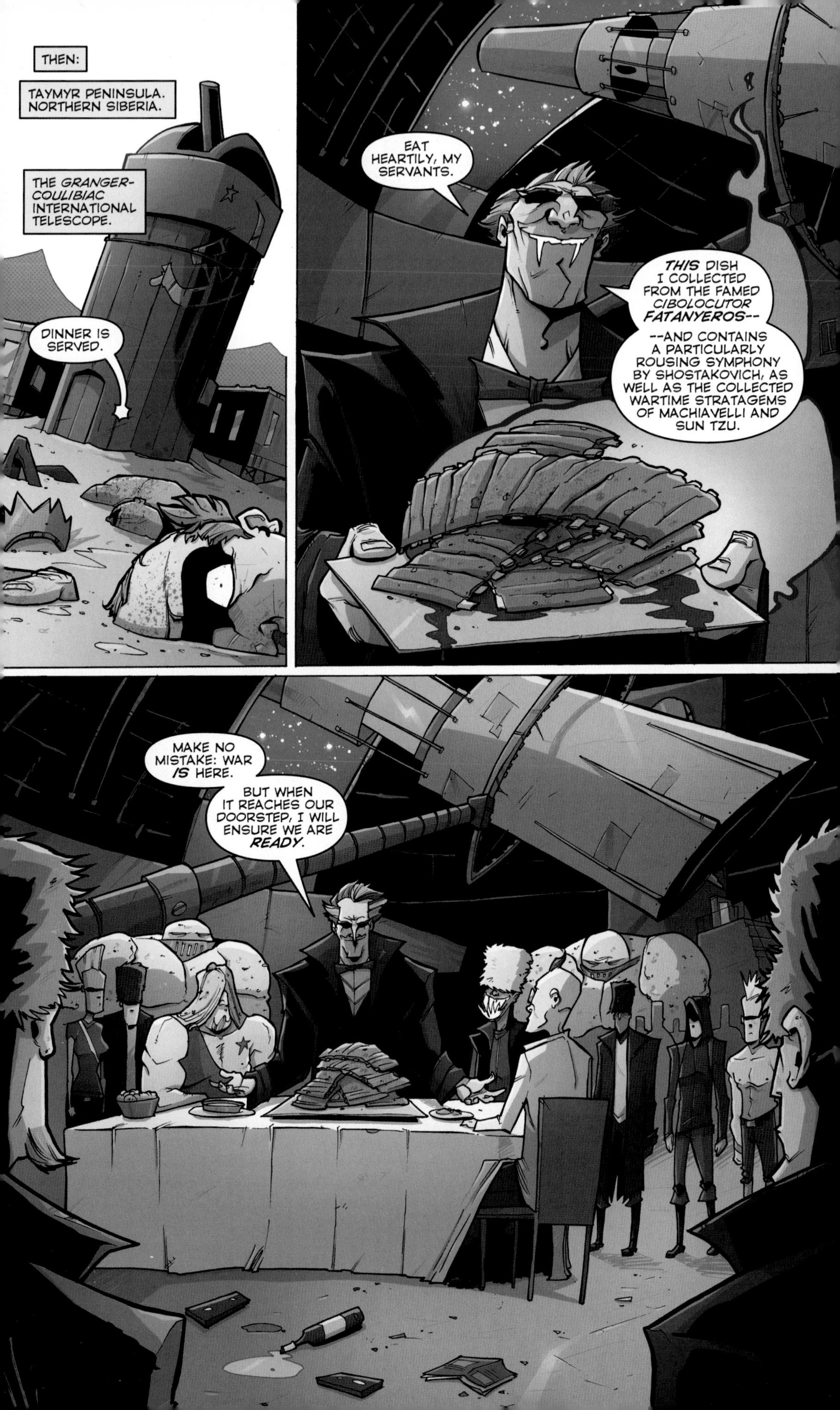
THEN:
TAYMYR PENINSULA. NORTHERN SIBERIA.
THE GRANGER-COULIBIAC INTERNATIONAL TELESCOPE.
DINNER IS SERVED.
EAT HEARTILY, MY SERVANTS.
THIS DISH I COLLECTED FROM THE FAMED CIBOLOCUTOR FATANYEROS--
--AND CONTAINS A PARTICULARLY ROUSING SYMPHONY BY SHOSTAKOVICH, AS WELL AS THE COLLECTED WARTIME STRATAGEMS OF MACHIAVELLI AND SUN TZU.
MAKE NO MISTAKE: WAR IS HERE.
BUT WHEN IT REACHES OUR DOORSTEP, I WILL ENSURE WE ARE READY.

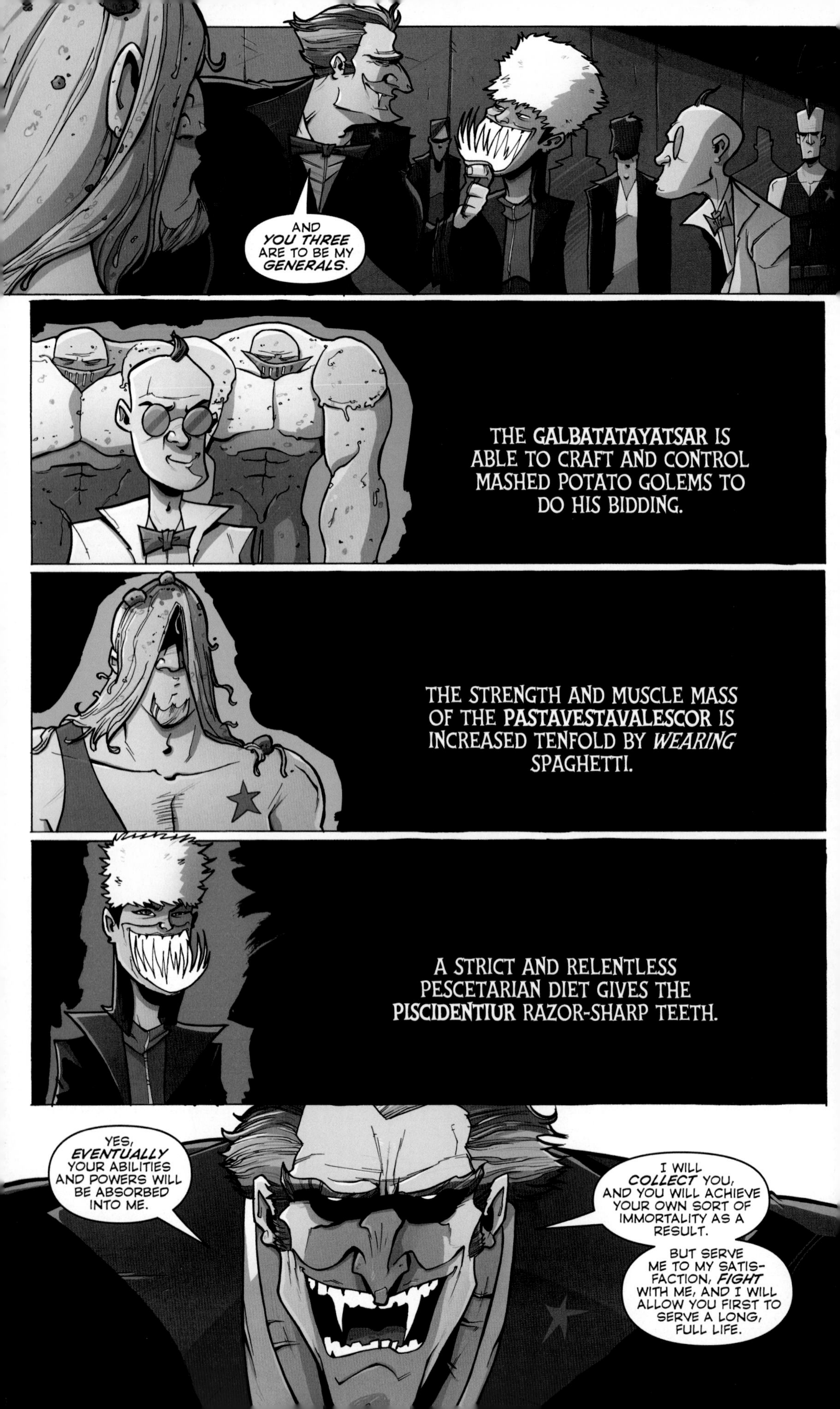

AND *YOU THREE* ARE TO BE MY *GENERALS*.
THE **GALBATATAYATSAR** IS ABLE TO CRAFT AND CONTROL MASHED POTATO GOLEMS TO DO HIS BIDDING.
THE STRENGTH AND MUSCLE MASS OF THE **PASTAVESTAVALESCOR** IS INCREASED TENFOLD BY *WEARING* SPAGHETTI.
A STRICT AND RELENTLESS PESCETARIAN DIET GIVES THE **PISCIDENTIUR** RAZOR-SHARP TEETH.
YES, *EVENTUALLY* YOUR ABILITIES AND POWERS WILL BE ABSORBED INTO ME.
I WILL *COLLECT* YOU, AND YOU WILL ACHIEVE YOUR OWN SORT OF IMMORTALITY AS A RESULT.
BUT SERVE ME TO MY SATIS-FACTION, *FIGHT* WITH ME, AND I WILL ALLOW YOU FIRST TO SERVE A LONG, FULL LIFE.

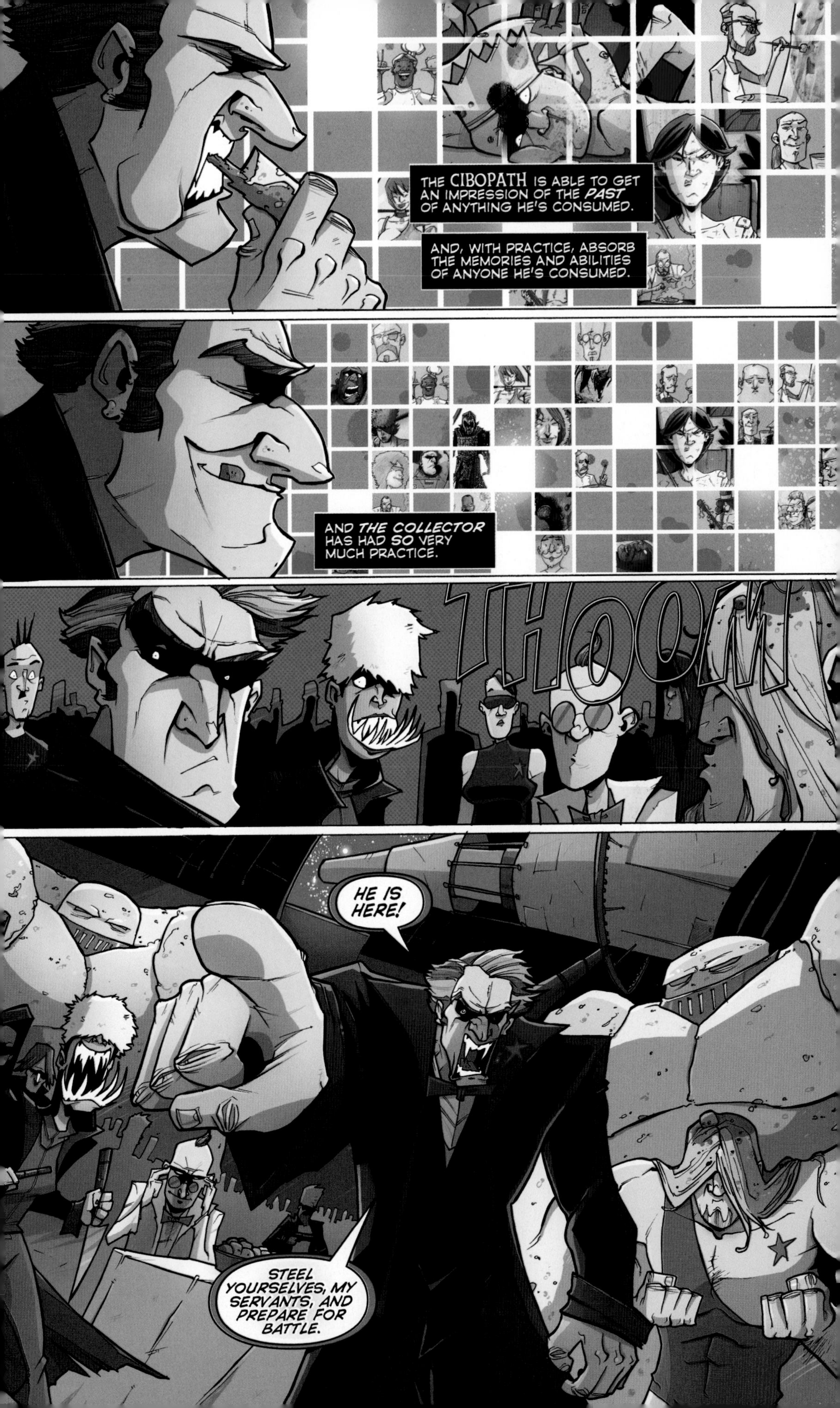
THE CIBOPATH IS ABLE TO GET AN IMPRESSION OF THE *PAST* OF ANYTHING HE'S CONSUMED.
AND, WITH PRACTICE, ABSORB THE MEMORIES AND ABILITIES OF ANYONE HE'S CONSUMED.
AND *THE COLLECTOR* HAS HAD **SO** VERY MUCH PRACTICE.
THOOM
HE IS HERE!
STEEL YOURSELVES, MY SERVANTS, AND PREPARE FOR BATTLE.

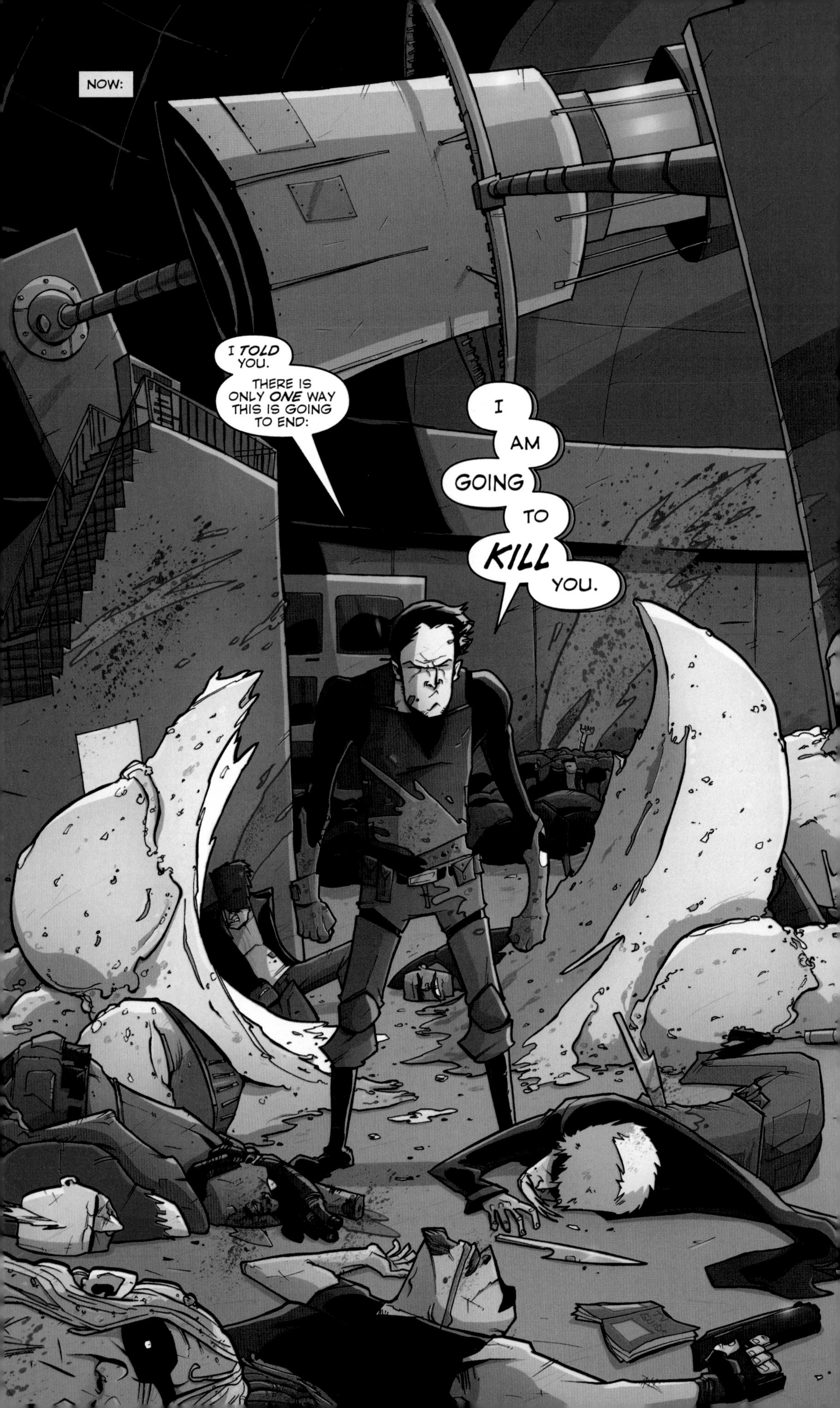
NOW:
I TOLD YOU.
THERE IS ONLY ONE WAY THIS IS GOING TO END:
I AM GOING TO KILL YOU.

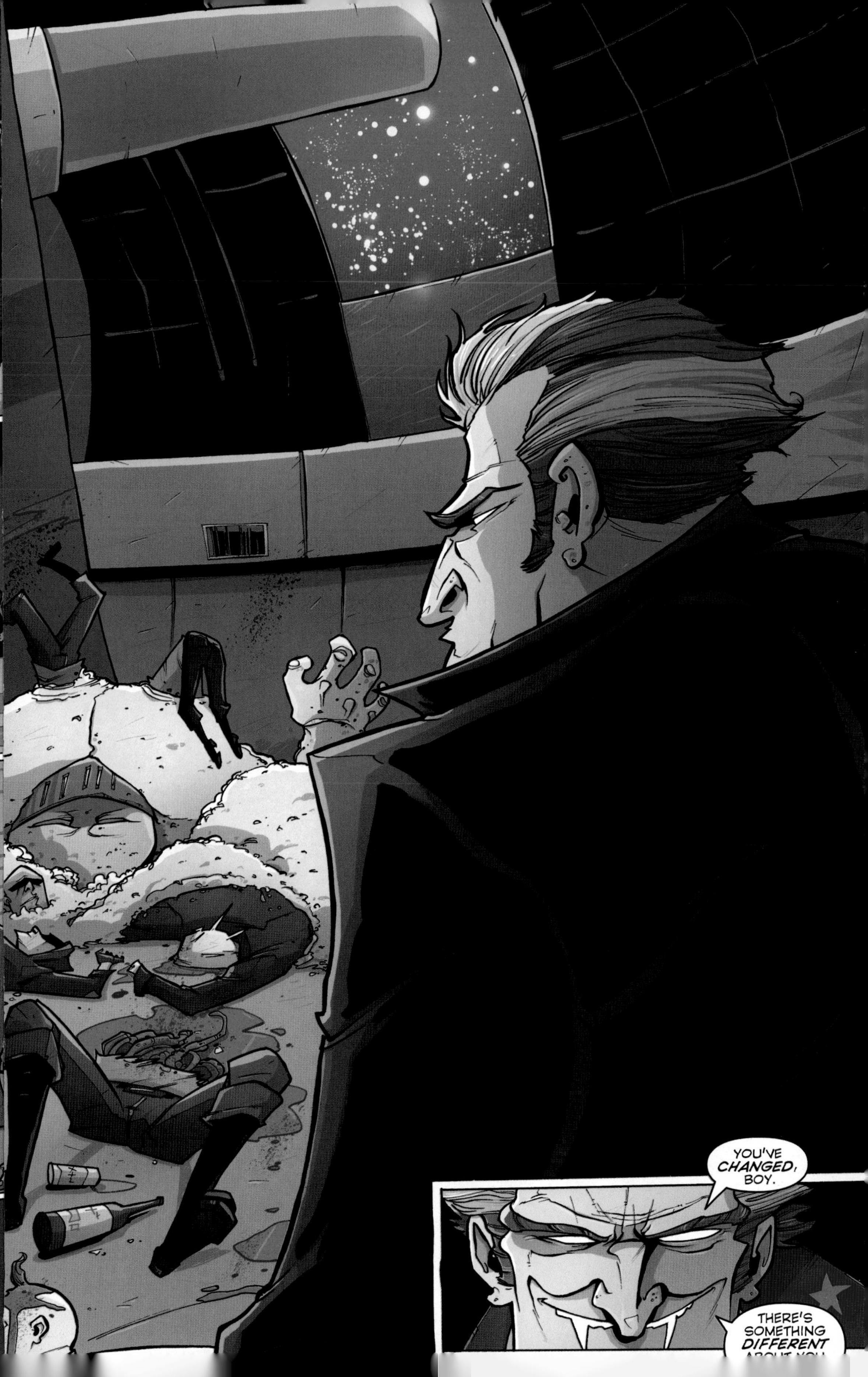
YOU'VE *CHANGED*, BOY.
THERE'S SOMETHING *DIFFERENT*

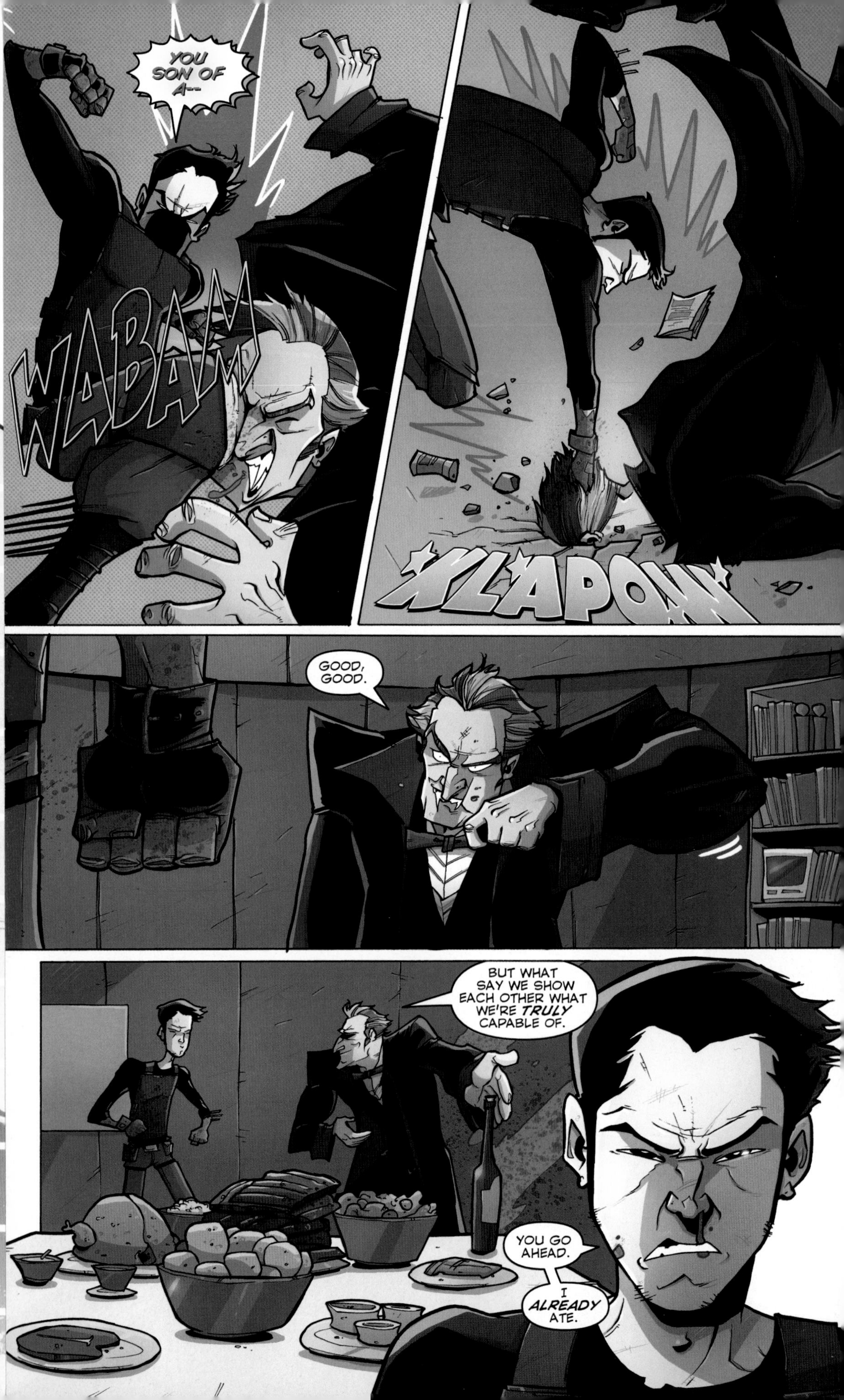
YOU SON OF A--
WABAM
XLAPOW
GOOD, GOOD.
BUT WHAT SAY WE SHOW EACH OTHER WHAT WE'RE *TRULY* CAPABLE OF.
YOU GO AHEAD.
I *ALREADY* ATE.

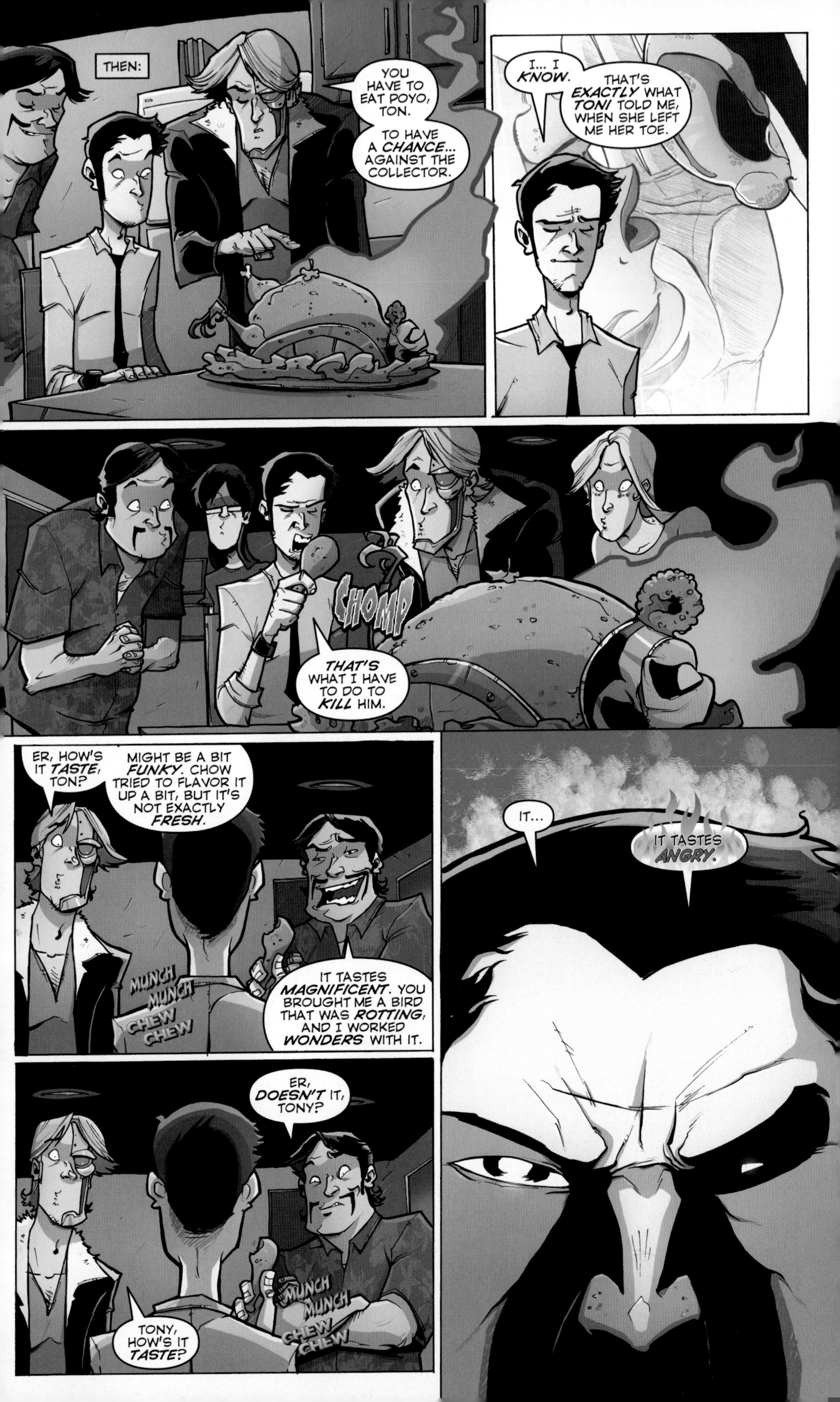
THEN:
YOU HAVE TO EAT POYO, TON.
TO HAVE A CHANCE... AGAINST THE COLLECTOR.
I... I KNOW.
THAT'S EXACTLY WHAT TONI TOLD ME, WHEN SHE LEFT ME HER TOE.
CHOMP
THAT'S WHAT I HAVE TO DO TO KILL HIM.
ER, HOW'S IT TASTE, TON?
MIGHT BE A BIT FUNKY. CHOW TRIED TO FLAVOR IT UP A BIT, BUT IT'S NOT EXACTLY FRESH.
MUNCH MUNCH CHEW CHEW
IT TASTES MAGNIFICENT. YOU BROUGHT ME A BIRD THAT WAS ROTTING, AND I WORKED WONDERS WITH IT.
ER, DOESN'T IT, TONY?
MUNCH MUNCH CHEW CHEW
TONY, HOW'S IT TASTE?
IT...
IT TASTES ANGRY.

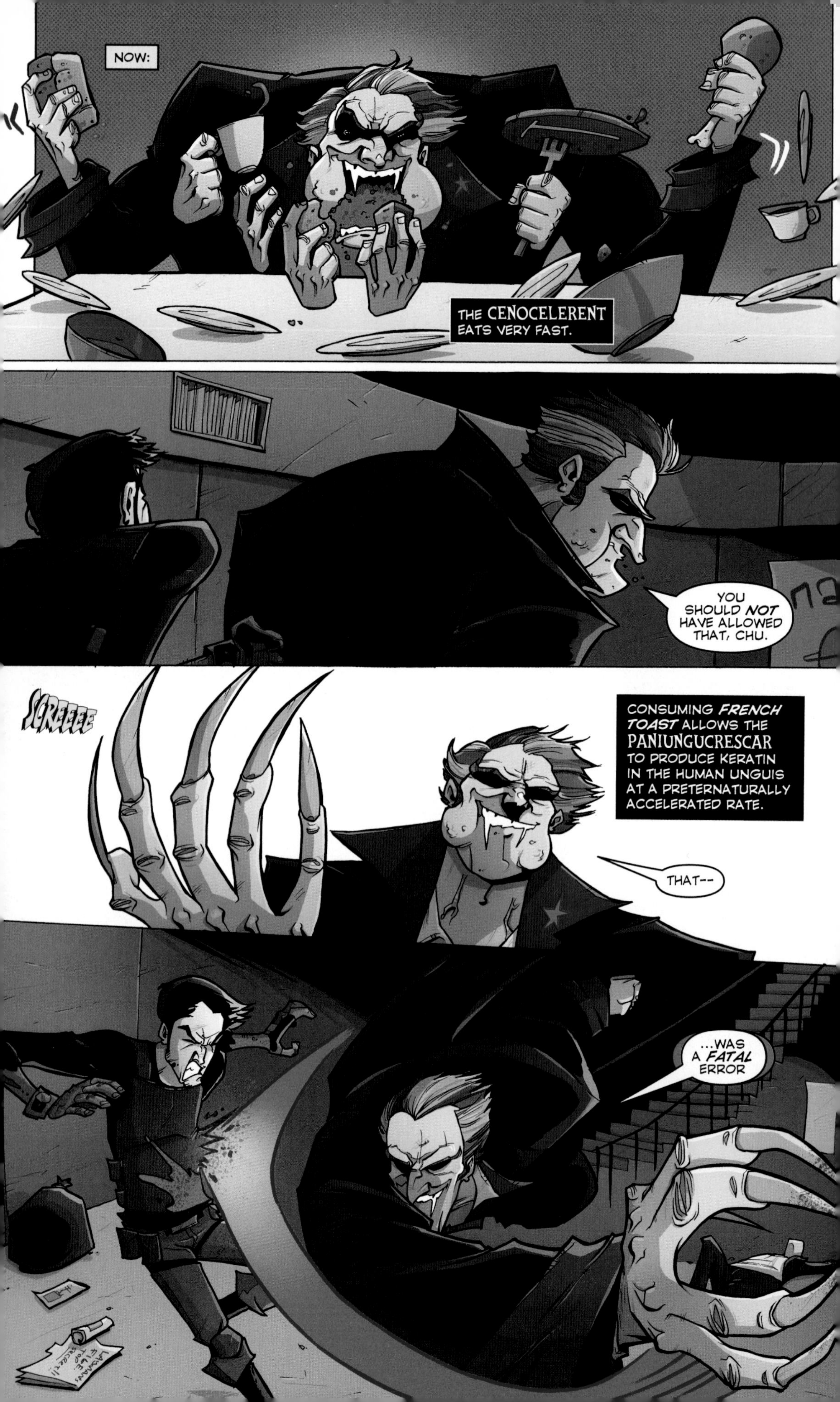
NOW:
THE CENOCELERENT EATS VERY FAST.
YOU SHOULD *NOT* HAVE ALLOWED THAT, CHU.
SCREEEEE
CONSUMING *FRENCH TOAST* ALLOWS THE PANIUNGUCRESCAR TO PRODUCE KERATIN IN THE HUMAN UNGUIS AT A PRETERNATURALLY ACCELERATED RATE.
THAT--
...WAS A *FATAL* ERROR

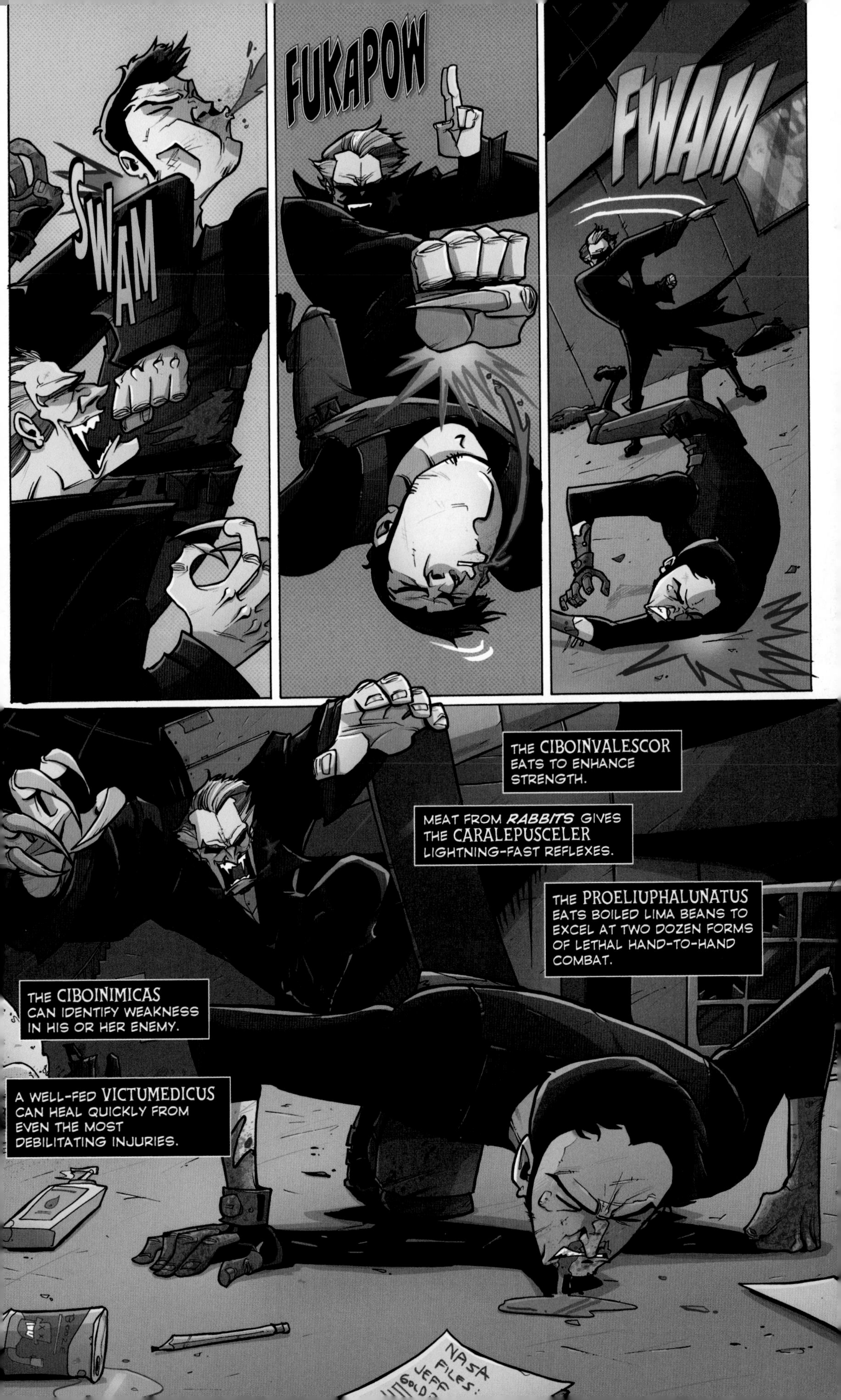
SWAM
FUKAPOW
FWAM
THE CIBOINVALESCOR EATS TO ENHANCE STRENGTH.
MEAT FROM RABBITS GIVES THE CARALEPUSCELER LIGHTNING-FAST REFLEXES.
THE PROELIUPHALUNATUS EATS BOILED LIMA BEANS TO EXCEL AT TWO DOZEN FORMS OF LETHAL HAND-TO-HAND COMBAT.
THE CIBOINIMICAS CAN IDENTIFY WEAKNESS IN HIS OR HER ENEMY.
A WELL-FED VICTUMEDICUS CAN HEAL QUICKLY FROM EVEN THE MOST DEBILITATING INJURIES.
NASA FILES: JEFF

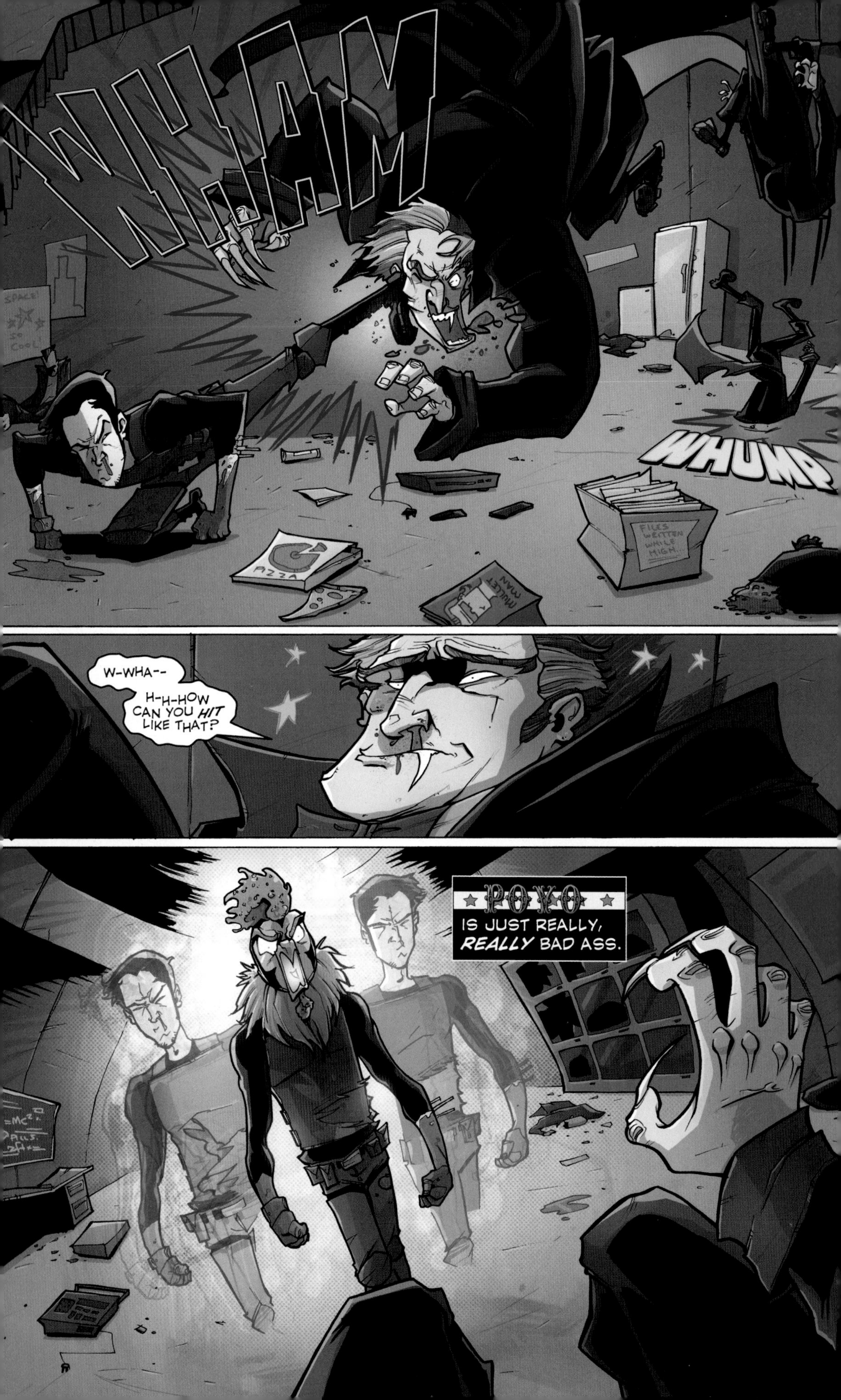

WHAM
SPACE! SO COOL!
WHUMP
FILES WRITTEN WHILE HIGH...
PIZZA
MULLET MAN
W-WHA--
H-H-HOW CAN YOU *HIT* LIKE THAT?
POYO
IS JUST REALLY, *REALLY* BAD ASS.

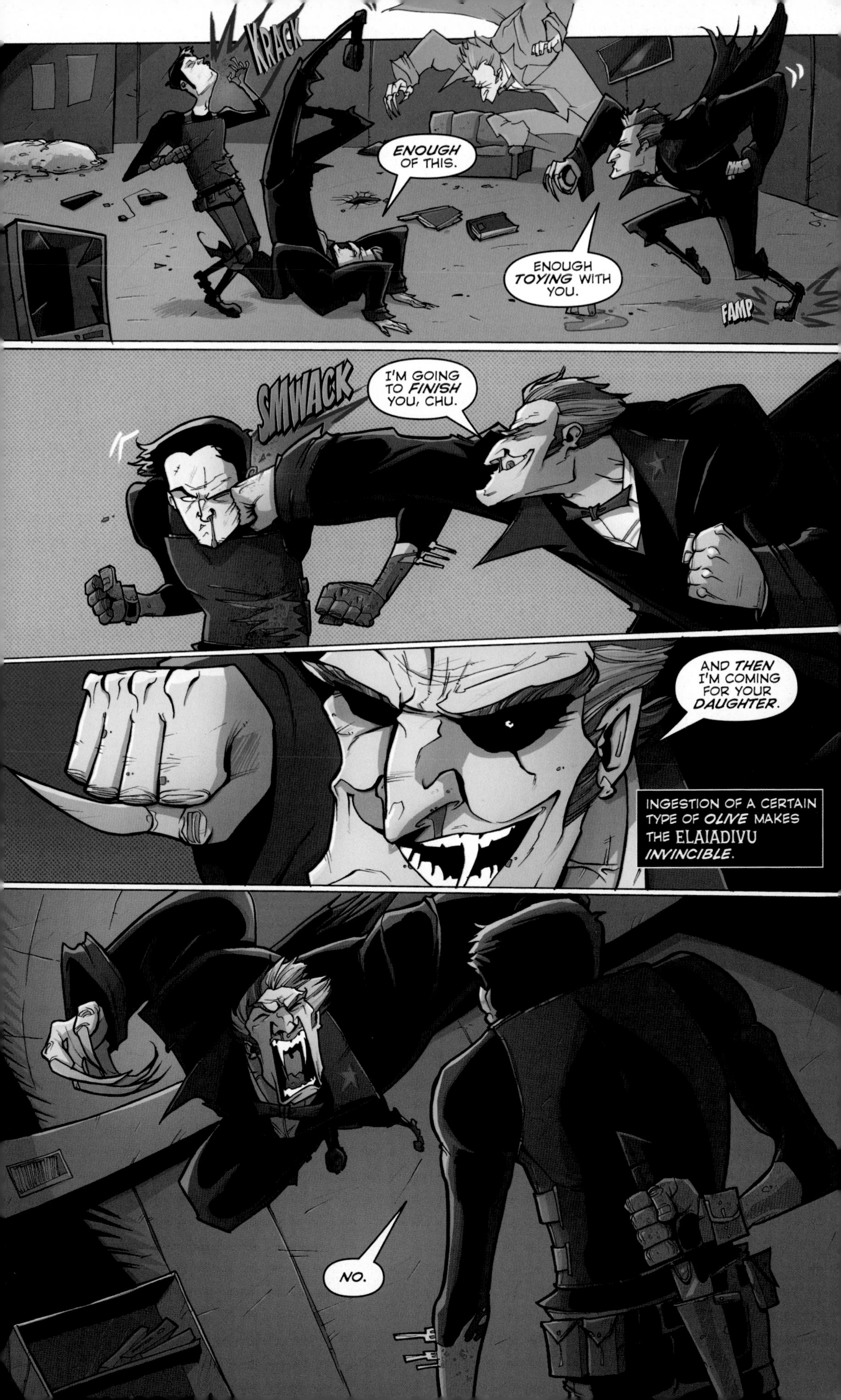
KRACK
ENOUGH OF THIS.
ENOUGH TOYING WITH YOU.
FAMP
SMWACK
I'M GOING TO FINISH YOU, CHU.
AND THEN I'M COMING FOR YOUR DAUGHTER.
INGESTION OF A CERTAIN TYPE OF OLIVE MAKES THE ELAIADIVU INVINCIBLE.
NO.

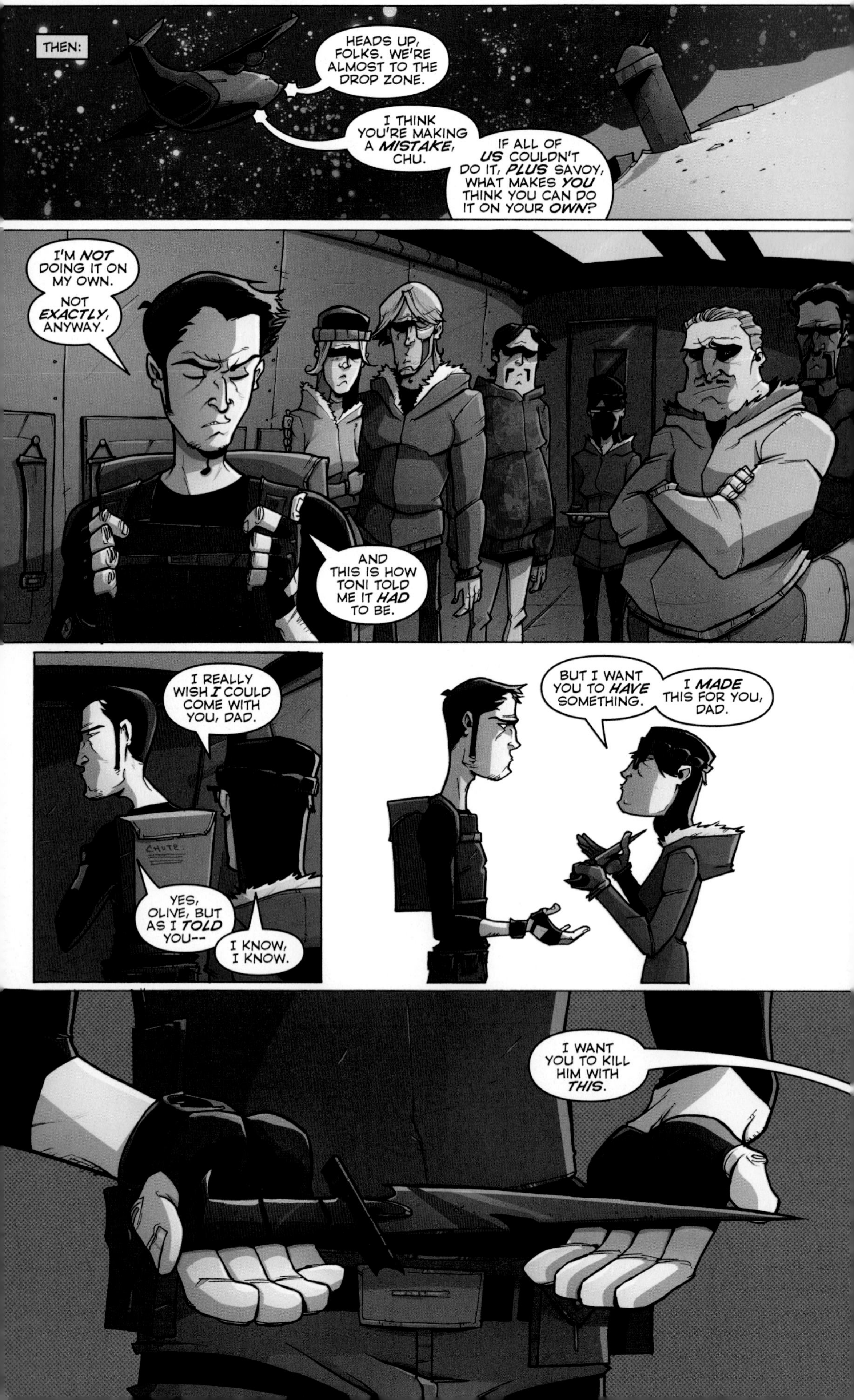
THEN:
HEADS UP, FOLKS. WE'RE ALMOST TO THE DROP ZONE.
I THINK YOU'RE MAKING A MISTAKE, CHU.
IF ALL OF US COULDN'T DO IT, PLUS SAVOY, WHAT MAKES YOU THINK YOU CAN DO IT ON YOUR OWN?
I'M NOT DOING IT ON MY OWN.
NOT EXACTLY, ANYWAY.
AND THIS IS HOW TONI TOLD ME IT HAD TO BE.
I REALLY WISH I COULD COME WITH YOU, DAD.
CHUTE
YES, OLIVE, BUT AS I TOLD YOU--
I KNOW, I KNOW.
BUT I WANT YOU TO HAVE SOMETHING.
I MADE THIS FOR YOU, DAD.
I WANT YOU TO KILL HIM WITH THIS.

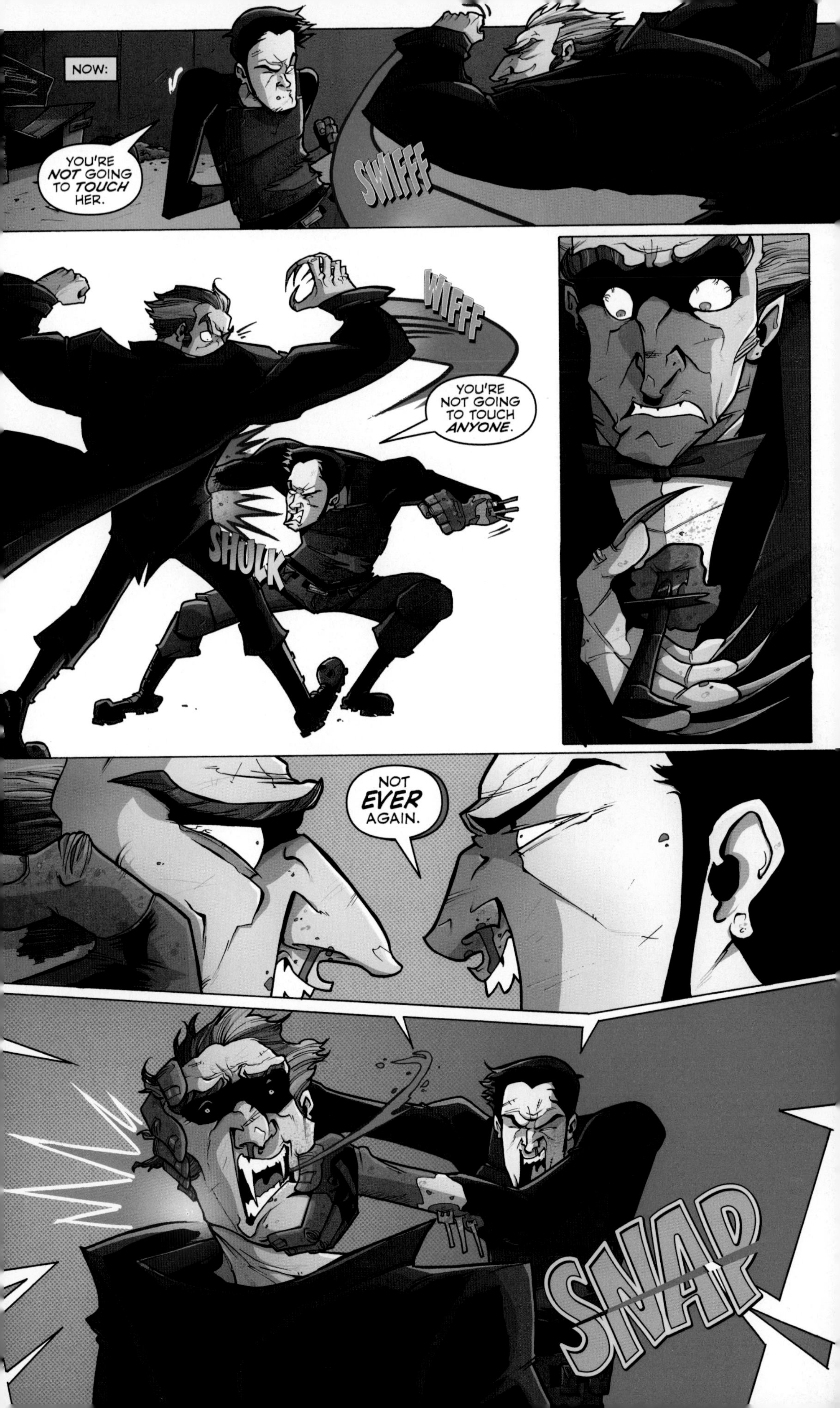
NOW:
YOU'RE *NOT* GOING TO *TOUCH* HER.
SWIFFF
WIFFF
YOU'RE NOT GOING TO TOUCH *ANYONE*.
SHULK
NOT *EVER* AGAIN.
SNAP

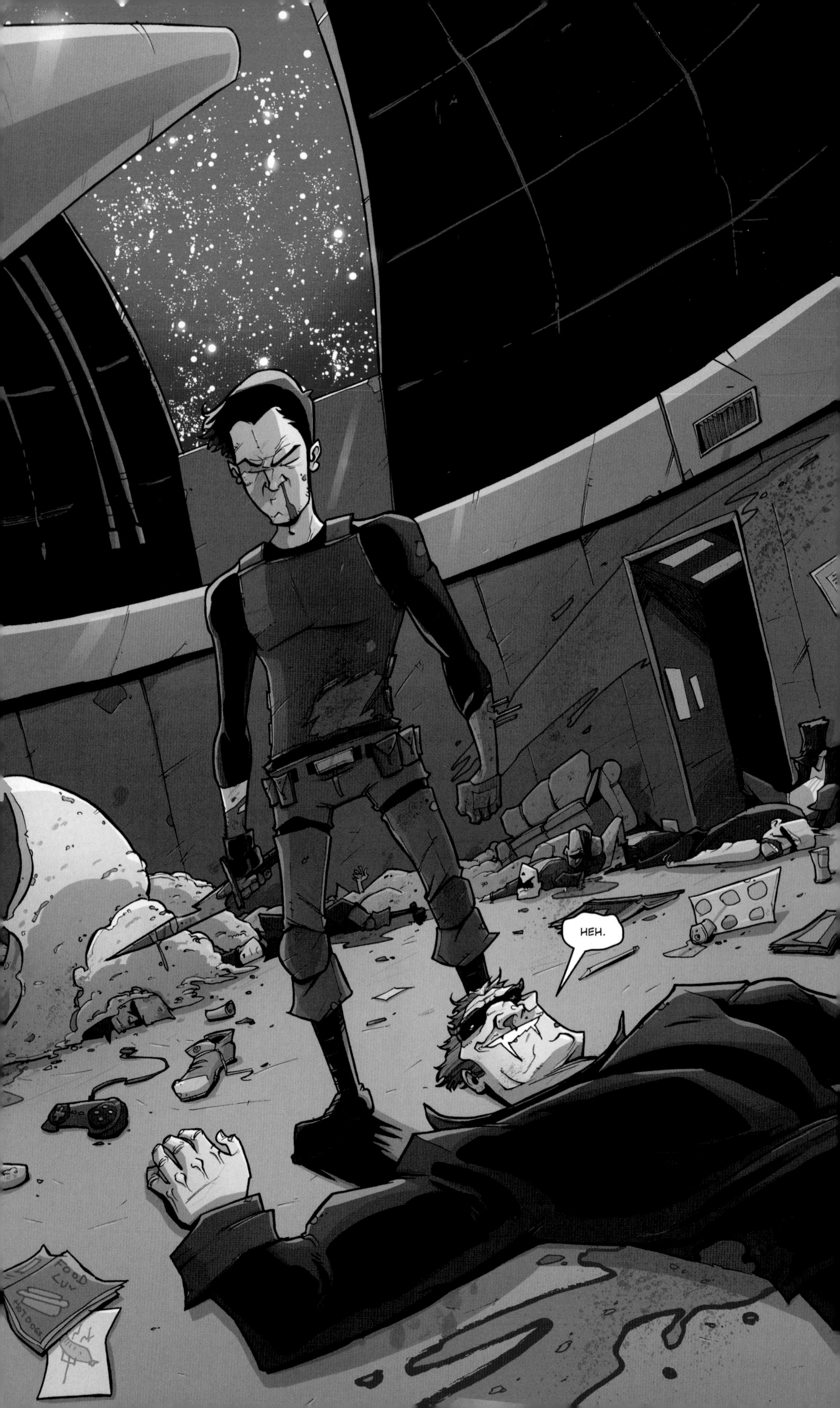
HEH.
FOOD
LUV
HOT DOGS

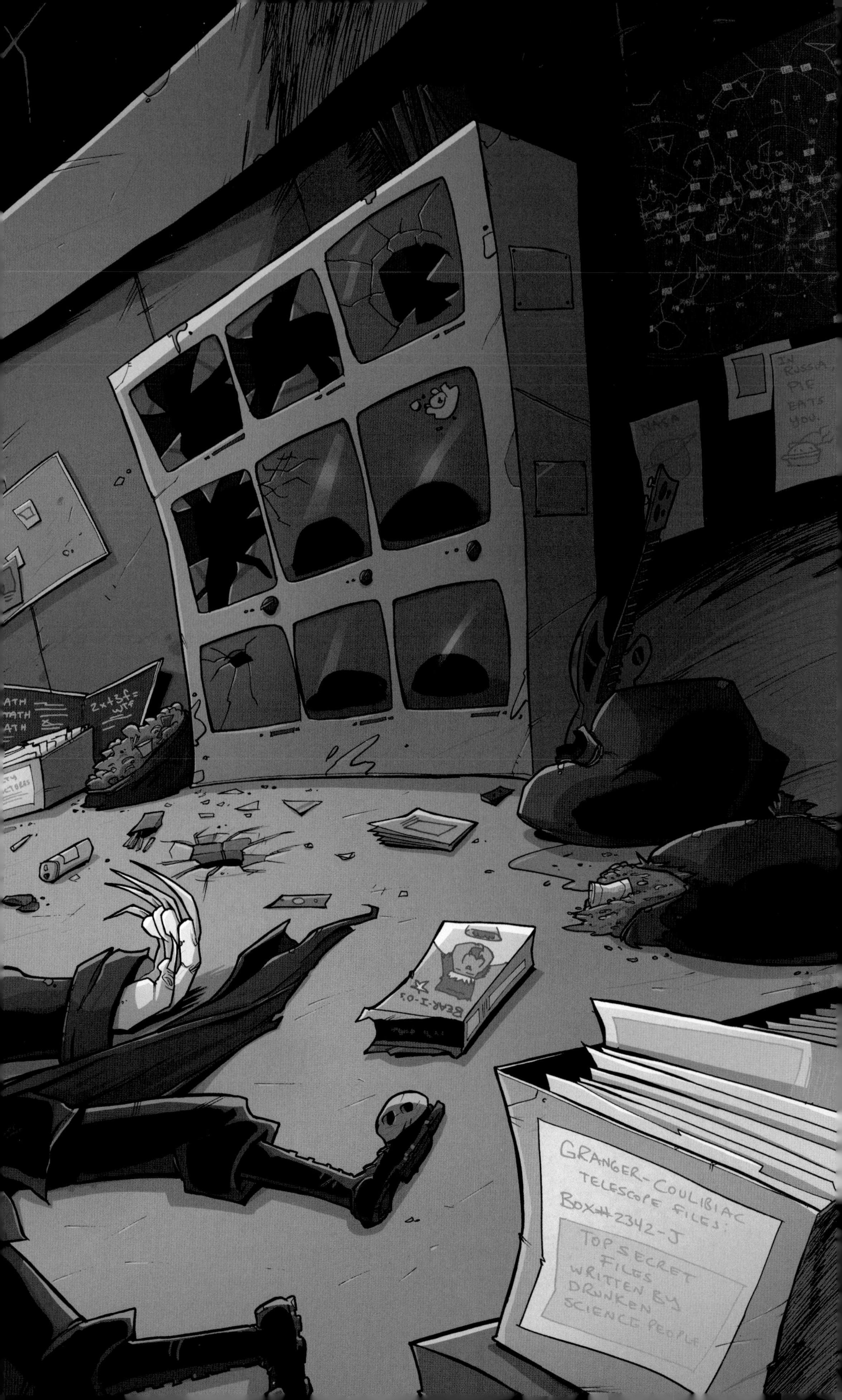

IN RUSSIA, PIE EATS YOU.
NASA
2x+3f = WTF
BEAR-I-03
GRANGER-COULIBIAC TELESCOPE FILES: BOX#2342-J
TOP SECRET FILES WRITTEN BY DRUNKEN SCIENCE PEOPLE

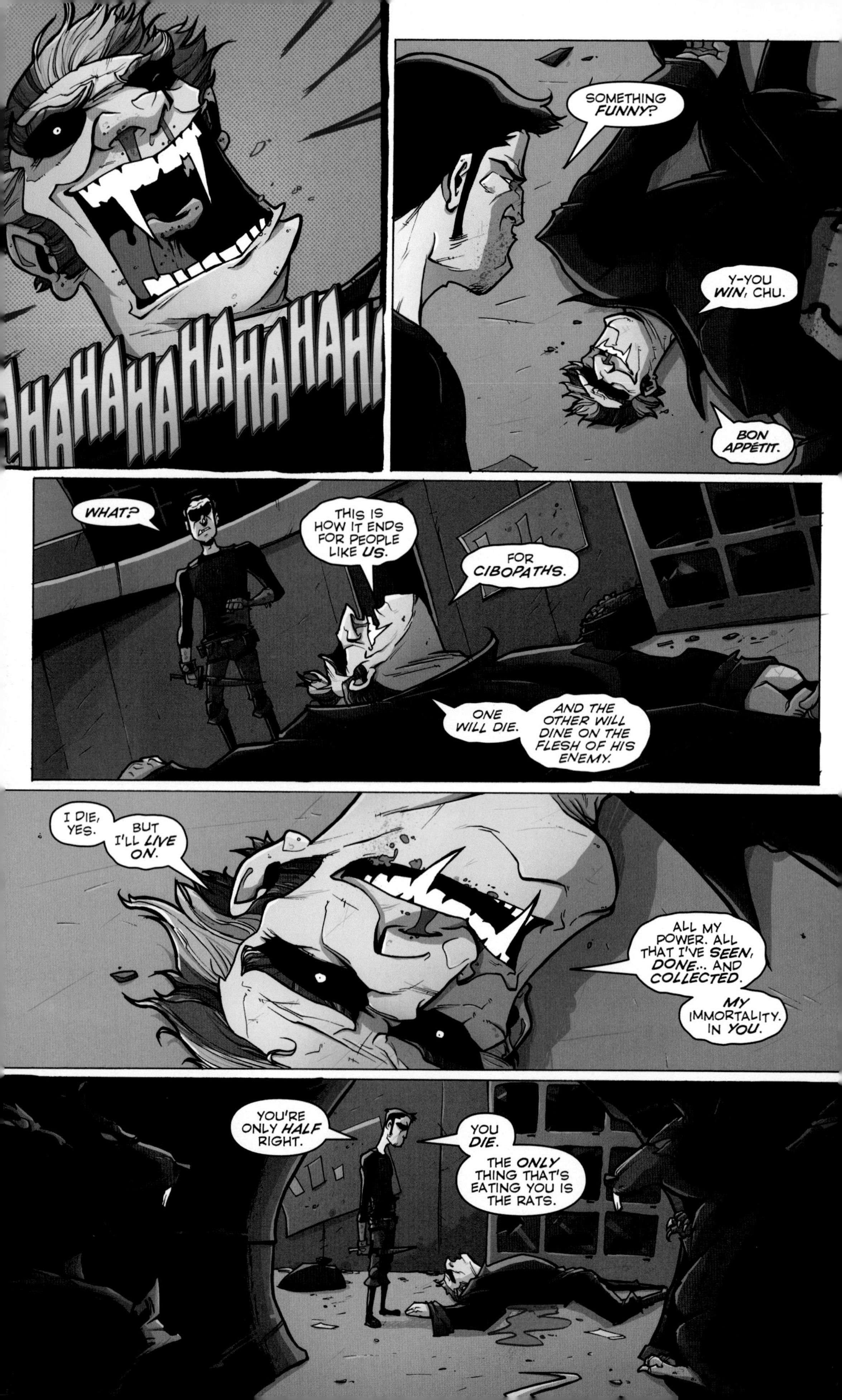
HAHAHAHAHAHAHAHAHAH
SOMETHING FUNNY?
Y-YOU WIN, CHU.
BON APPÉTIT.
WHAT?
THIS IS HOW IT ENDS FOR PEOPLE LIKE US.
FOR CIBOPATHS.
ONE WILL DIE.
AND THE OTHER WILL DINE ON THE FLESH OF HIS ENEMY.
I DIE, YES.
BUT I'LL LIVE ON.
ALL MY POWER. ALL THAT I'VE SEEN, DONE... AND COLLECTED.
MY IMMORTALITY. IN YOU.
YOU'RE ONLY HALF RIGHT.
YOU DIE.
THE ONLY THING THAT'S EATING YOU IS THE RATS.

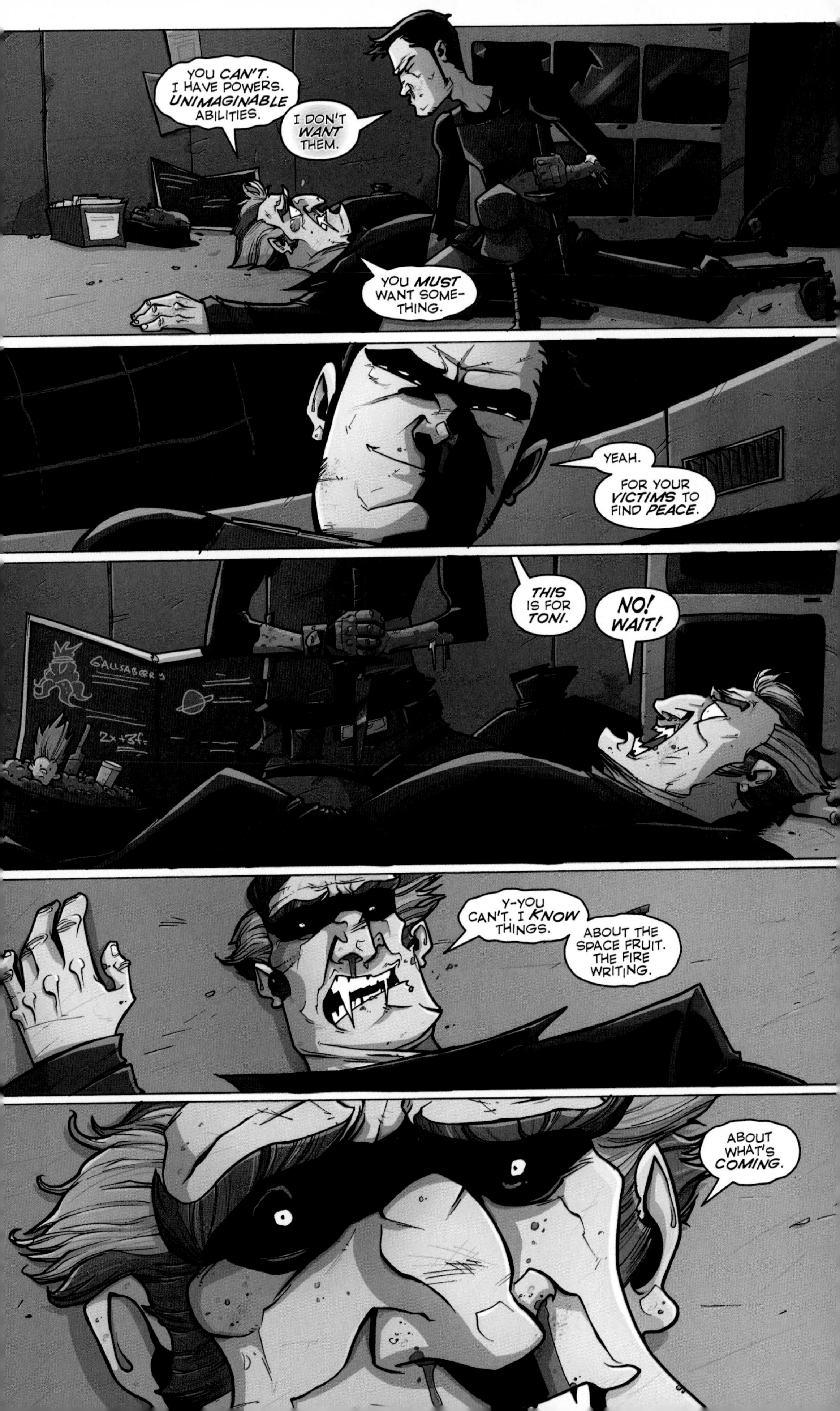

YOU CAN'T. I HAVE POWERS. UNIMAGINABLE ABILITIES.
I DON'T WANT THEM.
YOU MUST WANT SOME-THING.
YEAH.
FOR YOUR VICTIMS TO FIND PEACE.
THIS IS FOR TONI.
NO! WAIT!
Y-YOU CAN'T. I KNOW THINGS.
ABOUT THE SPACE FRUIT. THE FIRE WRITING.
ABOUT WHAT'S COMING.

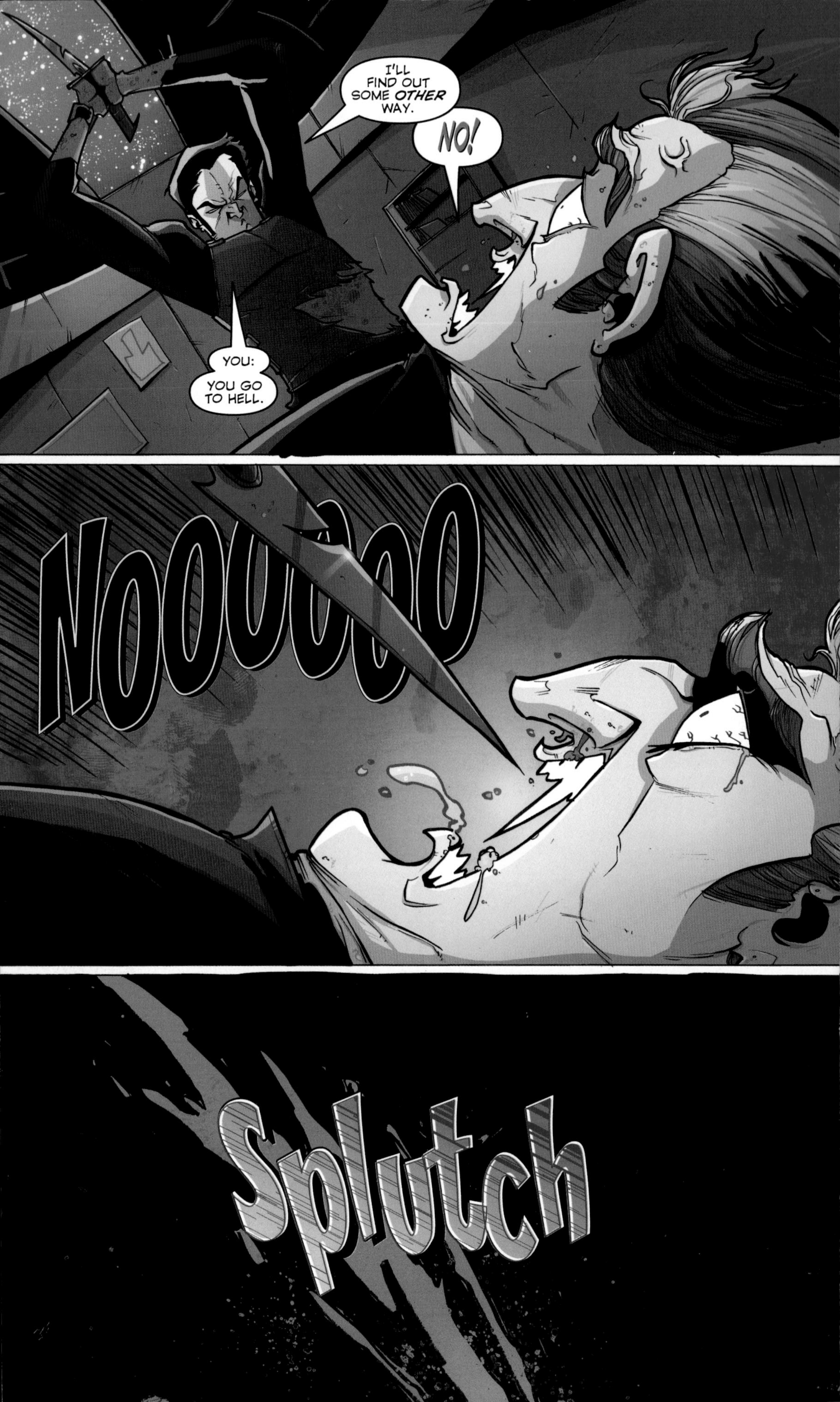
I'LL FIND OUT SOME *OTHER* WAY.
NO!
YOU:
YOU GO TO HELL.
NOOOOOO
Splutch

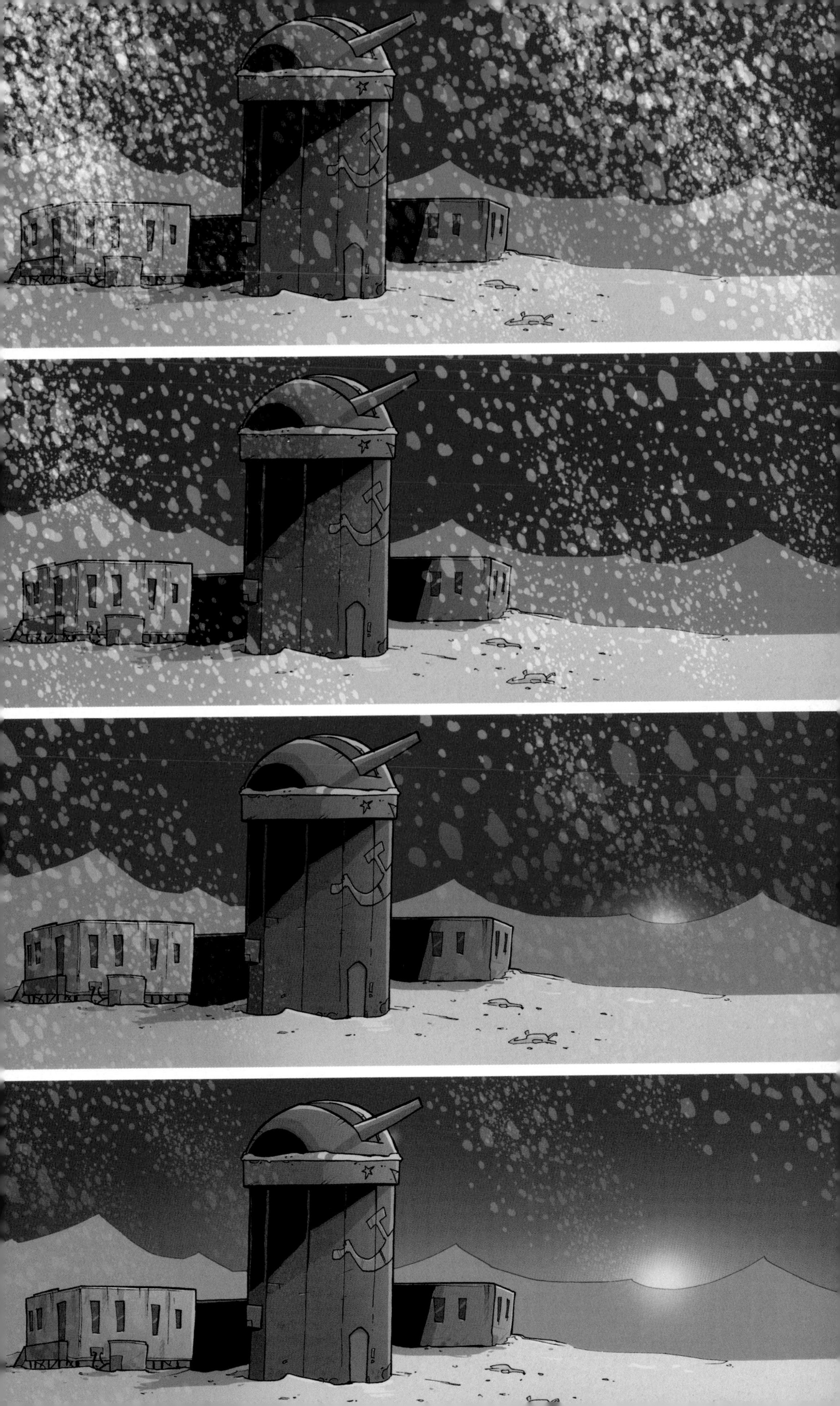

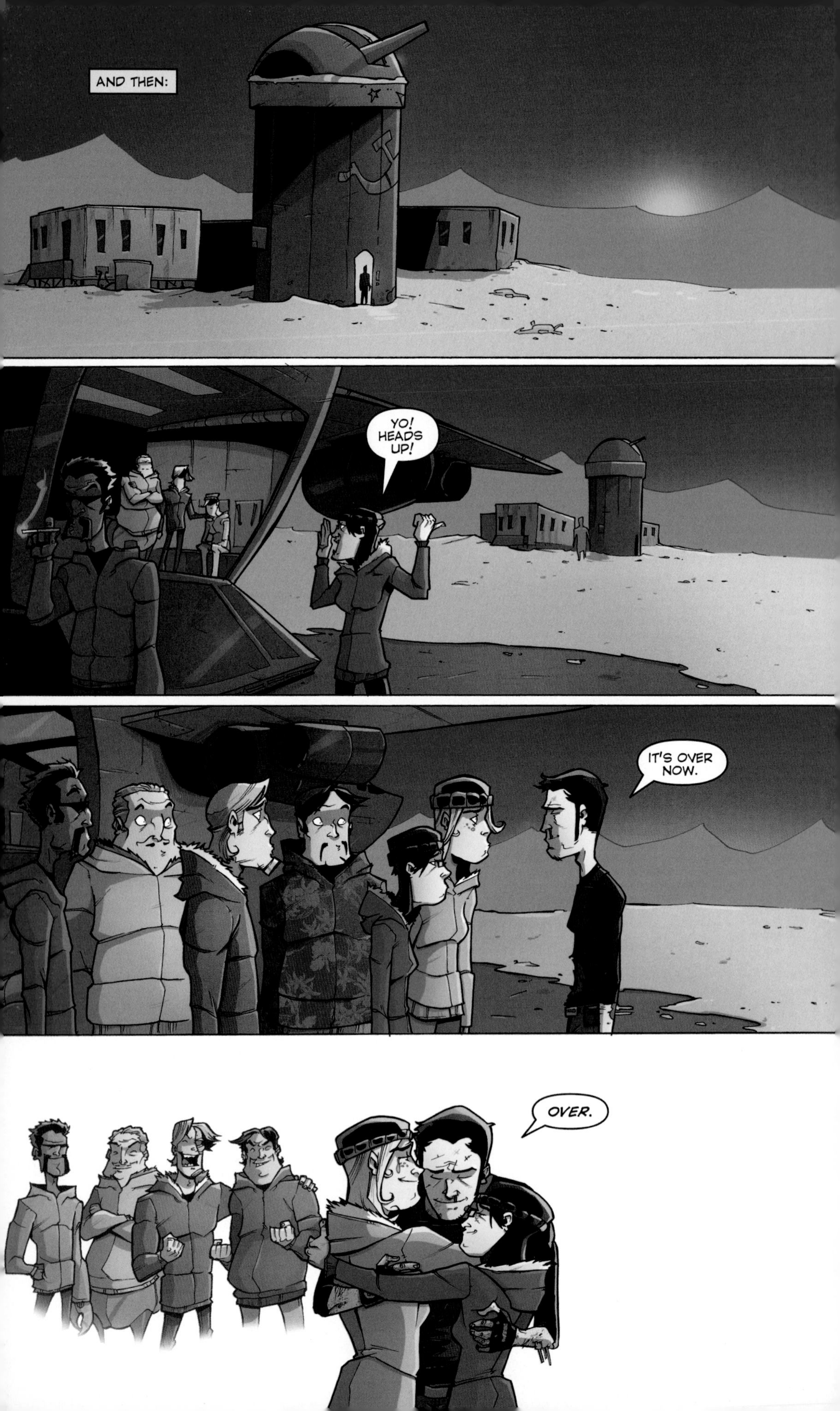
AND THEN:
YO! HEADS UP!
IT'S OVER NOW.
OVER.

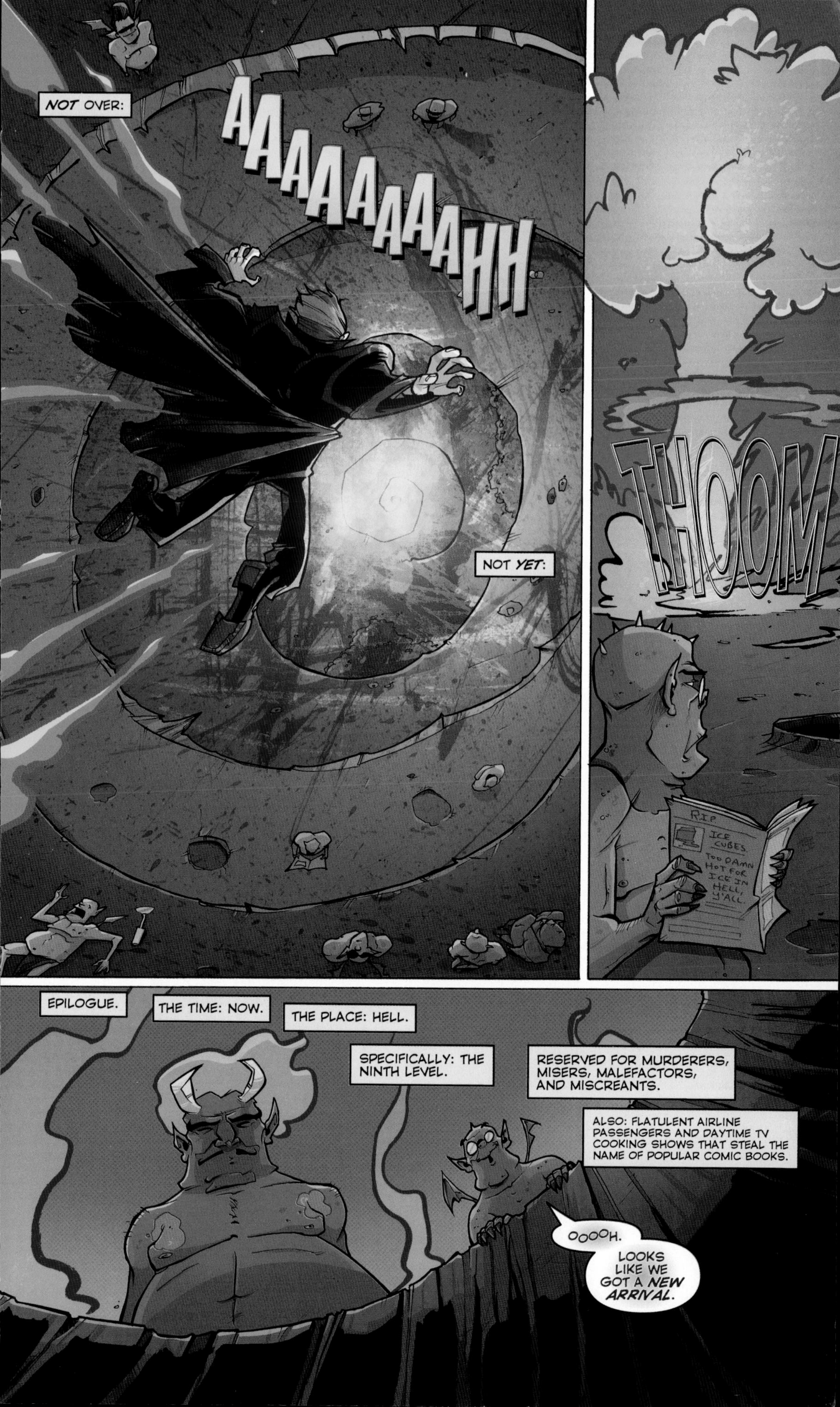

NOT OVER:
AAAAAAAAAAHH
NOT YET:
THOOM
R.I.P.
ICE CUBES
TOO DAMN HOT FOR ICE IN HELL, Y'ALL.
EPILOGUE.
THE TIME: NOW.
THE PLACE: HELL.
SPECIFICALLY: THE NINTH LEVEL.
RESERVED FOR MURDERERS, MISERS, MALEFACTORS, AND MISCREANTS.
ALSO: FLATULENT AIRLINE PASSENGERS AND DAYTIME TV COOKING SHOWS THAT STEAL THE NAME OF POPULAR COMIC BOOKS.
OOOOH.
LOOKS LIKE WE GOT A NEW ARRIVAL.

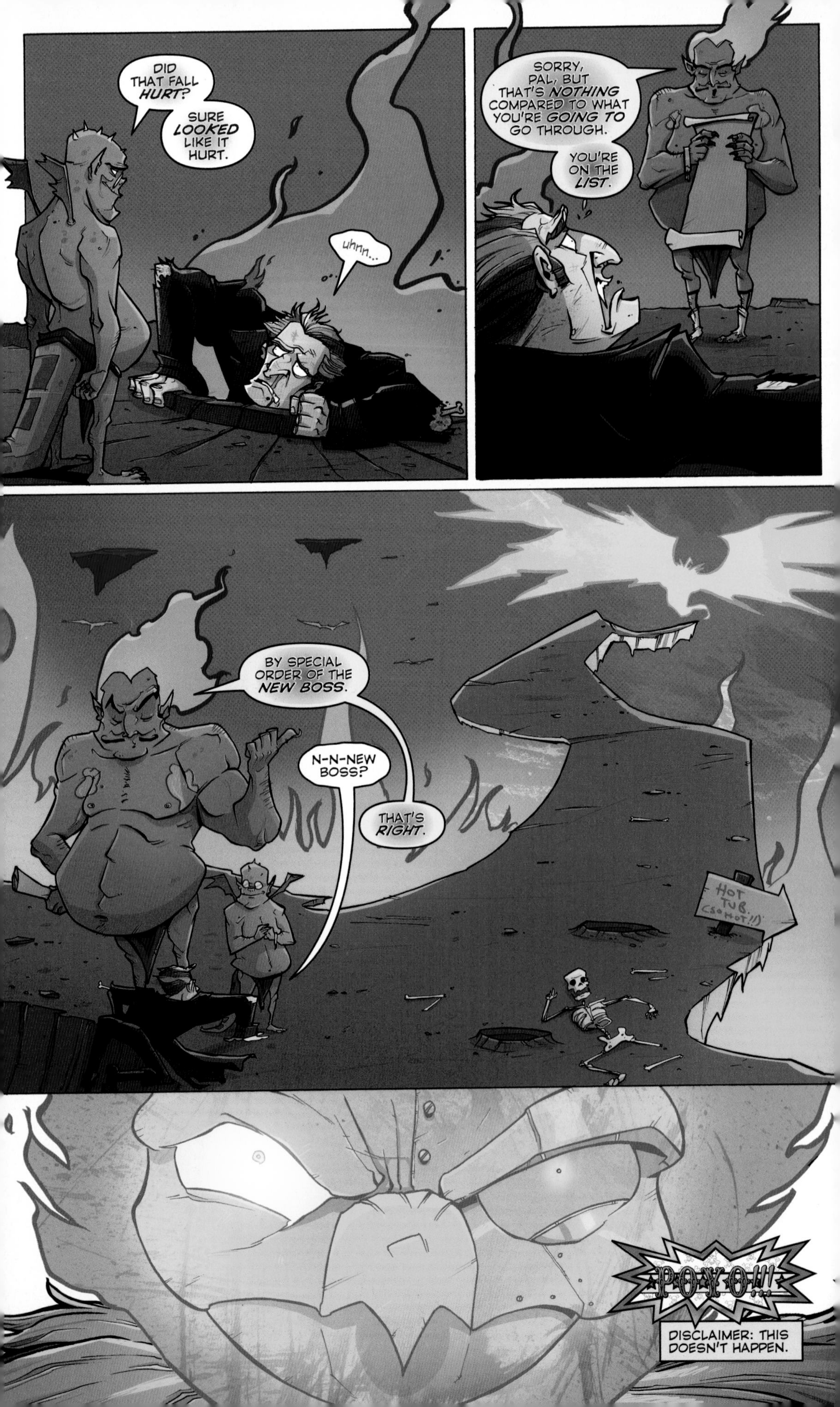

DID THAT FALL *HURT*?
SURE *LOOKED* LIKE IT HURT.
uhnn...
SORRY, PAL, BUT THAT'S *NOTHING* COMPARED TO WHAT YOU'RE *GOING TO* GO THROUGH.
YOU'RE ON THE *LIST*.
BY SPECIAL ORDER OF THE *NEW BOSS*.
N-N-NEW BOSS?
THAT'S *RIGHT*.
HOT TUB (SO HOT!!)
POYO!!!
DISCLAIMER: THIS DOESN'T HAPPEN.